FOR WHAT IT'S WORTH

Cordurouy

ISBN: 979-8-9887424-0-1 (Paperback)
ISBN: 979-8-9887424-1-8 (ebook)

This book is a work of fiction. Any references to real people, including quotations, are fictitious. Other names, characters, places, and events are products of the author's imagination, and any resemblance to actual events or places or persons, living or dead, is entirely coincidental.

Book cover design by Anna Dorfman.
Interior design by Rafael Andres
Printed by Cordurouy LLC in the United States of America.
First printing edition 2023.
Cordurouy Books
665 Valley Dr
Hermosa Beach, CA 90254

www.cordurouy.com

If Stupidity got us into this mess,
then why can't it get us out?
—Will Rogers

PROLOGUE

11:13 p.m.
Wednesday, May 17, 2006

The Sockolosky estate was half an hour north of Tulsa on rural side roads with neither streetlamps nor painted centerlines. It was remote, and there were few sounds besides birds, crickets, cicadas, and toads chirping a transcendental orchestra each night. You had to use your floodlights after dark to ensure you wouldn't smash into a deer bouncing across the road and accidentally kill both yourself and the graceful but witless beast. Deer had infested the area over the decades, and with hunting forbidden on private property, the animals had found a murder-free oasis in which to multiply and thrive in serene tranquility. Bobcats, wolves, and coyotes had once confidently roamed those lands, too, but since they were driven out, humans and cars remained the white-tailed deer's only predators throughout most of the Midwest.

A ruthless man had built the Sockolosky estate nearly a century before from the spoils of oil money. The home was constructed using the most ostentatious design standards at the time: four marble columns centered in front of oversized, carved wooden front doors overlooking a circular driveway, set behind a sprawling water fixture centered on a manicured lawn. The inside of the house encompassed 12,000 square feet, with seven bedrooms, two maid's quarters, two kitchens, and four fireplaces. Magazines once featured the home as an architectural staple of Oklahoma oil days when the house shone.

A dark-maroon Jetta rolled to a stop on the small shoulder of that remote road a few blocks before the estate's gate, and out stepped an angry man who hadn't ever shown the world his anger: Earl Derkatch. He wore sizable pentagon-shaped prescription glasses with a thin metal frame, and his trimmed white beard covered most of the engrained acne scars on his face. Earl was in his late fifties, but he looked like he could've been a decade older. His most identifiable physical aspect was that he had only one arm, his right. He had a belly, but he had been in proper boxing shape in his prime years before he lost his left arm and got old. Earl exited his vehicle, surveyed the road in each direction to ensure he was truly alone, and then pulled a black ski mask over his head. He wasn't a very adept or experienced criminal, but he had anger, tenacity, and persistence—all critical requirements in the field. Above all else, he had a lot of questions.

Two dogs ran up from the other side of the fence, barking at him loudly. Earl removed a wrapped fast-food hamburger from his jacket pocket, set it on his car's hood, and unwrapped the cheap meal. He took the patty from between the buns, split it in half, removed a pill from his front pants pocket, and broke the pill into pieces. He jammed the crumbled medication into each burger patty half and passed them through the fence to the dogs, who both gratefully inhaled them. He wiped his palm on his jeans to rid his hand of grease and then pulled a black leather glove onto his right hand, using his teeth to pull the glove over his palm.

Earl's left arm ended just above where an elbow would have been, and he had altered his jacket to fit his dimensions neatly. Dressed in jeans, boots, a glove, a ski mask, and a dark denim jacket, Earl took a heavy wool blanket from the backseat of his car and tossed it with a solid throw to hang over the top of the fence and pad the barbed wire for his ascent. Then he pulled out a small folding ladder from the backseat and closed his car door. He extended and positioned the ladder and then took another hard look in each direction of the quiet, unlit road. It was springtime in the Midwest, and the sky was absent of stars or moonlight, as storm clouds had been brewing for the past few hours. It wasn't raining yet, but a brutal storm was likely. In Oklahoma, there is no such thing as a light drizzle. You either have a downpour with heavy winds and tornado sirens or nothing. He worked slowly, waiting ten minutes for the dogs to feel the Ambien. Both hounds wandered to a nearby knoll and lay down to nap.

Earl summited the ladder steps and carefully swung one leg over the padded barbed wire fence. Then he used his other leg to kick over his ladder to the ditch behind his car. Holding a padded section of the railing with his right hand, he swung his leg over and jumped across, plopping onto the grass.

"Aargh, son of a bitch!"

He rubbed his right knee and hamstring in agony and then tugged to bring the blanket off the top of the fence. The barbed wires snagged at the blanket, tearing through its wool fabric. He shook the blanket a few times to dislodge it, carefully pulled it down, and set it on the ground for his return climb, which he knew would take much more effort without a ladder on his side.

The aging amateur criminal hobbled to the left side of the house, limping like a wounded animal with each step. Earl knew the place was deserted that evening because Bob Sockolosky was hosting a benefit for the governor at the Mayo Hotel downtown to raise money for the governor's reelection campaign. It was in all the local papers. Those events always went late, so it was possible the head honchos might even get drunk and tired enough to sleep at the hotel after the event wrapped. Bob's two kids were off in boarding school, his wife had left him a few years before, and he no longer paid for any live-in help on the property. The house was Earl's for a few hours, but he didn't need that much time. A safe had drawn Earl there: a safe in Bob's office on the first floor, hidden behind a painting. Earl had heard mention of that safe several times—where it was and local rumors about what Bob had squirreled away inside it—and Earl had become obsessed by it.

Earl had conducted his amateur sleuthing for a few months, and that night he finally built up enough courage to do something about it. If you have a safe, the last thing you should do is make anything about it common knowledge. Still, Bob Sockolosky was an arrogant showboat, even posing for a photograph in front of it for an architectural magazine after he first got married. Earl expected to find documents locked away—damning proof of corruption between Bob and some politician or criminal. There had to be something, at least as far as Earl was concerned, for Earl had the benefit of righteous intuition on his side. His intentions were pure enough, and that was how and why he convinced himself that he was a hero for breaking in, not merely a lowly common criminal. Rumors had spread about extortion, bribes, kickbacks, and misappropriation of government funds, but the authorities never made a case, and nothing was ever done. As far as Earl knew, Bob Sockolosky was probably laughing and smiling with the governor at that very moment, scheming to skim millions more over champagne and caviar in a swanky hotel ballroom.

But again, Earl was no master thief, and doing anything physical with one arm had its disadvantages. He had been teaching history at a local high school for the past twenty-three years. In his younger days, though, he had apprenticed for a locksmith in Stillwater from the age of sixteen. Then he attended Oklahoma State University while continuing to work for the locksmith. He got his degrees and then, when he turned twenty-six, finally quit the locksmith job to move up to Tulsa to teach advanced history classes to high school students who rarely cared about who won the Battle of 1812 or who Otto von Bismarck was. Earl still remembered the skills he learned while apprenticing. Few people in Tulsa knew anything about his adolescence and the decade he spent honing his skills as a professional lockpicker. After seeing the safe in the magazine photograph, Earl bought the same make and model for his own home and practiced on it for a few weeks, so he was confident he could crack the safe within five minutes and be back to his car within fifteen.

Earl approached a side door that led to one of the kitchens and pulled a tension wrench from his jacket pocket, which he used to pick the simple deadbolt. Once in the kitchen, he closed the door behind him, returned the tension wrench to his jacket pocket, and pulled out a small LED flashlight to guide himself through a hall and toward Bob's office.

The office was more august than expected. Earl observed several bookcases filled with legal volumes, almanacs, and first editions; a full bar built into a mahogany wall; a Persian rug in the room's center; and a few leather chairs facing a big, oversized desk with a giant hourglass on top of it. The room had a few paintings on the walls, and Earl recognized the one from the magazine article. It was an original modernist work from the 1930s by Max Ernst, with shapes that Earl couldn't fathom, but he still knew it was worth a great deal. The painting looked heavy, and Earl took a few moments to peruse it and decide exactly how he'd properly remove it from the wall with only one hand. Earl laid the flashlight on Bob's desk to illuminate the painting. Then he moved into position in front of the canvas. He settled for holding the right side of the frame with his right hand, the left side with the nub of his left arm, and he positioned his right knee at the bottom of the artwork to scoot it up and unlatch it from its hooks on the wall mount. He carefully lowered the image to rest on the ground and then dragged it to the side so he could get to work on the safe.

If Earl had been confronting a state-of-the-art safe, he might have had to resort to using a drill or heavy tools, but this safe was an 86-pound Amsec with a combination lock. If your goal is to fend off petty thieves who are brandishing simple run-of-the-mill crowbars, this type of steel box will keep them at bay just fine. A professional locksmith, though, can easily crack such contraptions with just one hand and a good ear. It was a simple enough process—no need for a stethoscope or anything like you've seen in the movies.

Earl spun the dial with a slight amount of trepidation. He took his time, slowly rotating the dial one way, then another, back in the other direction, and finally—*click*. The steel bolts retracted. He pulled the lever, and the door released. Earl exhaled noisily and then heavily panted like he'd been holding his breath for an hour, sweat dripping from his forehead. He shook his head and said, "All right, let's see what we've got here." He wiped sweat from his brow and then grabbed the flashlight from the desk and popped it into his mouth, aiming into the safe's dark interior.

He pulled items from the safe one at a time and laid them on Bob's garish desk. There were some manila file folders, none of which contained anything about finances or government entanglements. There was Bob's will, his children's birth certificates, corporate documents, and tax filings—nothing out of the ordinary. Then something in the back of the dark steel box caught Earl's attention, something he had seen before: a small, black velvet bag tied closed with a lace cord, the way sweatpants are closed with a drawstring. Earl carefully placed the documents and manila folders back into the safe and removed the velvet bag. He scrutinized it with his hand, feeling the contents and knowing it was his last chance to salvage the risky evening of virtuous intrigue by finding proof of Bob's crooked dealings. He imagined the evidence being so significant and urgent that newspapers would praise him; he imagined the culprits being promptly removed from office and charged with crimes, so no one would mind that he broke into a home to find his evidence. It was the childish pipedream of a man so consumed by his conspiracy theories that he could fabricate any confirmation bias necessary.

Earl loosened the drawstring, carefully poured the bag's contents onto the desk, and then gasped at what spilled out. Four sparkling blue diamonds rolled onto the desk, each around the length of a long fingernail. Earl knew nothing about fine jewelry, but it was clear enough that they could be worth millions, which almost guaranteed they were connected to money laundering or an otherwise nefarious activity. Earl was sure he would find the answers if he just looked hard enough. He paced the room facing the desk, considered his options, reconsidered and second-guessed, and then repeated the process. He glanced from the safe to the painting, then to the window, and finally back to the diamonds. A stout ceramic planter on Bob's work desk contained a Juniper bonsai tree, and small rocks roughly the same size as the diamonds lined the base of the planter. Earl took four of the stones from the planter, put them into the velvet bag, and stashed the bag in the far back of the safe.

He had just closed the safe, locked it, and exhaled deeply when he heard a car moving up the driveway. The noise shook him. Could it be Bob returning home early? Or maybe someone had identified him breaking in and called the police. Maybe there was an alarm system after all, but a silent one. In that split second, every possibility occurred to Earl, and he realized he wasn't built for the bold life of a cat burglar. He should have stuck to his day job, teaching high school kids lessons they would forget a week later. He was not one for danger and could feel his stomach tensing into knots.

Earl rushed to the office window behind the desk and peered out the blinds. What he found didn't provide him any comfort. A black SUV had passed the gold entrance gate and was steadily rolling toward the house, already nearing the circular driveway. It was Bob's Lincoln Navigator. He had made it home early after all. Earl looked around the room, panicked, and then picked up the four diamonds and hurried into Bob's windowless bathroom attached to the office. He turned on the light and scanned the room, looking for a practical solution. In the toilet, of all places, something caught his attention. There it was, in all its disgusting glory: a floating condom in the water basin, surely well used. One man's trash is another man's salvation, or something like that.

Earl set the four blue diamonds on the sink counter and hunched over the toilet, looking at the clear rubber in excited disgust. Then he looked at the door, calculating whether he could flee through the hallway and out of the kitchen unnoticed. But then he remembered his age, his bad knee, and his gnawing fear of being shot running from a stranger's house. Oklahoma is one of those states where just about everyone owns a gun. It was a near certainty that Bob owned one, and Earl wanted to die from old age, not from the bullets of someone defending his home from a one-armed, ski-masked vigilante.

Earl looked at the floating johnny, knowing he might have only another minute or two until Bob Sockolosky discovered the presence of an intruder, at which point Earl would undoubtedly be searched and the diamonds would be found. He bit his lip while staring angrily at the receptacle of human spawn circling the vessel of human waste. Then he did the unthinkable. Earl Derkatch reached into the toilet bowl, apprehensive at first, then quickly, as though he were ripping off a Band-Aid. He snagged the condom from the water and tossed it into the sink. Making haste, he sprayed liquid soap on top and inside of the sheath and turned on the faucet to give it a quick cleansing rinse, as though something like that could ever be sterile again, let alone after being in a toilet. Once satisfied that it was clean as it could be, he held it upside down to empty it of water. Then he placed the four diamonds from the counter into the contraceptive. He tried to squeeze all the air out of it and tied the end into a knot like a balloon, which is not so easy to do with just one hand. Earl looked into the mirror with a grimace, not sure if he was about to cry or vomit. Then he tilted his head back, lifted the condom above his head, and placed it into his mouth. He tried to swallow it like a drug mule coming in from Tijuana. The slamming of the house's front door made Earl panic again as he completed a problematic gulp.

Earl quietly turned on the sink faucet and splashed his mouth with water before fully swallowing the contraband into his heaving, unwilling belly. Then the nasty task was complete: he had safely stored the treasure inside himself. He sighed, turned off the bathroom light, and committed to waiting five minutes for Bob to go to bed. Then he would try to sneak out. The best-case scenario was that Bob would be tired and go straight to his room upstairs. That was most likely, Earl reasoned. After all, what purpose could Bob possibly have for going into his office so late? However, if Bob did go into his office, he would find the painting on the ground, check his safe, possibly discover the diamonds were missing, find Bob in the bathroom, and put two and two together. Earl prayed that would not be the case.

The minutes passed slowly. Finally, Earl summoned the courage to begin his escape. Quietly and tentatively, he turned the bathroom doorknob and stepped into the office. It was dark, and the painting was still on the floor where Earl had left it. He didn't see signs of anyone, so he took another step.

Wham!

Something struck Earl in the back of his head—something as brutal and unforgiving as a metal baseball bat. Earl toppled forward, put his hand out to brace his fall, and landed, unconscious, on the floor.

Earl opened his eyes to find himself seated and tied to one of the leather chairs in the office, except now the lights were on, two men in suits stood before him, and the safe door was open again—his worst-case scenario. The back of his head was throbbing, and he could tell there would be an enormous lump and a lasting headache. His ski mask had been removed, so Earl's pathetic, defeated face was on full display. One of the men was Bob Sockolosky, and the other was Walter Murphy, one of the vermin who worked for Bob. He likely drove Bob home, since Bob stunk of scotch. Bob poured himself a fresh glass and then pulled out a pipe and a match. He unhurriedly filled the pipe with tobacco, lit it with a match, and puffed intently. Then he sat at his desk across from Earl. Earl noticed the velvet bag on the desk, empty again, with the four Bonsai rocks sitting next to it. Despite his probable concussion, he knew that they knew.

"Good morning," Bob said sarcastically. "So who are you? What are you doing in my house?"

Earl remembered he had carried no identification with him. He had at least been wise enough for that, though he knew all they had to do to identify him was go down the road and find his car. His wallet, car insurance, and even lesson plans were all there. "Oh, uh, I was just passing by, and I thought I heard someone screaming, so I jumped over the fence and came in to make sure everything was okay. Which it looks like it is. So I can get out of your hair now if you'll just…"

"You broke into the safe and stole some diamonds just to make sure everything was all right? That's why you were in the bathroom? Making sure things are okay?" Walter had a whiny voice, but it still scared Earl.

"Yes. I do this all the time. I have excellent hearing, and if I hear someone crying out for help, I come running."

"Where the fuck are the diamonds?" the whiny voice screamed back.

"I don't know anything about any diamonds, and I, uh…" Earl didn't know what to do or say, but he knew he was not getting out of the situation without further confrontation. Walter smacked Earl across the face. The slap stung his cheek and flared up the throbbing sensation on the back of his head.

"Listen, fucker! This won't end well for you if you play this game. You have one chance." Bob held up the empty velvet bag for Earl to see. "We know they're not on you because we searched you when you were knocked out. Tell us where they are right now, and we'll let you go. Simple as that. We'll forget about this entire ordeal. Call it a night."

"Obviously, those diamonds were obtained illegally," Earl retorted. "Otherwise, you would have called the cops, and they'd be asking the questions right now."

"It wasn't me." Bob flailed his arms and stood to pour himself another scotch, agitated. "It was a one-armed man."

"I really don't appreciate jokes about my arm."

Bob nodded at Walter and took a long pull from his stiff drink. "You know, I have a feeling I saw you the other night. Were you at the casino?"

"Maybe that was someone else with one arm," Earl responded defiantly.

"Right. So that's your final answer? Not going to tell us where my diamonds are?"

Earl smiled like one of his smart-ass, trouble-making students who thought they could get away with anything. "You can't keep me here forever."

"I don't have time for this," Bob said. "I'm going to sleep. Kill him. Search his body; search his car. I'm sure it's the one parked down the road. The diamonds are here somewhere. Bury him in the spot out in Okmulgee where they're pouring concrete."

Earl gulped, and Walter pulled a revolver from a shoulder holster and pointed it at Earl.

"Not in here, you doofus," Bob said. "You'll ruin the rug. It was fifty grand. Take him out in the backyard and do him on the grass. And put a tarp in the back of the Navigator so you don't get blood on everything this time. Try to be smart, Walter. I'm exhausted. Meet me back here in the morning with the good news that you found my diamonds."

Earl felt genuine despair and prayed silently.

Bob walked to the door, paused, and then turned back to Earl. "Say. Where are my dogs?"

Earl shrugged stupidly, and Bob shook his head, heading toward the door.

"No, wait!" Earl called desperately. He figured there would be more back-and-forth, but Bob left the room.

CHAPTER 1

7:59 a.m.
Monday, May 15, 2006
(two days earlier)

The last day of my senior year in high school was one for the record books. Looking back all these years later, I believe the trouble started on the Monday of the last week of school. Life was so straightforward until then. But one event led to another, and to another, until everything snowballed and life got complicated. For what it's worth, here's how I remember it.

I pulled into the Will Rogers High School parking lot in downtown Tulsa. It was the last week of classes, so I wasn't worried about being on time, and I was blasting "Heart Attack" by Sum 41 on my car's stereo. It was two months shy of my eighteenth birthday, and I was ready to graduate that Saturday and become a free, full-fledged adult man. Soon it would be college and then a career, responsibilities, and all that nonsense. I was on the last leg of my tour through adolescence. The young are perpetually burdened with eager confidence and blind certainty of their own self-importance, and I was no different.

The sky was overcast that morning when I left home. Before heading to school, I stopped by the drive-thru at Daylight Donuts and picked up two small sausage rolls—a local pig-in-a-blanket type thing with a bit of cheese. By the time I parked next to Hernandez's El Camino in the school parking lot, it was raining hard; thick droplets came down in a torrential downpour, creating an omnipresent white-noise chorus of whooshing and splashing against the pavement. Hernandez and I had been best friends since grade school. His full name was David Hernandez, but everyone outside of his family just called him Hernandez. We usually parked near each other on the far end of the lot—in a corner as far from the main school door entrance as possible. So that's what I did that day.

The bell for class rang as I pulled into my parking space, and I was alone in the rain aside from two other late students parking their cars. Carrying my little brown paper bag of sausage rolls, I shuffled toward a side entrance with rain rinsing my hair, shirt, and socks. My feet sloshed through the already deepening puddles; I knew I'd have to deal with wet socks the rest of the day.

My homeroom that year was an easy computer elective that many students took to pad their GPA. I sauntered through the computer lab door and dropped a napkin and one of the sausage rolls on Angelica's workstation in the front row. Our teacher was absent, so we had free rein to socialize. Angelica thanked me by delivering a sweet smile. Her big, brown eyes were encircled by thin, round glasses, and her lips glistened from a thick layer of lip gloss. Despite wearing a trendy t-shirt from Hot Topic, she looked amazing. We had been friends since elementary school, and I had always had a crush on her, though I never dared to do anything about it. She set her pen down, and I noticed she had signed her name over and over on a page of her notebook, like she was practicing her signature. In any other circumstance, this would seem like the behavior of a psychopath, but she was a high school girl, and that's just what high school girls did.

"Oh, my gosh, thanks, Jon Ryan. You are the sweetest." She picked up the sausage roll from the napkin and took a small bite, then closed her eyes and muttered, "Mmmmm, so good. Thanks again, babe."

"My pleasure. How was your night?"

"It was good. I read a few chapters of that Salman Rushdie book I've been reading. What about you?"

I tried to remember what I had done the previous evening. "Um, my parents had a date night, so I just ordered a calzone from Mazzio's and watched an old movie called *Night on Earth* by Jim Jarmusch."

"I've never heard of that. Is it any good?"

"Oh, yeah. It's one of my favorites. Winona Ryder's in it, from when she was, like, twenty years old. I'll lend you my DVD."

"Thanks, love, I'd like that. Are you going to the concert tonight?"

I hated how she often called me "babe" and "love," even though she had been dating some other guy for the past year and a half. It's not like I was actually her love, so I didn't understand why she said those things. But though I didn't like it, I would have felt worse if she stopped being so sweet and flirty toward me altogether.

I responded, "Yeah, I'll see you there."

"Okey dokey. Thanks again for this, babe."

I walked to the back row of the class, where my station was, and ate my savory morning pastry while I powered up my machine. With light linoleum floors below, fluorescent lights and dropped ceilings above, and no windows, the classroom wasn't the most nurturing educational environment one could imagine. Not where any human belongs so early in the morning, at least. Our school had upgraded that year to Dell Dimension XPS 600s running on Windows XP, fully equipped with fancy, new, flat-screen monitors. The classroom was short but wide, with three long rows of computer stations fitted with little dividers, forming what looked like miniature cubicles. Most of my classmates had headphones on and were already playing *Call of Duty 2* with each other on our local LAN network by the time I logged into my device.

Cameron, the kid who sat beside me, eyed my sausage roll hungrily, removed his headphones, and said, "Thanks for bringing me one, too, jerk-off."

I shrugged. "What have you ever brought me, man? Hey, what map are you guys on?"

I finished my breakfast in three successive scrumptious bites, then logged in to the game. Cameron always killed me. He had a quirky and goofy personality but was also incredible at first person shooter video games. We had known each other for years. He was a bright, nerdy guy with whom I had spent much time in middle school. He was obsessed with dinosaurs when we were kids, but in first period that year, Cameron cared only about proving how much better he was at video games than we were. We were still friendly toward each other, but I never hung out with him outside of class anymore. He didn't go to sports games, parties, or most places I would have seen him. I ran into him at the movie theater a few times, and sometimes he came into the video store where I worked, but that was about it.

Our first-period teacher was Ms. Allen—a squirrelly old broad, if you can still say that. She was peculiar and hard to read, but I liked her, and I think most of her other students did too. She wasn't mean, and she didn't fake-smile or anything, like some of the phonier teachers at school did. Plus, she never flunked her students as long as they put in some effort. When students were having a tough time in her class, she would sit next to them and walk them through the assignments. Ms. Allen was warm and motherly in a lot of ways. Her curly, frizzy, fun hair used to be brown but was slowly turning gray. She was about a hundred pounds overweight and always wore these big, long, flowery, pastel dresses that a grandma might wear. I could picture her bringing my family a pot of stew or a casserole for a Sunday dinner, which I found both comforting and disarming, even though I wouldn't want to share a meal with her. Maintaining an A in her class all year hadn't been hard.

Her class was my homeroom throughout the twelfth grade: my first class of the day both semesters. I loved it because I could usually show up a few minutes late without her noticing, as she always stayed in the faculty lounge getting coffee and a bagel after the bell—presumably flirting with Mr. Donavan, another overweight computer teacher. A lot of teachers would not allow you to come in even a minute tardy without writing you up, but Ms. Allen never even knew as long as you made it to your seat within seven or eight minutes after the bell.

I appreciated those few minutes considering how early I had to wake up to get there; the first class of the day started at eight o'clock. From first to twelfth grade, eight o'clock butts in seats. Perpetually. Which meant being up and out of the house by 7:30. I've never been a morning person, so this schedule always felt overly sadistic. I thought 9:30 or 10:00 would be a healthier time to congregate and learn. The extra hour or two of sleep would have been a godsend for our growing bodies, and I'm sure the teachers wouldn't have minded starting a bit later too. Even now, I don't know what psychopath benefits from depriving kids of sleeping in, but I am sure somebody must. Possibly, Ms. Allen agreed with this hypothesis and regarded her late start time for first period as some sort of empathetic reparation.

By the final week of high school, senioritis had taken full effect, as grades and graduation were already determined. By that point, there were no more tests and no more homework. Most seniors had already registered for and enrolled in college (I had a solid B-average GPA and no involvement in any sports, clubs, organizations, nonprofits, or anything that could help with college applications aside from a two-year stint in the debate club and a part-time job as a video store clerk). Attendance was required simply because of a codependent routine—the school needed high attendance to receive as much money as possible from the state, and the students needed to graduate. It was a case of calendared necessity. And we had to be there bright and early. The teachers were just as excited to soon be rid of us as we were of them. When we completed our assignments, Ms. Allen let us play computer games as long as we wore headphones. So our class plugged in and played matches against each other while she tackled crossword puzzles at her desk. In return, she got a quiet and respectful class; we were grateful to her for the playtime.

When the bell rang, I went to my locker to recover my backpack and jabbered with some friends for a minute. Then I went upstairs to second period, speech class with Mrs. Woolery. All we were doing that quarter was watching movies, so I'd sometimes be able to take a little nap in her class. I remember that day clearly: I was excited about speech class because Mrs. Woolery had promised we'd start watching *Rear Window*. She popped in a VHS tape and casually mentioned that the video rental store had been out of stock of the Hitchcock version, so she opted to rent the remake with Christopher Reeve instead. I almost shouted at her for thinking that was comparable. I worked at a video store and was a real movie buff. I was about to explain that I could have brought a copy of the movie in if she'd only asked, but the scrawny pill addict next to me, Blake, told me to chill out. Blake was funny, and we often cracked jokes when Mrs. Woolery wasn't paying attention. He was kind of short with a young face, and his style was a cross between preppy and bohemian: he wore collared shirts from Hollister and American Eagle along with hemp and Puka shell bracelets and necklaces. His hair was always shining like he'd woken up early to put half a bottle of gel in it. I took his advice and put my head on my desk for a brief nap while the movie played. I hate when a movie is so great that it's remade for the sake of making more money on the same thing all over again. The redux is almost always terrible.

I liked Mrs. Woolery. She was young and attractive with blond hair—a straight-out-of-teacher-college type with wide eyes still full of optimism. But a few years after I graduated, I heard from one of my old classmates that she was caught having an inappropriate relationship with a male student, so she got fired and divorced. Hearing about a male teacher fiddling with kids was always disturbing, though not shocking, but hearing about a female teacher covertly dating a male student was rare. I presume she was charged with sexual battery or something, but I still can't say if this was the truth or mere rumor. I probably didn't hear about it at the time because that's not the type of thing our newspapers liked to write about back then, and the kid's parents likely wanted it kept quiet too. I wonder why she never made a pass at me if she was into that sort of thing. I mean, I was an attractive enough kid back then—though slightly short and overweight. But then again, maybe she did, and I was just too naïve and self-absorbed to notice the signals. Women were a great mystery to me in those days, as they still are now, but not in the ways they are to a teenage boy. I liked girls and thought they were beautiful, but I knew little about how to talk to them beyond how I spoke to my buddies.

Back then, most of my energies went toward having fun with my friends, drinking, and smoking. I minimized schoolwork and effort in any way I could, cut corners wherever possible, and did only the bare minimum. Yet I would spend an inordinate amount of time on other projects, like figuring out how to beat a drug test. Our school had recently mandated a random drug screening policy for anyone active in sports or extracurriculars, including kids in marching band and the debate club, if you can believe it. The drug tests were random, and once your number was up, you were informed during first period that you'd need to take a drug test in the nurse's office later that day at lunch. I wasn't into hard drugs or anything, but I smoked weed occasionally on weekends with my friends and knew marijuana could stay in your system for weeks after smoking it. So I went to work devising a surefire method to pass.

The most challenging part of the drug test was that the tube you had to pee into had a marker with a specific color that notated the temperature of the pee when it hit the glass tube. If you tried to fill the tube with someone else's urine, which was often stored at room temp or refrigerated, the pee would not be warm enough. So the temperature feature was a failsafe that helped them nail you.

To get around the system, I bought a thermometer and a plastic container with a sort of straw thing at the end that I could tape to my leg along with a hand warmer. I ran a few tests at home to see exactly how fast the hand warmer raised the temperature of liquid in the container. I practiced enough times to know that between five and seven minutes after I applied the hand warmer, the pee would reach the ideal human body temperature of 98 to 99 degrees Fahrenheit.

When, in the first semester of my senior year, my name got pulled and I was informed I'd have to take a drug test that day, I asked a friend who didn't smoke weed if he would wee-wee into my container, which he did without hesitation. Then at the beginning of lunch, I went to the bathroom and taped it and a hand warmer to my upper thigh exactly five minutes before entering the nurse's office. She had me use her office bathroom to pee into the tube, and she left the door open to ensure there was no funny business. I urinated with my back to her so I was able to discreetly fill the tube with my friend's pee, which was warmed to the correct temperature by then, and I passed her little test. That meant I at least didn't get suspended from school or booted from the debate club.

It's worth explaining to those who weren't there or simply don't remember that in early 2006, we were still a year away from the invention of, or even announcement of, the iPhone. I felt I was at the forefront of the technological age because I had a flip phone. It was two years before the app store was launched and three years before Uber was a company. Avoiding DUIs and DWIs in those days—before ride-sharing apps existed—was a more complicated endeavor. I would be lying if I said no one in my friend group ever made the unforgivable choice to drive while intoxicated, but at least nobody ever got hurt within our small circle. I regret some of our dumb decisions, but we were the products of our environment…or insert some other apt excuse. We were in the middle of the millennial generation, the last generation to grow up without today's heavy screen usage or conveniences. We didn't grow up putting brand-new iPads and iPhones on our Christmas lists like the spoiled tech-addict brats of ages since. I played *RoboCop 3* on Sega Genesis, *Goldeneye* on N64, and *Metal Gear Solid* on PS2. When we were seniors in high school, we'd barely upgraded to *Halo* on XBOX 360. That was the progression—none of it comparable to the number of games available and amount of time we stare at our magic phones today. We went through middle school with Michael Jordan and Barry Sanders posters on our bedroom walls. We played outside, and nobody tracked where we were all the time.

Now please don't take me to be one of those old grumps that says things like, "Things were better back in my day," or "The youth today are useless, mindless assholes." We were assholes too. Stupidity is a defining feature of youth, and we were no different. Things were undoubtedly simpler, though, and that's my point. The world was different, and it was a sweet spot in time between never-ending wars and an absolute information state. We were in elementary school during the Oklahoma City bombing and in fifth grade during the Columbine shooting, the first notorious school shooting. Back then, mass shootings in America weren't really a thing. We were in junior high on September 11. Gradually, the world got ghastlier, and people got more suspicious. Even the *Batman* movies got very dark. Our childhood idols like Kurt Cobain, Tupac, and Chris Farley were all dead by the time we got to high school. Who do you look up to once all your heroes are just fading memories?

At the time of this story, I'd just watched the two music documentaries *The Devil and Daniel Johnston* and *Dig!* Both documentaries were about artists that suffered various addictions and mental health issues that caused them to spiral out into obscurity and irrelevance until some people decided to make documentaries about their lost potential, and they both resonated with me more at the time than they probably would now. Our teenage angst at that time was further fueled by early internet mental illnesses and the peak of a nationwide opiate epidemic. At lunch we regularly traded for Xanax, Vicodin, and OxyContin. We downloaded thousands of songs illegally off LimeWire and Napster and then burned CDs for each other to listen to in our cars. We were still figuring out what the internet was or could be; it was unregulated and without social media sites other than the unimposing, relatively harmless Myspace. The show *Jackass* was still in its prime and was ushering in a new world of filming yourself doing insane and homoerotic stunts for no reason other than the laughs and the eyeballs.

When you see small children today staring at iPads in their strollers, it's tempting to insist that excessive screen time is the reason for their obsessions and antisocial tendencies as they grow up, as if their behaviors are abnormal or new, just as previous generations griped when television, the radio, and the printing press sprung into existence. There may be some truth to the notion, but only the millennial generation came of age during the tumultuous time when the World

Wide Web as we know it was being spawned. Back then, by happenstance, teenagers often and easily viewed the most terrible things on the web and file-sharing sites that are relegated to the dark web today, like videos of people being executed and porn involving rape, pedophilia, and incest. I believe our generation is more fucked up and desensitized than today's constantly plugged-in toddlers with antisocial tendencies.

Once, in junior year, my friends and I stayed the night at our buddy Weasel's house, and Weasel passed out drunk while sitting on his couch watching a movie with a bowl of Froot Loops on his lap. Hernandez took the bowl of cereal, dipped his testicles into the milk, and then returned the bowl to Weasel's lap. Later that night, Weasel woke up and finished eating his Froot Loops while we all laughed at him, and Hernandez said things like, "Hey, how do my balls taste?" We found it funny, but Weasel was furious when he realized what had happened. Still, the rest of us laughed. The thing is, I can't imagine my dad and his friends would have displayed quite that level of homoeroticism in the boyish pranks of their youth. The birth of the internet and the rise of shows like *Jackass* undoubtedly influenced us. Weasel didn't talk to us for a week after the cereal incident, and going forward, we agreed to hardline rules concerning our pranks toward each other.

In some sense, that time was a new Wild West. Bottom line: life just differed from today. So I'll leave it there.

I woke up when the bell rang to signify that second period was over, and I was thankful that I'd missed most of the first half of the second-rate redo of *Rear Window*. Then I adjourned to third period—the last class before lunch— which was AP History, also on the second floor near my speech class. History was my favorite subject, and my teacher, Mr. Derkatch, was my best teacher during high school. He encouraged class discussions, and they usually managed to be interesting enough that the entire class would take turns chiming in. But during the last few weeks of school, even in his class we watched movies. It was the obvious option, given we were so close to the end of the school year and the seniors' grades were already foregone conclusions. If we didn't understand what the Cold War was by then, we were likely never going to. At least he chose better movies than those we watched in speech class, and he sometimes took requests and let us decide what to watch.

Mr. Derkatch had a gray beard and was a big guy, tall and heavy. And he was missing his left arm, like someone had cut it off just above his elbow. Rumors circulated about how he'd lost it, but he never talked about it in class. I figured one of the rumors must have been true. Someone told me he lost it while saving a child from an alligator in Louisiana. Hernandez said he heard Mr. Derkatch used to be an international art thief who got caught stealing something in Iran and had his arm cut off as punishment because that's how they do things there. Mr. Derkatch could have just told us what happened, but I think he enjoyed keeping it a mystery. He was a kind but tough sort of teacher. It was an AP class, so we had fewer assholes than the on-level classes did, but still, now and then, some wiseass made fun of his missing arm, like saying, "One hand washes the other." Mr. Derkatch would send such offenders straight to the principal's office, and Principal Trout took that type of misbehavior very seriously. He'd give at least two weeks of in-school suspension for mocking a disability, which meant you had to do all the same classwork and come to school, but you sat in a little room all day by yourself—high school's version of solitary confinement.

Mr. Derkatch had given me a copy of *Time as History* by George Grant that previous Friday, and I had perused some of it over the weekend. I kept having to go back and reread pages multiple times, and I still barely understood what it was saying. It was a collection of a series of lectures by George Grant, a Canadian philosopher, concerning Nietzsche's views of how humans understand time and history. Philosophy is such a funny occupation. You can build an entire career from supposing and re-supposing what someone in history might have meant about vaguely written opinions a hundred or even a thousand years ago. Our species has already ruminated on every idea and theory possible; all we do now is take turns describing what those ruminations mean. The idea of arguing what *time* really is seemed peculiar to me. The book said something about thinking about how we think apparently—if that gives you any clue.

In any case, I was not enjoying the book that much, but I was determined to finish it because I appreciated that Mr. Derkatch thought to give it to me. I liked nonfiction, but back then that sort of philosophical stuff felt too abstract to be exciting. The last book I had read that year, Ben Yagoda's biography of Will Rogers, had been the most interesting book I had ever read, so it set a high standard for me. It's still one of my favorite books. Often called "Oklahoma's favorite son," Will Rogers was from the Tulsa area. He lived the most incredible and fascinating life, so I liked that our school was named after him.

I sat in the far row, next to Mr. Derkatch's desk and near the front of the class, so I could be engaged in his lectures. He was kind but never one for idle chat. If you had something to contribute to a class conversation about a specific history topic, that was the time to speak. That day, after he called roll, I told him, "Thanks again for lending me that book. I don't understand it all yet, but it's fascinating. I can bring it back to you this week when I finish it if you want."

"It's okay, and I think you should keep it. You'll understand it in *time*." He laughed at his corny dad joke and then pushed play on the movie.

For once, I was excited to watch a movie in class because I had suggested the film: an Errol Morris documentary about Robert McNamara. The rest of the class seemed interested enough. Mr. Derkatch turned off the classroom lights, and we all watched the first forty-five minutes before the next bell.

CHAPTER 2

11:03 a.m.
Monday, May 15, 2006

Then it was lunch, the most crucial hour of the school day. This was a public school, mind you, so lunch wasn't ever anything to write home about, but at least you got to see your friends, and I like to think the lunch ladies did their best with the ingredients they had access to. There were nearly 800 kids in our class alone, so they split lunch into two services, and my friends and I were in the early one. Nobody is ready for lunch at 11:00 a.m., but when you force people to start their day so early, they won't complain about what time you let them eat and see their friends. Going off campus for lunch was against the rules, but around once a week my buddies and I would sneak out and drive down the road to grab some fast food just to get off school grounds for a while. It was also an excellent opportunity to smoke a joint and return to school toasty.

That day we ate in the school cafeteria. It was still pouring rain, so going outside didn't even sound appealing. Crispy chicken sandwiches and french fries were on the menu. I got my rations and brought my tray filled with the state-sanctioned serving size portions to our usual circular table with eight bolted-in, hard, round, plastic seats—no back rests on the seats, as they didn't want to make us too comfortable. Three guys and three young ladies were already at the table when I arrived—our typical crowd. Hernandez, Fonz, and Weasel sat to my left, and Tera, Alisha, and Naomi were on my right.

Hernandez was a chubby, first-generation Mexican American. His parents moved here from Oaxaca when he was five years old. His dad was a preacher at one of the million Baptist churches around town, and his mom was a housewife involved in church activities. He had two sisters: one was older, and one was his twin. We had been best friends since the fifth grade, and he drove the El Camino I always parked next to. Hernandez had bought the El Camino as a piece of junk, stripped it down, and rebuilt it himself. He was always handy with tools and cars and helped me change the oil in my Ford Bronco.

Weasel had a baby face, but the hair on the top of his head was already thinning by junior high. By senior year, he had a balding patch on the back of his skull like an old man, but he still had the face of a young boy. We spent many of our evenings senior year at Weasel's house playing drinking games since he lived with only his dad, who seemed to always be away on business. I couldn't say what his dad did for work, but he looked a little like a poor man's version of action film actor Jason Statham, so I always imagined he was a secret agent or something. Weasel's real name was Sean, but everyone in our class had called him Weasel since the seventh grade, strictly because there were already enough people named "Sean" in our grade—and he had a bit of a weasely personality.

Fonz was taller than the rest of us and looked the oldest. If we went to the right gas station at the right time, he could sometimes pass off his fake ID to buy us beer. Most nights, though, Fonz would handle the Hey Mister, which is what we called the practice of walking up to a guy in a gas station parking lot and saying, "Hey, mister, would you mind buying us some beer if we give you the money?" The practice was effective about half the time, especially when Fonz did the asking. His family had moved to Tulsa from Michigan before he was born, but his grandparents were originally from Portugal. His last name was Fonseca, so everyone in school called him Fonz—even the teachers. He shaved every day, but he'd have a five o'clock shadow by the end of soccer practice.

The rest of us looked like we were still little boys compared to Fonz. He and I would quote movie lines together a lot, usually from *Spies Like Us* or *The Jerk*, but half the time when you said something to him, his response would just be, "Nice." You can use a lot of different inflections with that word and get a million different meanings, but when he said it, I usually found it funny. Fonz's family moved to a friendly gated community when we were in tenth grade, and from then on, they had the most impressive house of all our families. By 2006, most people had switched from dial-up internet to DSL. Still, Fonz's family was the first in our group to acquire the faster home internet. We accidentally downloaded nude photos to his family computer off LimeWire a few times before we knew how to use the "clear history" function and a few other basic commands. In some circles, Fonz may have been considered a poser since he was obviously from a wealthy family yet always wore torn-up jeans with Air Force Ones and thrift store t-shirts sporting band names like Wu-Tang Clan and Incubus, and he had one stud earring, but our group didn't care about the dichotomy. He was our buddy, unapologetically.

Fonz, Weasel, and I grew up in the same neighborhood, and we all had brothers four years older than us who were also best friends, so we were sort of born into our friendship. We were similar in all the ways that seemed to matter back then. We had similar senses of humor, and we liked many of the same things. Growing up, we played hide-and-go-seek, laser tag, and backyard football. We had injured each other and lied to each other's parents for each other. We shared secrets that no one else would ever know. Hernandez and I didn't play any sports, but Fonz was the goalie for the high school soccer team, and Weasel was on the tennis team; they were both talented athletes who probably could have played in college if they'd wanted it badly enough.

Regarding Alisha, Tera, and Naomi, we never invited them to sit with us, but they did so every day, rain or shine. We had become pretty close friends during ninth grade, so they just stuck around, I guess. Sometimes they'd drink with us at Weasel's home.

Naomi was short and cute and had even been my first kiss back in fifth grade. I was waiting for the school bus at her house one morning, and she told me to close my eyes. Then she surprised me with a kiss right on the lips. Things never evolved from there, and by high school she told me I was more like a brother to her. Anytime a girl tells a boy that he's "like a brother" and she "doesn't see him that way," it's just a lovely way for her to compliment and insult him simultaneously. Naomi had been dating some cowboy all of senior year, and they both chain-smoked menthol cigarettes anytime we weren't in school. Since her boyfriend wasn't in our lunch period, she sat with us. She lived near me, and both her parents were realtors who worked together and were friends with my parents.

Our classmates considered Alisha and Tera both to be Indians, but in different ways. Alisha's family had immigrated from India, and both her parents worked for competing companies in the oil industry. She was thick and short and always had the best comebacks and funny stories. I thought she was hilarious from the first day I met her.

Tera's parents were both of the Cherokee Nation tribe, and she had two slightly older sisters who partied with us occasionally. On separate occasions in the past two years, Weasel, Hernandez, and I had each hooked up with Tera, but none of us were dating her. She didn't see any of us as romantic options, but she thought we were fun.

Of us guys, Fonz was the only one with a steady girlfriend: Elaine. But she was also in the other lunch group, so we really only hung out with her after school or between classes at the lockers.

"*Hola*, boys and girls," I said.

"Jon Ryan," Fonz identified me as I took my seat.

"Hey, Jon Ryan," the girls said, almost in unison.

The good and bad aspects of having a short first and last name and a last name often used as a first name is that most people call you by your full name. Nearly everyone in school called me Jon Ryan instead of just Jon.

"Did you hear about the football guys' prank this morning?" Weasel asked me.

"No. What was it? Are they stealing our thunder already?"

Fonz shook his head. "No. I just wrote out the rules last night. Nobody else could've known about our game unless the girls told them. But I think senior pranks are a pretty well-known practice. A rite of passage, per se."

Weasel smiled at the way Fonz said "per se."

"What'd they do?" I asked.

"They broke into the school early this morning," Weasel answered. "They put, like, a hundred baby chickens in the teacher's lounge. It's pretty funny, actually. I heard before school started, someone opened the door, and all of the chicks got out, and they were chasing them around for, like, an hour before they rounded them all up. It's making students and teachers alike laugh. Rave reviews. The bastards."

"Amateurs," Hernandez answered glibly. "How do you even get a hundred baby chickens? That's got to be, what, like, five hundred dollars or something? What the hell kind of prank costs five hundred dollars?"

Alisha answered to remind us that we boys weren't the only people at the table. "Jackson's family is rich, but they probably borrowed them from the plant or from Austin's family farm. And it's probably more like two hundred dollars if they bought them. But like I said, they probably just borrowed the chicks and returned them, you know?"

We all nodded as though we understood perfectly.

"Did any of the chickens get hurt? I mean, if they left them there all night without food and water, can't they die?" Fonz asked with heroic sympathy.

"God, you're such a pussy," Weasel declared. "They broke in after midnight, and the teachers started getting in around six. That's six hours, max. The chicks are fine. It just sucks that we have competition now. I like Jackson and them, but I honestly thought they were too dumb to pull off something like this. But it's a solid prank. They had to break into the school and everything. People might remember this."

I glanced over my shoulder to another round table in the corner where a few football players and a few girls were enjoying lunch. Jackson laughed and gave a high-five to Will, another guy on the team who was twice my size. We had all been close with them until high school, which was when they started hanging out exclusively with their team members and cheerleaders, along with the other popular kids. By senior year, we'd run into them only if we were at a party that the entire school was invited to. Fit, blond-haired, and blue-eyed, Jackson had been a backup quarterback, but they let him start a few games during senior year. He was among the most popular kids in school, but a few of us knew his secret: Jackson self-medicated with high doses of Xanax. There are periods in your life when you need different things. There's a whole swath up front when all you need is your mother's milk. Maybe there's a time in college when you just need light beer, weed, and pizza. At that moment, and for the next dozen years or so, all Jackson needed was Xanax. His eyes were usually red and glossy, and he was always smiling.

As I watched him laugh, I grew angrier, especially since he was sitting next to his girlfriend, Angelica. The same Angelica to whom I'd given my pastry in the computer lab that morning. I had always liked her. In eighth grade, we sat next to each other in three classes so spent half our days with each other. She always flirted with me and even said things to me like, "If neither of us is married by the time we're thirty, we should just get married to each other." And I agreed, even though I didn't want to wait that long, but by never making a move, I put myself in a friend zone I would never escape. I guess I always thought that for two people to date, they should be obviously mad for each other. If there's any doubt or hesitation or even shyness from either person, then the relationship is probably not worth it. Looking back, I see I was the one who was culpable for not trying harder.

The reason I was mad at Jackson was that one night, about halfway through junior year, I was standing next to him at a party, and I pointed to Angelica and told him that I had a crush on her. By the next week, I heard they'd started dating—the bastard. I don't think he even noticed her until I pointed her out at that party. I couldn't really blame him, I guess, since I had never even made a move, and she seemed to like him. He was a good guy and indeed was lovely to her. All that said, I was still jealous, so I resented him. I didn't want him to have anything to do with our senior pranks, our last attempt to be remembered at that institution.

The four of us guys—Fonz, Weasel, Hernandez, and I— had been talking for months about how all the preceding graduating classes had legendary and unforgettable senior pranks. Two years before us, a group of seniors broke into Broken Arrow High School, one of our football rivals, and stole their championship trophy from their trophy case, painted it, and left it upside down in a toilet in our school's upstairs hallway bathroom. Allegedly, they all peed on it too. People still talk about that escapade. Another year's senior class released eight pigs in the school. They numbered them by painting one to ten on their backs, but skipping two of the numbers, so it seemed as if there were actually ten pigs, which caused a fair amount of confusion when rounding them up. Before our time, there had always been a ballsy and fantastic group of guys that did something risky and memorable just before graduation.

Every senior class wants to be remembered, just as every person wants to be remembered. But most students know that outside a small circle of friends and family, most people will forget their parts in that place in time—they'll be just another brick in the wall and all that jazz. A Homeric prank was a rite of passage that seemed constantly just out of reach—fervently desired but difficult to conceive. We kept acting as if we could easily outdo any previous class's antics without question, but in the end, we had done nothing about it, and neither had anyone else in our class, at least not until that Monday morning with the baby chickens in the teacher's lounge. Every caper concept we put forth sounded like a dumb stoner idea and didn't come close to some of the epic senior pranks we'd heard about—classics like using a crane to put the principal's car on the roof or chaining tapped kegs to the flagpole. We needed our white whale.

"How are we looking on the rules? It's now or never," I demanded.

"Like I said, I wrote them up last night, and I have them right here. Be cool," Fonz said defensively as he removed a crumpled piece of paper from his backpack and unfolded it onto the table. "I present to you the official prank rules."

Weasel grabbed the paper first and quickly skimmed it.

"It says we each get one prank. And we'll all help each other?" Weasel was already trying to confirm all the finer points instead of just reading it aloud for us.

"Yes, just read—" Fonz began.

"And it says that we each pitch in a hundred dollars. What are you, a Saudi Prince, Fonz?"

"Will you just read it, asshole? Yes, it has everything we discussed on Friday; why would anything there be confusing you? It's perfect." Fonz took the paper from Weasel's grip and delivered it to Hernandez, who studied it, smiling menacingly. Once he finished, Hernandez passed it to me. I tried to smooth the crumples as I spread the paper in front of us so we could read it together. Neatly handwritten by Fonz, it read:

The Official Top Secret Prank Rules

1. Engaging in acts that cause permanent property damage, alteration, or destruction that can be construed as vandalism shall be disqualified. If the prank is viewed as harmless and silly, it shall be allowed.

2. Any prank that results (intentionally or not) in any physical harm to any person or animal will result in disqualification (except for toy poodles because they feel no pain and are, in fact, evil incarnate).

3. Each of the four participants shall commit $100 to the pot as a winner take all. All participants will vote at the end and cannot vote for themselves.

4. Each participant shall have one (1) prank and one (1) specified evening to pull it off. The other three participants will assist in any way the prank master of the evening decides. There must be some video or photo evidence of each prank for posterity.

5. Saturday before graduation, all votes for "best prank" must be cast. Will re-vote until there is at least a three out of four majority. Pranks should be judged on merits such as creativity, difficulty, originality, and, of course, how many people the prank makes laugh.

6. We, the undersigned, agree with and will be bound by the above rules.

At the bottom of the crumpled piece of paper scribbled with our potential path to notoriety, four lines awaited our signatures.

"What's with rule one? Did we discuss that?" I asked. The girls were curious, and Alisha snagged the paper so they could read it while we boys talked it out. Alisha, Tera, and Naomi whispered and giggled as they read over the file, and we continued to argue the finer details.

"I did some research online over the weekend. Senior pranks aren't really viewed as cute or funny if they're just vandalism or involve animals getting hurt. So rules one and two address that. Otherwise, we just end up with arrest records and fines we have to pay to the school," Fonz explained.

"That makes sense." I took out a pen, grabbed the document back from the girls, signed it, and then passed the paper and my pen to Hernandez. Hernandez signed it and handed it back to Weasel.

"We want to play too," Tera nagged. Both Alisha and Naomi nodded and mm-hmmed along with her.

"Yeah, we're part of the group. Let us compete. There will be more money in the pot to win," Alisha added, but we dismissed the girls outright.

"Ladies, this is more about bragging rights than money. We've been talking about this for weeks, and it has to be just the four of us. Sorry," Fonz explained sympathetically.

Weasel signed the paper, and then Fonz signed it last. He filed it away by cramming it into the bottom of his backpack with a sturdy fist.

"Sorry, ladies. You'll have to do your own. This is a boys-only endeavor," I said. They all pouted and then quickly left our table in what felt like performance-anger to sit with Jackson and the football players, as some seats had opened up at their table. They probably wanted to ask those guys if they could help with their next prank instead. The indecency.

"Do you think the girls are actually mad at us?" I asked.

"No way," Weasel answered. "They've heard us talk about this for the past month, and today they say they want to be included? You kidding me?"

"The rules are pretty specific," Fonz added. "We all have to be involved in each prank and help each other. Four people fit in a car, and we can't have a busload of drunk chicks trying to sneak around and be incognito. It wouldn't work. They'll get over it."

"Yeah," Weasel agreed. "What would their pranks be anyway? Dyeing their hair a silly color?"

This made me chuckle, and I nodded.

"So how do we start? Is there an order, or should we do odds and evens?" Hernandez asked.

"If you guys are amenable to it," Fonz said while uncrumpling another sheet of paper and flattening it on the lunch table. Then he began scribbling out his idea for the itinerary. "I was thinking of this: tonight we have the concert, so we take the day to brainstorm. Tomorrow night Hernandez goes first. Wednesday is me. Thursday is Weasel, and then Friday is Jon Ryan." Fonz finished writing out the schedule as described in his neat penmanship. "And we can each put our hundred dollars into the pot when we see each other tonight."

I was a little relieved to go last, as I didn't have any decent ideas for a plan yet, so I just nodded and said, "Sounds good," as did everyone else.

"Awesome. So it's all set," Fonz declared, and we sat there for a moment with boyish grins that implied we each had gloriously nefarious ideas brewing. However, all we actually had were dumb ideas of reenactments of better, more memorable pranks that had come before us.

"Man, our legendary senior pranks—I can't wait. Or at least mine will be hilarious. Hernandez will probably go with that silly hair color idea," I teased.

"Yeah, right," Hernandez replied. "I have my idea all set for tomorrow. I just need to stop by Home Depot after school and pick up a few supplies."

"What's your plan, Hernandez? Fill us in," Fonz said.

"No, no, no. The rules don't say I have to tell you what we're doing; it just says you all have to help. You'll see. It's layered, like a complex psychological experiment," Hernandez said.

"Our crew and the 2006 graduating class will be remembered in infamy. I love you guys," Weasel said. We took bites of our food in silence, ignoring his edict of affection and making him feel awkward.

"So who's driving to the concert tonight?" I asked.

"I think Weasel should drive," Fonz answered.

"Guys, it's just that it's our last week of high school, and I want to make sure that it's memorable. We'll all go to different colleges, and who knows if we'll keep in touch." Weasel was imploring us to indulge in some emotional soap opera, but we weren't interested. He was right, though. We'd all registered at different colleges and would probably see each other only on holidays from here on out. "But the four of us, we're solid, right?"

"Yeah, man, it's all good," Hernandez said, patting Weasel on the shoulder. "I agree. Weasel drives tonight. We should probably get to the casino around six. The tickets say doors open at five. It's an early show since all their fans are geriatrics."

"Like, we can go through anything," Weasel continued, unfazed and still desperate for some melodramatic male bonding. "We'll always still be boys, you know? We can go through anything together. Like when I hooked up with Natalie. That didn't affect us, so I don't think anything will."

We all scrunched our foreheads in confused surprise, and Hernandez was immediately livid. "You did what with Natalie? You mean my sister Natalie?" Hernandez demanded, prepared to punch Weasel in the nose.

"Oh, um, I thought we talked about this already." Weasel's face was the epitome of regret. "Didn't we?"

"You hooked up with my sister? What does that mean? Tell me you're joking right now. Please." Hernandez looked like he was ready to take a swing.

"I thought you knew, bro. I'm sorry. My bad. I was drunk on your birthday, and it just happened. It was a mistake. An honest mistake." Weasel was trying hard to weasel himself out but couldn't find the right words.

"She's my twin sister. That is not cool. It's like another version of me."

"To be fair, she's a skinnier, hotter, female version of you," Weasel answered, like he was correcting a teacher's answer in class.

Fonz and I glanced at each other and then both closed our eyes in a silent laugh.

"Man, you don't hook up with your buddy's sister. Everyone knows that. This is completely out of line. This is unforgivable." Hernandez stood up, and I wasn't sure what his next move was or if his sermon was over.

Weasel spoke calmly, trying to mend the situation. "You need some time to process. I get that. It was just the one time, I promise, and I apologize. I was trying to make the point that we're boys, and nothing can affect that."

"That's ironic, then. You're a genuine piece of shit, Weasel. I don't know how I can even look her in the face at dinner tonight, *ese*." Hernandez was always using Mexican slang to make himself seem hard. He turned to me for support. "He did this on purpose—all of it."

I shook my head and said solemnly, "Weasel's too self-absorbed to be malicious."

Hernandez nodded his head along with me. "Weasel, I can't even look at you. I'm out of here." Hernandez violently snatched his lunch tray and stormed off. I knew he'd cool down in a few hours and that we'd all be laughing about it by later that evening, but still, it was a classic Weasel move in every way.

"Hernandez kind of has a point, man. You don't bang your buddy's sister," I told him after Hernandez exited the cafeteria.

"Well. Now I know. Is this common knowledge? When would I have heard about this? She liked it. It was even her idea."

Fonz and I roared, and Weasel grinned.

"He'll cool off, man. Water under the bridge," Fonz said.

"Yeah, why did you decide to tell him that shit today? You said it like it was no big deal, but I don't think any of us knew you hooked up with Natalie. That's so fucked, man. That's hilarious. Some real sociopath-type shit," I said, chuckling.

Weasel put his hand to his chin and puffed, "Hmm. I could have sworn I had already told him about it. Or I thought Natalie told him. Honest mistake, I guess."

That made Fonz snort. "Bro. Always being such a weasel. At least it's on brand."

"Well," Weasel answered, "at least he doesn't know I hooked up with his older sister too."

Fonz and I laughed, and I said, "What? Are you trying to bang his whole family or something?"

Weasel laughed his obnoxiously high-pitched, weaselly laugh. "Yeah. His mom and dad are up next. So are we set on the pranks, or is Hernandez going to be a bitch and chicken out now? Did he sign the contract or not?"

"He signed it. We all signed it, and we're all legally obligated now. He's up first tomorrow night, and he'll be down for it. Just apologize to him at the concert or something," Fonz explained like a trained arbitrator.

After lunch, I had English class and then math. I had a B in both. English was easy for me, but I'd had to cheat on my math final the previous week to keep my grade point average up. Someone in the period before me had lent me their notes from the last test with all their work and equations, and the teacher hadn't noticed that I was just copying them down on my test. I always thought it funny how math teachers said things to us when we were growing up like, "You won't have a calculator on you all your life. You need to learn this stuff." Then, as if on cue, smartphones were conveniently invented a year after we graduated, and basically everyone on the planet has had a calculator on them ever since. Plus, I have never once in my entire adult life utilized a formula from my high school or college math classes.

After math, I went home and took my golden retriever for a run, as it had stopped raining for a while. Stringer Bell was technically my little sister Heather's dog. She got him as a Christmas present when he was still a tiny puppy, and then, as many kids do, she lost interest and barely gave him the time of day, let alone proper playtime or exercise. He was a typical golden retriever, always happy and wanting to play, so I felt terrible for him. She had given him the cute name Bubbles, which happened to be the name of a character in *The Wire*, so I started calling him Stringer Bell, and it stuck. Eventually, we all called him that. Junior and senior year, I tried to take him for a run once a day when I could, or at least for a long walk off-leash on the dirt trails near our house. Sometimes I brought a soccer ball to kick while running with him. I never let him take it from me because I was nervous he would pop the ball with his sharp teeth, and I didn't want him to deflate it. It's funny the things you remember. Stringer Bell is long gone now, and I've had other dogs since, but I still think about him sometimes, about how happy he always was to see me and how I never let him play with that soccer ball. It makes me laugh to think that after all the nice things I did for him, he might have just seen me as the guy who wouldn't let him play soccer. Like, maybe he was born to play it. I could have been sitting on a classic Air Bud-type situation without realizing it. Who knows?

One hot summer day when Stringer Bell was still a cute puppy and before Heather lost interest in him, she and I were outside playing with him, running around as we used to when we were kids—back when playing was the ultimate human experience. That week, our parents had gotten a small, plastic kiddie pool for our fenced-in backyard for Stringer Bell to play in. The first time we filled it up with water, Stringer Bell started splashing and digging like he was searching for a treasure, making Heather and me laugh. We had been running around in the dirt barefoot all day when Heather jumped in the tiny plastic pool and started kicking water, splashing along with Stringer Bell.

She was just a kid having fun with her puppy, but I told her, "Hey, get out of there with your dirty feet."

She didn't get out, but she did stop splashing to look at me defiantly. "Stringer Bell is in here barefoot too."

"Yeah," I agreed. "But he doesn't know better, and he's drinking out of there. What if I put my dirty feet in your drinking water?" I barked at her like she should be ashamed of herself, and she bowed her head and quickly stepped out of the plastic pool, knowing I was right. Stringer Bell looked at her with melancholy puppy eyes; he had been having fun before I got all self-righteous and stopped the fun for his supposed benefit. It wasn't that Heather didn't care about Stringer Bell. She was just too young to train or treat a dog properly. Dogs don't know what they need, just like kids don't.

Five years younger than me, Heather was a real straight-A dweeb who was nosy and prying and always told our parents everything, so I was careful about what I admitted to her. I guess she was too busy getting me in trouble to play with her dog. It was as if she enjoyed seeing our parents mad at me. Maybe it pleased her to feel like their favorite child. We're closer to each other now than we were then. She was always a bright kid who read many books, but she was also a little stupid in some ways; she understood little about how life operated outside of her friend group and our family.

After walking Stringer Bell that day, I showered and got ready for the concert. Our parents worked at the same oil company and usually got home around six. I would be gone by then, so I told Heather to let them know I had gone to the concert and should be home around 10:00 p.m. Hernandez and Fonz worked together at Fuddruckers as line cooks making burgers, and I had been working at a video rental store for the past two years, but we all got the night off for the show. Weasel was free because he didn't have a job; I don't think he had one until college. I had actually taken two weeks off to make room for all our graduation activities. Taking two weeks off the job wasn't easy to schedule, but my manager was a sweet old lady who covered my shifts and told me to enjoy and remember my end-of-high-school moments. "You're only there once," she would say sagely.

At 5:30, Weasel pulled into my driveway to pick me up. He was smoking a joint. "What if Heather saw you smoking, man?" I exclaimed. The laws on smoking pot were strict back then, so we had to be careful around tattlers.

All he said was, "Well, let's go."

I got into Weasel's car, and we headed to the Hard Rock Hotel & Casino in Catoosa, a casino owned and operated by the Cherokee Nation. Catoosa is famous for the Blue Whale, an endearing twenty-foot-tall, eighty-foot-long blue metal whale statue that is one of the few surviving interesting attractions of old Route 66 and that the locals call the Big Blue Whale. Hernandez was still furious with Weasel, so Fonz was driving with Hernandez separately, and we all planned on meeting up at the casino before the show to smoke and bury the hatchet. We had tickets to see Three Dog Night perform at the casino and knew some other kids in our class were also planning to be there. Going to the show was more of an excuse for a social occasion than anything. Three Dog Night was already an old act by that point, and it wasn't like we were groupies. Still, they had a few classic hits we liked.

CHAPTER 3

6:28 p.m.
Monday, May 15, 2006

Weasel drove a black 2002 Honda Civic with a manual transmission, and he didn't exactly take excellent care of it. He paid to have all the windows tinted and a top-of-the-line after-market subwoofer system installed in the trunk, but those were the only parts of the car he spent any money on. When Weasel played loud rap music, you could hear the bass shaking his car from a block away. The car was filthy. He never cleaned the inside.

Weasel got the Honda Civic when he turned sixteen, even though he didn't know how to drive a stick shift, so we all did our part to help him learn. Fonz, Hernandez, and I spent half an hour in an empty parking lot showing him the basics one day, and then we made him drive around town by himself while the three of us followed closely behind him in Fonz's car to make him nervous. We'd pull up behind him at an intersection, and whenever he would inevitably stall and kill the car, Fonz would lie on his horn, honking obnoxiously. Hernandez and I would stick our heads out of our windows and yell at him like we were irate strangers in a hurry to get someplace. To us, it was hilarious, and we spent about two hours driving around town like that. Weasel would do fine shifting from first gear to second and then from second to third, but almost every time he came to a stoplight and had to shift from neutral back to first gear again, the car would kick forward, stall, and die. And we would be right behind him every time, honking and shouting mercilessly while horrified strangers looked on from their cars like they thought we were the worst people. Tough love and trial by fire worked, however, and by the end of that day, Weasel had stopped stalling and was proficient at driving a standard.

As Weasel drove to the casino, it started lightly raining again. Luckily, the venue for the show was indoors, so the rain didn't matter, but it worsened the traffic, and we arrived later than we had planned. When we pulled into the parking lot, Hernandez and Fonz found their way to Weasel's Civic and hopped into the backseat. We all gave Fonz our hundred dollars to hold until the prank contest was over, and then we got down to business. We were excited to try the weed and psychedelic mushrooms I had procured a few days prior. The weed was the best cannabis available to our crowd. Our dealer, an older guy named Pete, claimed all his products were shipped in from California via FedEx, and we thought that sounded like some big-time Tony Montana shit. Both substances, weed and mushrooms, were policed and prosecuted at the time, especially in Oklahoma—a state that still holds a few ridiculous legal records, like most life sentences for marijuana in the nation. Such being the case, when we were growing up, partying often felt like an episode of *Fear Factor*, but for all the wrong reasons.

In Weasel's car, I rolled two large blunts and then divvied up the mushrooms. We each forced the terrible-tasting fungus down our throats, chomping it painfully and washing it down with a few warm beers Weasel had in the car. It was advised that we should each eat about an eighth, which is 3.5 grams, but I had mistakenly bought 20 grams, so the four of us each ate an even five. I now know that five grams is far too much for any one person, but back then I thought a larger amount would make for an enjoyable six- to eight-hour trip. The concert would be over within two hours, so we planned to either bum a ride home or call a taxi rather than attempting to drive during an extreme mushroom trip.

We finished consuming the shitty-tasting mushrooms, which would still take another hour to kick in, and I lit up one of my blunts. Hernandez had cooled off and stopped being so mad about Weasel and his sister, but he still didn't want to discuss it or even talk to Weasel. He tolerated Weasel's presence, which we understood was the first step toward reconciliation. As the driver and DJ, Weasel was playing Jurassic 5 on his car's bass-heavy speaker system as I lit the blunt, and then he switched it to Three Dog Night to help set the pre-show mood. The band's lineup had changed throughout the years, but they had not stopped touring since the late 1960s, which I thought was terrific. We were all red-eyed and properly sedated when we finished the blunt. Hernandez and Weasel were friends again and had forgotten why they were fighting in the first place. When we opened the car doors and let the hotboxed air spew into the parking lot, a few older couples stared at us with judgmental disdain. Hernandez put on some dark sunglasses, smiled at one couple, and confidently said to them, "Evening, folks. Feeling lucky?"

Weasel locked his car, and we strolled toward the casino entrance to find the show. When we entered the lobby, we paused for a minute to take in our surroundings. From our stoned vantage point, we observed the depressing amalgam of a few hundred older people slowly playing slot machines while ignoring each other. They stared at their "lucky" machines replete with jangly music, beeping, and the sound of whirring spinning wheels to give them a false sense of excitement and fun—upbeat sounds like you hear at carnival games. The old folks were frighteningly addicted to their flashy slot machines in much the same way we would all become addicted to screens and phones just a few years later. I did a double-take when I noticed my history teacher, Mr. Derkatch, sitting on a swivel chair playing slots. He was easy to spot, but he missed me. I was too stoned to say hello.

We walked through the lobby, passing its four bars and two restaurants. One restaurant served burgers and bar food, like chicken strips. The other was a pizza joint. I caught a whiff of a supreme pizza being pulled out of an oven, and my eyes closed instinctively to dissect the ingredients. Ever since I was fourteen, all I wanted out of life was to own a small Italian bistro and pizzeria with my very own brick pizza oven. I have always loved those huge pizza ovens. I can't tell you why. But a good pizza can be reason enough—just ask anyone with half a tastebud. None of my lineage is Italian, but I love Italian food and the Americanized spins on it. I had no delusions of culinary grandeur. My goal was never to open some Michelin-star Italian joint in New York—just a one-location spot for pizza, lasagna, spaghetti, and paninis in a suitable location where I could serve a decent, humble meal. Mostly, I wanted out of my hometown. I was afflicted with that common youthful urge to start fresh somewhere new and see a bit of the world. I wanted to be a foodie Steve McQueen.

We reached the venue entrance, presented our tickets, and entered about fifteen minutes before the music started. The opening act was a band I had never heard of, and they were playing their last song before clearing the stage for the main event. It was a general admission show with no assigned seating—standing room only. I prefer that to sitting in designated seats at concerts. Maybe the music hits you differently when you're standing, or perhaps it's just the freedom to move around that I enjoy.

We squeezed past all the old-timer fans, got as close as we could to the stage, and found other cliques of students from our school drinking from flasks and looking rowdy and ready for fun. The mushrooms still hadn't taken effect, but we expected a shift in consciousness at any moment. I don't think the other kids were on mushrooms, but for all I know, they might have been. The football guys were there, as well as some other kids I recognized and said hello to while we waited for Three Dog Night to emerge. I saw a few different groups of young people I assumed were our counterparts from nearby high schools, but mostly, the average age of the audience was over sixty-five.

The band made their entrance. The first two songs they played were newer songs, not their big recognizable hits, and the lead singer looked old enough to be my grandfather. Then they played "Never Been to Spain," and everyone in the audience cheered and sang along, especially every time the lyrics mentioned Oklahoma. I took the song as a sign that it was time to spark up the second blunt to help push the mushrooms into effect. The trickiest part of a mushroom trip is when it first kicks in because you have to convince your brain to give up control and go for the ride; the weed would help with that acclimation. I pulled the blunt from my pocket and lit it, and then I took my time taking three or four puffs before passing it on to Hernandez on my left.

Just as Hernandez placed the blunt to his lips and was about to inhale, a security guard brushed past me and put his hand on Hernandez's shoulder. Then the guard took the blunt from Hernandez and physically escorted him out of the audience. We knew that certainly wasn't a good sign, but there was nothing we could do about it, so we kept singing along and acting like we didn't even know him. I'm sure he would've done the same if the roles had been reversed. At the time, we thought the security guard had just thrown him out of the concert. But later, we learned he took Hernandez to the hallway and had an officer arrest him for possession. Never once, before or since, have I ever seen someone get arrested for smoking weed at a concert. The authorities usually turned a blind eye in that scenario. I don't know why it happened— maybe because we were in Oklahoma during an era when such things were still done, or because we were in an Indian casino, or because the crowd was mostly older, or because the venue was indoors. I can't say for sure, but Hernandez was handcuffed, taken to jail, and charged with possession of a controlled substance. The timing was fortuitous, as the security guard nabbed Hernandez a moment after I handed him the blunt, so I felt relief along with a slight sense of regret and responsibility, but not too much. The worst part for him would be the headache of dealing with bureaucratic legal drama while his heavy dose of mushrooms kicked in. He was in for a strange evening.

When next the band played "Mama Told Me Not To Come," everyone sang along. We'd forgotten entirely about Hernandez by that point. Reality became what was right in front of us. If anything, I was a little disappointed that the last blunt of the evening was confiscated. We found Tera and Alisha, and they danced next to us. Angelica even joined in and danced with me for a song. More than an hour had passed since we ate the mushrooms, and I could feel a tingling sensation roll over my brain and take hold of the wheel. Fonz squeezed back through the crowd toward the bathroom, and I realized I had to pee also, so I followed him and left Weasel dancing with the girls. Of the bathroom's six urinals, only the one next to Fonz was vacant, so I walked up to it and shouted to him, "This must be where all the dicks hang out!" My delivery was either pitch-perfect or the mushrooms had kicked in with an ultra-giggly phase because when Fonz heard me say this, he bent forward, laughing hysterically, and even peed on his shoes a little. I unzipped at the urinal next to him and continued my bit while peeing. "Ooh, this water is cold. And deep." Again, Fonz lost it and scrunched his face as he let out a crazed, cackling howl. None of the older men in the restroom laughed. They just eyed us suspiciously, and I am sure they could smell the perfume of marijuana on us.

"Nice," Fonz said, then returned to giggling.

We both finished peeing, zipped up, and went to wash our hands. I said in a more serious tone, but still loud enough so everyone else in the bathroom could hear, "You know, it's a shame they captured Hernandez. He'd robbed sixteen banks before they caught up to him."

Fonz giggled at this but didn't laugh as he had at my first few jokes—at least, not pee-on-yourself kind of laugh.

"Poor Hernandez," Fonz said. "I wonder what his dad will say. The guy is a preacher."

By the time we returned to our spot in front of the stage close to our classmates, the drugs had fully taken hold of our brains, and we might as well have been at a factory in space that created classic rock transcendence. The concert lasted for another hour, but it felt like no more than eight minutes. We weren't dancing anymore. We just bounced our heads along to the music and swayed, entranced by the stage's beats, lights, and energy. Those old geezers put on a hell of a show.

Fonz's girlfriend, Elaine, arrived late, found us, and offered to drive us all home later since she was sober. Tera suggested we stop by for a drink after the show since her parents were out of town. Four other cars were parked at Tera's house when we arrived. Elaine parked her vehicle on the street next to Tera's mailbox right as Weasel put *The Soft*

Parade album by the Doors on the speakers. Weasel, Fonz, and I begged Elaine to let us stay in the car and listen for a bit.

"Okay," she agreed. "But turn the engine off. Just don't let the battery die. If you guys end up staying here for long, start the car every twenty minutes or so. And don't drive anywhere. You're all fucked up."

"Babe, we'll talk about this later," Fonz told her, giggling. Shouting this at her around other people, as if something serious were happening between them, was an ongoing joke of his. There was never a follow-up later, and she usually just rolled her eyes. Fonz found it funny, and either I had grown to appreciate it or the drugs had because I found myself chuckling.

Elaine laughed and nodded, then she kissed his cheek and closed the car door. As she went into Tera's house to visit with other drunk teenagers who had gone to the concert, we turned up the music. Fonz and I each smoked a yellow American Spirit cigarette, and the next thing we knew we had listened to the entire album. Fonz started the car to make sure the engine wasn't dead, ran it for a few seconds, and turned it back off; then we went inside the house. About ten of our classmates were playing drinking games and talking. We'd eaten far too many mushrooms, and the vibe shift from Three Dog Night to the Doors and then to loud, drunk, idiot kids was too much to bear.

Jackson was there. He was very drunk and came over and shook my hand, smiling like he had just won the World Series. "Jon Ryan! What's up, bro?"

"Not too much, man. We took some mushrooms and saw Three Dog Night."

"Oh, man, right on! I was working so I couldn't make it. It was the shit, though, right?" He swung his hand out again, prompting me for another handshake. I obliged. I hated when young, amateur drunks wanted to agree and shake hands over and over like some lightweight bro trope. Sometimes they'd get excited and want to shake your hand five or six times in a single conversation. I could already sense our situation was heading in that direction, and one or two handshakes per conversation was my limit. I backed away slowly while flapping my arms like a bird and stepped into the backyard by myself.

Fonz, Hernandez, Weasel, and I had all been drinking together since we were fourteen, when Weasel's older brother bought us nasty dark beer that came in black tallboy cans and had 20 percent alcohol by volume (ABV). He had to buy it at a liquor store since only liquor stores were allowed to sell beer stronger than 3.2 percent ABV in the state. I can't remember the name of that beer, and I'm not sure if it's even made anymore. I remember it tasted gross, and after drinking two or three of them, we'd be slurring and stumbling around. By senior year, we could handle ourselves like experienced alcoholics and didn't act like drunk little boys who wanted to agree with everyone and shake hands a million times.

In the backyard, I lit a fresh American Spirit and walked around Tera's large, fenced-in property. I was startled when a big, beautiful, brown horse stuck its head over the fence to neigh hi to me.

"Hello, there," I said. The horse responded to me with another neigh, though louder this time. I nodded and continued talking to it. "You won't try to shake my hand ten times, will you, horse? No, you won't. You're a smart horse. What's your name?" The horse just stared at me like it knew I was on drugs.

I looked around the backyard and, at the far end, spied a fishing boat covered with a tarp. Behind it sat a camper trailer that looked like it had been there a thousand years. One song from the Doors album repeated in my mind, and then the nighttime didn't look so dark. The moon was out, and the lighting was fine, but the mushrooms made everything brighter. A glow surrounded the moon; it looked how I imagine headlights at night look to someone with astigmatism. Clouds shaped like fuming, frowning faces scattered the sky. I had a sense that the chirping crickets had been singing the same song since time began. The horse watched me closely as I took in the sights and sounds around me. I looked up at the tree branches above me, and I swear the leaves were swaying to the rhythm of the Doors song in my head, even though I don't remember any wind. I rubbed my eyes and smiled, happy about my incredible mushroom overdose experience. When I opened my eyes again, the grass was smiling, the earth was breathing, and the horse was laughing loudly at me—I heard a real, human, female laugh. A deep, sincere, deliberate laugh. I looked at her, a bit surprised but also delighted.

"What's so funny?" I asked, smiling at her.

"Just horsing around," she answered. The beast had a gravelly old cowgirl voice like she'd been around the block a time or two.

"It's a nice place you got here," I said.

The horse looked around and nodded a slow, long nod. "It's not bad. You're friends with Tera, huh?"

"Yeah, she's a friend."

The horse neighed again, almost like it was upset by my answer. "Are you sleeping with her?"

"No! Ha ha, I mean..." I don't know why, but I was nervous about having such a personal conversation with the horse. It felt like being grilled by Tera's mother, I guess. "We've hooked up before, but it was over a year ago. I think she kind of did it out of pity, so I wouldn't be a virgin anymore."

The horse nodded again, and we both looked away from each other. I looked up at the moon and saw three angry clouds instantly turn into happy, smiling faces. I backed up to the porch, found an ashtray to put my cigarette out, and asked the horse, "So what were you laughing about?"

"Just thinking about a joke I heard yesterday. It's stupid. You won't like it."

I walked over and leaned my arms on top of the fence. The horse stayed still, staring at me as I implored, "Tell me. I like stupid jokes."

"Okay, fine. How do animals ask a llama's name in Mexico?"

"I don't know," I said, already smiling.

"Como te llama." The horse looked at me, waiting for a reaction, and I chuckled.

"That's good. I like that. You're all right."

Now, you may not believe I really had a conversation with a horse, but whether you believe it or not doesn't really matter. It happened. It's in the past, and as Friedrich Nietzsche said, "If you gaze for long into an abyss, the abyss gazes also into you."

The horse and I talked some more, and at one point, I ranted and raved about meatballs. I told her that when I was sixteen, I started cooking meatballs for my family once a month—not to serve in spaghetti, but to put in fresh French rolls from the local bakery. Everyone who tried my meatball sub sandwiches agreed they were off the charts. In fact, they were so good, I'm going to digress in my story to tell you the same recipe I told the horse, which is simple enough for a teenager to nail.

You start by sautéing one whole diced onion, four or five sliced garlic cloves, and two or three diced jalapeños. Once those brown, put them in a bowl to cool off. Then, in a big mixing bowl, place a pound of ground beef and a pound of ground pork—preferably grass-fed or whatever premium meat you can get your hands on. Add a cup of breadcrumbs, a cup of fresh ground parmesan, and some seasonings. You don't need too many herbs. Some salt and pepper is crucial, and then some ground red pepper, a fair amount of oregano, and a lot of fresh parsley does the trick. Use whatever amount of parsley feels right to you—and then double it. You need much more parsley than you think. That's key.

Next, add the cooled-off sautéed mixture to the bowl, using your hands to combine everything. Create racquetball-sized spheres with the mix and brown them on a hot, oiled cast-iron skillet, occasionally turning them for a proper char on all sides. When the meatballs are cooked to about medium and are the same browned color on all sides, place them in a baking pan. Bake them in the oven for fifteen to twenty minutes at 350°F, and heat up your sauce while they cook. Of course, you can make a homemade sauce, but when I was a teenager, I simply bought name-brand marinara sauces so I could focus solely on the meat.

Take the meatballs out before they overcook and get dry, and then add them to the sauce and stir. Let them cook in the sauce for at least another twenty minutes, and then start making the sandwiches. Cut a baguette lengthwise, and bake it for a few minutes until it's toasted. Then scoop about four meatballs and some sauce onto the bread. Add some sliced onion, pickled jalapeño, and a healthy amount of mozzarella, and you're all set. Half a baguette will fill you up, and you can freeze the leftovers for later. When I was a teenager, I refused to order meatballs at any restaurant because I knew they couldn't compare to mine.

But back to my story: other than meatballs, I forget much of what I told to the horse, though it felt very important and profound at the time. I just remember feeling silly and giggly for the first few hours. However, near the end of my exchange with the horse, I began feeling dejected and melancholy about high school ending, knowing my life was about to change and that I'd soon have obligations and responsibilities and a mortgage and all of that. I remember gently crying for a few minutes while petting the horse's neck while she consoled me, assuring me that more good times were still ahead.

Eventually, Fonz, Weasel, and Elaine found me in the backyard, and Elaine drove us all to our houses. I got home a little after midnight, and the place was dark. My parents and little sister were asleep, so I quietly searched the fridge and found a piece of lasagna my mom had saved for me. I microwaved it and took it upstairs and watched a movie. The lasagna tasted better than anything my mom had ever made. When the movie finished, I finally came down from my high and fell into a deep, coma-like sleep.

CHAPTER 4

8:03 a.m.

Tuesday, May 16, 2006

On Tuesday morning, I got to school late again. I didn't even have time to stop at the donut shop, but I remembered to bring my *Night on Earth* DVD for Angelica to borrow. My dad left for work at 6:30 a.m., and my mom left at 7:00 a.m. My mom woke me up before she left, but I went back to sleep as soon as she exited my room. The mushrooms had worn out my little mind, and I was exhausted. Why did school have to start so fucking early? Luckily, Heather wanted a ride to school and woke me up at 7:40 a.m., so I had enough time to throw on sweatpants and a shirt, jump in the car, drop her off at middle school, and make it to class five minutes after the bell. I hated those mornings so much that it almost made me hate my life. It's hard to be excited about life when you dread getting up each day.

Ms. Allen was still in the teacher's lounge when I found homeroom, so I gave Angelica the DVD and took my seat. I played video games through first period, slept in second period through the end of the *Rear Window* remake, and woke up in time to get to history class to watch the documentary I had suggested. By lunchtime, I was myself again. I found my usual seat with the usual crowd. It was sloppy joe day—the sandwiches were decent tasting, made with a little barbecue sauce in the ground meat. I devoured lunch within two minutes, and Naomi looked disgusted by the way I wolfed down my meal.

Hernandez gave me a fist bump after I took my seat. I used my right hand to continue pushing the sloppy joe into my mouth while I tapped Hernandez's fist with my left, and he said, "*Qué pasa, cabrón?*"

I swallowed a tasty bite and apologized. "*Hermano, lo siento.*"

He shrugged and smiled. When you're already in deep shit, you might as well enjoy it. He filled us in on his grueling evening of being handcuffed and taken to the Catoosa police station. His parents had to drive there to pick him up, not understanding why he was tripping so hard. They and the police officer assumed he had smoked some weed, but they did not know about the mushrooms. But, like us, Hernandez was as stoned as five grams can make you. His dad, the preacher, delivered some harsh but loving words, and his mother shook her head in disappointment. He said for a few minutes, she even cried. According to him, making his mom cry was the worst part of the entire evening.

He was famished when they left the police station, so they stopped at the Taco Bueno drive-thru on the way home. Hernandez said he ordered a dozen party burritos just for himself. Party burritos are tiny, but consuming a dozen is absurd. They ate at the dinner table when they got home, and as he ate his burrito, he moaned loudly in ecstasy like he was having an orgasm, shaking his head with every slow bite and growling, "Mmm, mmm, mmm. Oh, man." He remembers telling his parents repeatedly that the burritos were the most delicious burritos ever made as he dipped them into multiple side containers of salsa and queso. That went on for a half hour since he had a dozen burritos to make sweet, repulsive love to, and by the end, his lips were covered in bright yellow and red condiment oversplash. His parents watched his strange, starved space-out in abject horror. He eventually went to bed, and when he woke up sober in the morning, his parents gave him yet another lecture about needing to grow up. His experience sounded miserable, but the way he told the story made us all laugh.

"Yikes," I told him once he had finished his tale of woe. "I'm sorry I passed you that blunt, man. It was bad timing. I'm sure Three Dog Night will tour again someday, though, pal."

Alisha, Tera, and Naomi were the most supportive of him, saying things like, "You poor guy," and "Yeah, I wish it was Jon Ryan who got arrested," and other comforting words.

"What'd you guys end up doing after the show? Did the mushrooms make you hungry too?" Hernandez asked, changing the subject from his nightmare trip.

"A few of us went over to my place," Tera explained. "My parents are out of town until tomorrow. We played Presidents and Assholes, and everyone left by around eleven or twelve. Except for Colton. He stayed until, like, two." Tera snickered naughtily as she said the last part.

"Colton? Oh, you nasty girl," Weasel joked, and Tera punched him hard in the arm. Weasel flinched and rubbed his arm like he thought he was about to bruise on the spot.

"I do not feel like going to any more classes today, man. So many awful movies," Fonz said.

"We don't have any more classes today. Well, like half of fourth period, but then it's senior assembly," Naomi reminded us.

"Oh, thank God," Fonz said, rubbing his brow and temples like he had a migraine. "Those mushrooms really wiped me out. I want to go home and sleep for, like, three days."

"The senior assembly. Is that where they hand out awards for the bullshit we voted on?" Weasel asked, and Alisha nodded. "Cool. I wrote in Karl Malone on most of mine."

"The Mailman," Fonz grinned. "Nice."

"I don't think that's how it works," I said. "So, Hernandez, are you still game for the prank tonight? Or are your parents grounding you now that you're a felon?"

"Yeah, I've got something planned. Don't you worry your sweet little ass. Weasel has to drive us, though, so he's on designated driver duty tonight. I'm thinking we'll leave from his house around midnight. It's gonna be good. Very philosophical and deep. It has layers, man." Hernandez smiled deviously. "Wear something dark that you don't mind getting dirty."

"Your parents aren't pissed?" Fonz asked.

"Yeah, of course, they're pissed. I got arrested, *ese*. But I'm about to turn eighteen, and I move out soon, so they know they're gonna miss me. What happened doesn't really affect them as long as I get good grades in college. In fact, I think they're kind of happy about the whole situation because I'm going to have to go to AA meetings and take regular drug tests now. I won't even be able to smoke for, like, six months, so I'll probably be a genius the first semester of college."

"God, that's rough," Weasel answered, laughing maniacally. "I can't imagine tripping balls in a police station all night."

"It wasn't so bad, really. I think I made a friend in there."

Fonz winked at Hernandez. "I'll bet you did."

"No, really. I was at the peak of my trip in the drunk tank for about an hour before my parents got there. Some wasted guy told me he met God, and I kept asking him to tell me more about their conversation."

"You know, Jon Ryan made a friend last night too," Fonz responded. "I went outside at Tera's house and saw him having a full-on conversation with her horse, man."

This got a few laughs around the table.

"Yeah," I answered. "I think I kept asking her what her name was and told her how to make meatballs."

"Daphne," Tera answered. "She's so sweet. I'm glad you spent some time with her." Then she took a dainty bite from her sloppy joe.

"I think Jon Ryan was trying to take Daphne home," Fonz joked.

"Daphne's got more charm than the three of you combined," I said to the guys.

Lunch ended, and we all adjourned to fourth period for roll call. A few minutes later, we were released to the auditorium for the senior assembly, where we all found each other again and picked our seats in the bleachers. This was a day that all the honors kids looked forward to. Some of their parents even showed up to watch their little brats get recognized with meaningless certificates printed on thick paper and signed by the principal.

The first half hour of the assembly addressed how all the teams and clubs had performed that year. Then came awards for grades, attendance, honors, and all that crap. A few students who had gotten into prestigious colleges were asked to stand and wave, and you could tell they were embarrassed and wished their fancy Ivy League futures had been kept secret. Then began the superfluous awards, with a male and female winner for each. A kid named Erickson won "Most Talented." He did the moonwalk and lip-synced to Michael Jackson songs at talent shows every year, which was always a crowd favorite, so I wasn't surprised. The female winner for that category was Molly, a legitimately talented singer who deserved recognition because she had an amazing voice and had even been writing her own songs for the past year. I had voted for both of them.

Weasel yawned and said, "God, this is worse than watching women play basketball."

One of the math teachers went on stage to present the award for "Best Nose." No kidding. We had awards for ridiculous things like this to make as many folks as possible feel included. Even more shocking, she announced

Hernandez and a girl named Ashley as the two winners. Hernandez's frustration over the previous evening's affairs left his face, and he shot us a goofy, open-mouthed look in shock. Then he hurried down to the podium and took the microphone from the math teacher while Ashley looked on in confusion. Students didn't give acceptance speeches for these awards. Nobody had done it before, and as far as I know, nobody has done it since. But I guess Hernandez felt compelled, even though he had no speech prepared and was stuttering nervously, killing whatever potential there had been for him to get a quick laugh from his peers. "I, uh, I don't really know who to thank, but I think that—"

As Hernandez was struggling to find something clever to say, Weasel stood and shouted as loudly as he could, "Dave Hernandez has chlamydia!"

Immediately, the entire auditorium erupted into laughter, including some parents and teachers. Our principal, Mr. Trout, however, was not amused. He used two fingers to point at his own eyes, then at Weasel, to let him know he saw him and he had it coming. Even so, Weasel continued to stand and bow for a minute, basking in the applause.

Hernandez tried to come back with a smart retort but was still a stuttering mess. "Um, I do not," he said into the microphone. "I do not have chlamydia." He said it almost like he was asking a question, then gave the microphone back to the math teacher in embarrassment. The teacher and Ashley each took an extra step away from Hernandez, and, humiliated, he disappeared back into the bleachers to applause. He sat far away from our group this time. I thought the funniest bit was when a girl named Becca, who was sitting below us, planted her face in her hands because I knew Hernandez did, in fact, have chlamydia, and I knew Becca had given it to him. They'd both gone to doctors and received treatment already, but the joke was even funnier because it was true. The parents of the honors kids looked disgusted, but nearly everyone else loved the outburst. The teachers, burdened with being the event's organizers, tried to keep the show moving. Two more awards were presented. Then I felt a tap on my shoulder.

I turned to find Mr. Trout, our principal, staring at me menacingly. He signaled for me to come with him. Then he pointed to my friends. "You too, Fonz. You too, Weasel." Even Mr. Trout called him Weasel—that's how much of a weasel he was. The three of us followed Mr. Trout to his office, where Hernandez was already waiting. Mr. Trout led us into the room and took a seat at his desk while making the four of us stand and sweat. Mr. Trout had a lean build and was tall, or at least he seemed tall to me at the time. His head was bare and pink on the top, with remnants of thinning gray hair in a horseshoe shape around the sides and back.

"Sir, I didn't know Weasel was going to say that." Hernandez started talking without being asked. "I am just as outraged as you are. And in terms of the allegations, I—"

"Shut your mouth, Hernandez." Mr. Trout cut him off without apology. "I heard about some problems at a concert last night. It was off school property, but for the sake of this school's safety, we're going to conduct a sweep of all your vehicles and lockers for illegal substances to make sure nothing unlawful is occurring on school grounds. I've asked the school resource officer, Officer Dwayne, to assist me."

We stared at him, stunned, wondering how he knew about what happened at the concert the night before.

Dwayne, a fat man in a uniform, entered the office. He was an active, sworn law enforcement officer, and his role was presumably to protect the students from harm, but in this case, it was to search our lockers and cars for pot.

"Now, you can refuse the search. But if you do so, you will be suspended automatically, and you will not be allowed to attend graduation. If you allow the search and we find any illegal substances, you will be suspended, and whether to press charges will be up to Officer Dwayne's discretion. I wasn't planning to go through this hullabaloo during your last week of school, but after that outburst in the assembly, I think I need to make a point. Do you know what that point is, Weasel?"

"Eh, uh, I…" Weasel answered, unprepared for a pop quiz. "That…you're in charge here and you can do whatever you want?" Weasel answered sincerely. Sometimes he couldn't even hear his own sarcasm. It was just his nature.

"The point," Mr. Trout continued, "is that you still have a week of school. You haven't graduated yet. We let you seniors slack off a little this late in the game, but we still have rules and guidelines. You can't act like disruptive, unsupervised, druggy punks all of a sudden. Now I hope you weren't dumb enough to bring drugs onto school property, but we are going to find out. If you did, it shouldn't impact getting your diplomas, but it will mean your families will not be able to watch you walk at graduation. And I think that might upset them, so I hope you've all kept your noses clean."

"I have the best nose—spotless, sir!" Hernandez proclaimed, holding up his award for "Best Nose" signed by Mr. Trout himself, which made us chuckle.

Mr. Trout raised his voice and a vein in his forehead began to extrude. "This is not a game. Now let's get this over with. Hand your car keys to Officer Dwayne."

First, they scavenged our lockers but found nothing but typical items like books and backpacks. Then we moved to the parking lot, where Dwayne conducted a sweep of our cars one at a time. Fonz's car was still at the casino since his girlfriend had taken us home. Weasel, however, had returned to the casino early that morning to pick up his car, so the three of ours were available for the petty inspection. First Dwayne probed Hernandez's El Camino. He found a Playboy magazine under the driver's seat, but that wasn't illegal, so he moved to my Bronco, which was clean and empty. Finally, he examined Weasel's Honda Civic. The floorboards were covered in trash, so it took him a while to conduct the sweep. Dwayne and Mr. Trout seemed desperate to find something. Dwayne moved up the front seat and rubbed the fabric floorboard, where he found a small handful of marijuana seeds. He put them in a plastic bag and nodded as if he had just found something really damning. Then he searched the bottom of the center console, where he discovered a small glass pipe in which Weasel sometimes smoked weed; for Mr. Trout, unfortunately, that was more than enough.

Even though they had found no drugs in Weasel's car—only seeds and paraphernalia—they cited Weasel for drug possession. Mr. Trout informed Weasel's dad and officially suspended Weasel from his last week of high school. He was forbidden to walk at graduation. Weasel's dad was out of town for work, as usual, so at least Weasel didn't have to deal with the repercussions in person, but he had to have an upsetting phone conversation. His dad knew that being suspended for a pipe and a few seeds was outrageous, but he still yelled at Weasel for a minute and told him he needed to stop being so stupid.

The whole thing was sadistic and unnecessary, and I vowed to never forgive Mr. Trout. Even now, I don't understand what he thought he would gain from the suspension or how he could have possibly thought suspending Weasel improved the safety of the school. Weasel looked crushed, and we felt his pain nearly as much as he did, except our parents still got to come to graduation and watch us receive our diplomas. Graduation is a big day for parents, and we all knew that. The worst part was Dwayne's smug face as he held out the pipe in front of us. The ironic part was how the administration demonized us for using a harmless drug like pot when at least a few hundred other students were hooked on dangerous unprescribed painkillers and barbiturates. Dwayne didn't search for those types of drugs because, unlike weed, they didn't have decades of stigma attached to them and decades of propaganda working against them. Plus, catching someone using opioids with a random drug test was unlikely because after a day or two, those types of drugs flush from your system.

After Weasel was suspended, we said goodbye and arranged to meet at his house later that evening. I went for a run with Stringer Bell and then had dinner with Heather and our parents. When I got to Weasel's house around nine, the only other people there were Weasel, of course, and Tera and Naomi. The first few scenes of *Groundhog Day* were playing on the television in the background as they played Jenga at the dining room table. I wasn't surprised at the movie choice. There wasn't a lot of variety in Weasel's TV-watching habits. Sometimes he'd watch professional tennis matches, but he mostly liked to watch the same handful of movies repeatedly, and *Groundhog Day* was one of them. There's something strange about watching that specific movie on repeat when repetition is what the movie itself is about.

In one respect, I admired that he liked *Groundhog Day* so much because it really is an incredible movie. But I worked at a video store throughout high school, so I knew a thing or two about movies to play in the background on repeat. I usually worked alone during the evenings. Sometimes on busy days, the morning shift would stay a few extra hours to help with big lines, but most of the time, I was working nights solo. I would finish my duties and, once business slowed down, grab a sandwich at the deli next door and eat it while lasering in on a movie while it played on all twelve screens in the store. My all-time go-to film to view during work that year was *The Hitchhiker's Guide to the Galaxy*, which I'd probably watched two hundred times since it had come out on DVD that past September. One night I put on *Pretty In Pink*, a PG-rated movie I had seen before but remembered little about. I was busy shrink-wrapping used DVDs to place on sale, so I wasn't paying attention to the movie when a lady pushing a stroller started shouting at me. The scene playing on all the televisions featured several close-up shots of a woman's bare breasts. This surprised me, and I was also shocked that it offended her and her toddler. I apologized and stopped the movie right away, but she continued making a bigger deal out of it than was necessary until, eventually, she left. I guess back in the eighties, when that movie came out, the MPAA thought PG audiences deserved to see boobs once in a while. Who knew?

Other DVDs Weasel liked to rewatch were *Planes, Trains and Automobiles*, the box set of *Magnum P.I.*, and Dave Chappelle's comedy special *Killin' Them Softly*—I probably watched that one twenty times that year at Weasel's home. So my point is, it wasn't just *Groundhog Day* that Weasel had a weird obsession with.

I went to the kitchen and opened the refrigerator. "Hey, can you spot me some beers until Fonz gets here? He's bringing me a case." I removed a cold one for myself before Weasel even answered and then took a seat at the table. Jenga was a fun game to play as it was, but we made it more entertaining by writing drinking game commands on the wooden pieces with a Sharpie. When we pulled out each piece from the Jenga stack, we'd read something like "Take Shot," "Make a Rule," "Give 3 Drinks," and other commands I can't remember anymore. It was Weasel's turn to remove a piece from the stack without making the whole stack fall, and he was upset—not about the game or even about Mr. Trout suspending him. He was arguing with Tera about something else, and they both seemed very serious.

"The dude's a fucking loser. I don't know why you do that," Weasel berated her as he removed a wooden rectangle and set it on top of the Jenga stack. I was sitting on Weasel's left, so it was my turn next.

Before I went to work on the piece in the middle, I took a few sips of my beer.

"I don't know why it's any of your fucking business. He's nice. He's fun," Tera said, defending herself.

As they continued, I began to piece it all together. Tera had apparently mentioned that she'd been sort of dating an older guy we all knew named Jake. He was friends with Pete, the older kid we bought our weed and mushrooms from.

"The dude is five years older than us and still hanging out with high school girls. He's a fucking loser," Weasel shot back at her. "And didn't you say you hooked up with Colton last night? You're just being a fucking whore."

We all knew it was a mistake for Weasel to say that, and Tera knew it before any of us. Straight away, she slapped Weasel hard in the face, landing a loud smack that you could tell really stung. Weasel didn't react. He just shook his face a little and took a drink as I finished removing my piece and placed it on the top row of the stack.

"Don't you fucking call me a whore! I am not a whore. Except for sleeping with you, you asshole. And Colton was a mistake, too, but he was a better mistake than you were."

"I'm sorry, Tera. I shouldn't have called you that. I'm sorry." She scowled at him again and then shrugged, and we all knew things were de-escalating. "I just think he's a jerk and a loser and doesn't deserve you. That's all."

"I know, Weasel. You're like a good big brother sometimes, and other times you're an asshole."

"I do kind of agree with Weasel," I said reluctantly. "Not the whore part. But that guy should stop seeing high school girls. It's kind of fucked."

Tera pulled her purse onto the table and began rifling through it. It was a thin, rather flat, circular purse woven with beige, straw-like material and had woven straps to match.

"What is that?" I asked. "Is that for carrying tortillas? Can I have one to make a quesadilla?"

We all laughed, and Tera waved the air in front of her like she was getting rid of a foul smell. "Shut up." She snorted louder, realizing her purse really was the perfect size for delivering tortillas. "Why are you guys ganging up on me? I don't like it, and this purse is cute."

"It is. I like it," Naomi reassured her.

Fonz and Hernandez busted through the front door together, and we all cheered, happy to see them. They walked across the room, put their beers in the refrigerator, and asked if any of us needed a fresh one from the fridge. We all did. Then they found seats at the table with us.

"Oh, *Groundhog Day*. That's a surprise. You put this on every time you're sad, buddy?" Fonz asked.

"It's a great movie, and yeah, it's been kind of a rough day. I'm not sure if you remember, but earlier today I was suspended from school during the last week of class and banned from walking at graduation. Kind of sucks, you know?"

"Their loss," Hernandez joked. "You get to sit here and watch this same movie every day like you're Bill Murray living in purgatory. You're the lucky one."

Naomi pulled her Jenga piece and placed it on top of the stack. "Are you boys still going to do some stupid prank tonight? Do you need any help?"

"Oh, it's happening. But it's still just for the four of us boys, sweetie." Hernandez winked at Naomi when he said "sweetie" because he knew she'd hate it. Her lips curled, and her face scrunched up in disgust.

"Hey, Weasel," Fonz said. "Aren't you supposed to be our designated driver tonight? Should you be drinking?"

"Hey! Yeah!" Hernandez screamed. "You're supposed to be the driver for my prank, *ese*. We talked about it."

"That was before I got suspended, man. Give me a break, will ya? We can use my car if that's what matters—if you don't want your car on security cameras after your arrest. But you can drive. Shouldn't you be sober the day after getting arrested anyway? I guarantee your parents will stay up waiting for you tonight."

Hernandez sighed deeply at the inconvenience, but then he gave up and muttered, "Sure, yeah, fine. I get it. I'll drive. But we'll take your car."

CHAPTER 5

11:35 p.m.
Tuesday, May 16, 2006

Hernandez drank two beers around ten that night and then stopped imbibing altogether for the evening and made a pot of coffee. He insisted we slow down our drinking and have at least one cup of coffee each so we'd be sharp as tacks during his caper, but we were playing Sevens, Elevens, and Doubles and got pretty toasty. By 11:35, he was sober and bossing us around with vague intentions and grandiose delusions. "You guys are going to have to keep up and just follow whatever I say in the moment, okay? The rules say you all have to assist me, but it sucks going first because we've got to set a precedent. You hear me? You can't sabotage me. You all have to help."

"Yeah, yeah, yeah." Weasel was already drunk. "We hear you, *cabrón.*"

"So is it time to fill us in yet?" Fonz asked. "What's the plan? What's the prank?"

"Oh, you guys will see when it happens. Better that way. Trust me."

Fonz threw up his hands in frustration. "So we find out thirty minutes from now or now. Can't you just tell us? I'd rather know now if we're drugging Mr. Trout and smuggling him into Mexico in a shipping crate. What are we getting ourselves into? Can you at least tell us what you got today at Home Depot?"

Hernandez gave a coy grin that pleased nobody. "That I can do. I bought three gallons of paint, four paint rollers, four paint trays, painter's tape, sandpaper, and some tarps and plastic sheets. And a rope. A sick rope."

"So we're painting something," Fonz surmised brilliantly. "A night of physical labor. That sounds wonderful, Hernandez. Another rollicking idea. Good job."

Hernandez tilted his head like a dog trying to understand a new word.

"Don't you at least have to tell us some of the details?" Weasel enquired.

"That's not in the rules. They just say you all have to help me. As a matter of fact, I don't even want anyone to be able to tell that what we're painting has been painted once we're done. I hope some of you have painted a room or two before because we'll have to do an immaculate job. Can't be shabby in any way."

"Professionally painting. At night. When we're exhausted and drunk. That sounds like even more fun. Did someone bring a camera, at least?" Fonz asked.

I held up my thick, old Canon camcorder and set it on the table. "I did." I'm not sure why we thought documenting our shenanigans was an important or prudent requirement, but we did. I told myself that filming ourselves was artsy and labeled it as a sort of absurdist existential neorealism.

"I love painting. Sure wish we could help," Naomi teased, winking at Tera. "I just bought a book about famous painters."

"Oh? How many of those famous painters are women?" Weasel asked obnoxiously, with a snarky smirk like the Grinch. He was joking, of course, and I knew for a fact that he treated everyone in the world the same. I bet he actually could have named five famous women painters and was probably the only one of us who could. He just enjoyed riling the girls up sometimes and acting like a jerk because it came easily to him.

We all knew that Weasel had empathy and a kind heart deep down because of what had happened to his older brother, Matt. Weasel's brother was friends with Fonz's and my older brothers. All three were in the same class together, four years older than us. I think we were all aware that Matt was gay pretty early on, but he didn't come out publicly until the end of his freshman year in college down in Stillwater. Stillwater remained a cowboy town despite the big university there, and I think Matt dealt with a lot of bullying and harassment. At least I assume he did; we all assumed that.

Nowadays, many people living in the sticks are probably more accepting and kinder than they used to be. Even though it wasn't so long ago, country folks were a different breed back then and did not take kindly to gay people. During winter break of his sophomore year of college (our sophomore year of high school), Matt committed suicide by hanging himself. It was a very sad time, and I worry that by writing it down, I'm minimizing or simplifying Matt's life. Sometimes talking about something meaningful and sacred diminishes its specialness somehow. It becomes a mere typed list of information, like everything else. I'm telling you about it to show a different side of Weasel. He loved his older brother, and I knew for a fact that he would never make fun of someone if he thought he was really hurting them. He was a classic sheep in asshole's clothing.

We all went to the funeral, and then we didn't talk about his death ever again. We'd tell stories of funny times back in the day and share happy memories, like when he bought us all our first beers—those nasty, high-alcohol beers in tall, dark cans. Weasel's dad had always been aloof, but after his oldest son died in such a tragic way, I expect he blamed himself—for not being more supportive or present when it mattered or for not being a better listener, possibly. That was when Weasel's dad started working on the road a lot more, and he was hardly ever around by the time Weasel was a senior. His dad's reaction reeked of irony. In his sorrow about neglecting one son, he started neglecting the other one even more. No one knew where Weasel's mom was, not since he was a toddler.

I guess what I'm trying to say is that Weasel was always an equal-opportunity dick. He was an asshole to everyone. He'd make ridiculous arguments while portraying the role of a bigot, using his funny and sarcastic tone, but he was really just trying to shift the focus away from his true self. He had been suspended that day, and he had been drinking steadily since he got home, so I think we all knew what was happening and were already enjoying the turbulent mock debate about women painters.

"Shut up," Naomi said, trying to end the conversation immediately.

"No, really. Name five famous women painters right now, and then you can come to paint with us tonight."

"Shut up," Naomi said, waving her hand and laughing like she adored both him and his stupidity.

"I could name, like, a dozen famous male painters. I'll give you five just off the top of my head." He used his fingers to count them. "Michelangelo. Da Vinci. Picasso. Salvador Dali. Rembrandt. I could probably list thirty more. You can't name just one woman?"

"Georgia O'Keefe. Okay? Are you happy? There are famous women in everything. I'm not playing your game, you asshole." She was still smiling, and we had all forgotten about Jenga by that point. Naomi considered herself to be a staunch feminist, but she was still too timid to dish out good comebacks to typical male bullshit, and Weasel knew it. He was great at fucking with anybody, and you could tell he was enjoying the ribbing.

"Okay, name one more. Georgia O'Keefe's a good one, actually." Weasel broke character and cackled, and everybody laughed. "Name one more, please."

"I don't need to. Women can do anything, and I think you know that. I'm not engaging with your ignorance. Let's finish the game, or you guys can go paint your circle-jerk fort or whatever you're planning on doing tonight."

"Circle-jerk fort! Nice," Fonz said and laughed.

"Yeah," Tera replied. "Let's finish the game. The stack has to fall over for someone to lose."

"No, really," Weasel said in an overly sarcastic tone that was both hilarious and offensive. "Women have driven so much innovation and formed governments and invented things throughout history. No, wait, that's men. I was thinking about how men have driven history."

Fonz and I chuckled as Naomi snorted, fuming now because she needed to win the argument for the sake of women everywhere. But we all still knew Weasel was performing. "Just do me a favor," he continued. "Forget about painters and remind me of what things women have invented. Just name one thing, in all of human history, invented by a woman. Aside from the dishwasher. Off the top of your head, what is one thing a woman invented?"

"You're such an asshole." Naomi broke a reluctant smile and made a short, uncontrolled grunt as she enunciated the word "asshole." Then she said, "I don't want to talk about this anymore. Let's play the game."

"No, really!" Weasel was laughing and didn't know how to quit while ahead. "Just tell us one thing in history that was invented by a woman. Anything. You could guess."

Naomi gave him a soft slap to the face and turned away from him. "I'm over it." The slap was nothing like the provoked one I had seen Tera give him when I'd first arrived. Naomi's slap was gracious and playful. She walked to the kitchen and got herself a drink. "Does anybody need a beer?"

We all needed one.

***

11:54 p.m.
Tuesday, May 16, 2006

Hernandez transferred all of his painting supplies from the back of his El Camino and into the trunk of Weasel's car. Then Hernandez took the driver's seat as Fonz and I poured into the back and Weasel got into the front passenger seat. The sky was clear, and the weather was perfect. It was a pleasant night outside. Naomi and Tera had to go home, and they left with a quick, dismissive, high-pitched, "Byeeee," as we were packing up Weasel's car for our secret mission.

"So where are we going?" I asked, closing the back door once we were all inside.

"You'll see, *cabrón*," Hernandez answered as he started the car. He tried to put it in reverse but stalled, and Weasel laughed maniacally at him. Hernandez restarted the car and drove less than a mile before pulling into a lot adjacent to our high school, directly in front of the school's athletic facility and stadium. The car idled, and Hernandez lit a joint. "Some motivation," he called it. For us, smoking a joint was a sort of ritual to be done before tackling any arduous task that should definitely not involve cannabis. A sort of childish superstition we had inherited, like holding your breath while driving past a graveyard. It made no sense, but we continued the tradition like devout choirboys.

Hernandez turned up the sound on the beginning of "Atlantic City" by the Band a little louder than necessary and then turned it back down so we could talk. We passed the joint around and had our fill, hotboxing Weasel's Civic, as per usual.

"Didn't you say you have to start taking drug tests for, like, six months?" I asked.

"After court, yeah, for getting caught smoking your blunt yesterday. Shit's still in my system. I'll quit next week. Hey," Hernandez said, trying to switch to a vibe of laughter and cheer. "What does broccoli have in common with anal sex?"

We all shrugged, but Fonz bit. "What?"

"If it's forced on you when you're a kid, you'll hate it when you're an adult."

A few chuckles, but Hernandez was the only one to really laugh at his own joke.

"That's fucked up, man," Fonz responded, half serious.

"Okay," I said apprehensively. "So tonight involves breaking into the school, and it involves painting something well enough that no one even notices it was painted. I've got that right? Enough dancing around, you prick. You have to tell us the plan before we go in."

"All right, fine. You guys are no fun," Hernandez lamented, switching the car's engine off. "We're painting Trout's office. There's a skylight above his desk that's installed with regular screws. I've got a power drill. We'll use the ladder on the wall next to the athletic facility, go up to the roof, take off the skylight, and then rappel down with the rope."

"Rappel down?" Fonz asked, as if the mere mention of rappelling offended him. "What are we, Navy Seals? A rope? Seriously?"

"It's a ten-foot ceiling, and the skylight is right above Trout's desk, Fonz. Man up. You're, like, six feet tall and an athlete. Pull out your tampon and grow a pair." With that, Hernandez opened his door and exited the vehicle, extinguishing the joint on the ground by grinding it with the toe of his shoe. Hernandez popped the trunk and started pulling out painting supplies, so we followed suit by exiting the car and watching him work. Hernandez put the rope around his shoulders like he was Rambo and gave me two paint cans. Then he handed the paint rollers, rolling trays, sandpaper, and power drill to Fonz and gave Weasel a handful of plastic sheets and fabric, along with the painter's tape. Finally, Hernandez took the other paint can in one hand, closed the trunk of the car with his other, and said, "You boys ready for this?"

Weasel was still drunk, and he was the only one to answer with a monotonous, "Yeah, sure."

I slipped the strap of my camcorder around my neck like a heavy necklace. I turned the camera on and recorded a few seconds to show our supplies and the boys prepping for the secret paint operation.

Hernandez crouched down and darted across the street toward our school like a Special Ops soldier making a sneak attack across enemy lines. It was after midnight, and there wasn't any traffic or anybody out to spot us, so the three of us simply jogged behind Hernandez casually. Some nights an officer would drive around and patrol the school parking lot once an hour—Dwayne's nocturnal counterpart. He was an actual police officer, not designated solely to school security. We knew of him and had seen him doing his rounds a few times, but none of us had ever met him.

We made it to the bolted-in ladder on one of the concrete walls that Hernandez had mentioned and scaled it. We took our positions on the roof while we watched Hernandez slowly remove fifteen screws from the skylight. He placed each screw into a plastic baggy and left the baggy sitting next to the skylight's metal frame. I filmed Hernandez as he took the rope from his neck, went back to the ladder we'd scaled, and tied one end of the rope to the ladder using an impressive-looking knot. He then went back to the skylight, removed it, and gently lowered the other end of the rope onto the desk below. He had obviously meticulously practiced and prepared for his prank, which made me nervous, as I still had no clue what mine would be. Luckily, I had agreed to go last, so I had until Friday to figure it out.

Hernandez had used a legitimate sailor's knot to tie the rope to the ladder, so I was confident it would hold us. He grabbed the rope and began to descend. Slowly and carefully, he scooched down the rope until he was standing on Mr. Trout's desk. He was nearly tall enough to reach up and grab our hands from where we were kneeling on the roof. We handed down the paint supplies, and he organized them in a neat pile by the office door. Then we took turns climbing down the rope until we were all in our principal's office, wondering how long we'd be painting. It sounded like more of a chore than a prank, but of course, sometimes important things can seem like a chore in the moment. We just had to trust that Hernandez's idea was more fully baked than it seemed and that it would all come together in the end.

"Help me with this," Hernandez said as he handed me a dark two-foot-by-three-foot piece of fabric. "Hold it up to the window, and I'll tape it off."

I followed the instructions and held the fabric up over the window. It fit inside the window frame almost perfectly, and Hernandez used the painter's tape to secure it tightly to the windowpane.

"What the hell is that for?" Weasel asked, dumbfounded.

"We tape up the window so we can turn on the lights in here without people out there noticing. Haven't you guys ever pulled a prank before?" Hernandez asked, finishing his tape job. He walked to the wall by the door, switched the light on, and winked at us.

"What about the skylight? People won't see light coming from up there?" Fonz asked, which made Weasel and I grin. We loved poking holes in Hernandez's plans and seeing him react defensively.

"Pfft. No," Hernandez puffed back. "We're not hiding from aliens. No one'll see the light from the skylight, you moron. Either trust me or don't. This is my plan, boys."

I turned the camera on again and filmed some of our antics. "So we're not hiding from aliens? Should you repeat that for the camera, Hernandez?" I asked, and he pretended to be too busy to notice.

Fonz looked around in disappointment. "So you know when you have to clarify the prank ten times, it probably means that it's a bad prank, right? It sounds like we're painting Trout's office, and the goal is for him to not even notice that we painted it. I still don't think I understand, *amigo*."

Hernandez nodded. "That's because you're not a big-picture kind of guy, Fonz. The prank has layers, *ese*. I guess I shouldn't expect you guys to understand. It's too brilliant."

"What are we all missing then? Why is this a good prank?" Fonz asked him sincerely.

"It has layers, *ese*. I told you. I'm Indiana Jones, and you're the little Asian boy. Your job is to just help out."

"His name was Short Round," I interrupted. "Ya racist."

"So, Dr. Jones, why don't we paint his office pink or yellow or something that he might actually notice? That might be a prank. Maybe," Fonz offered, genuinely frustrated.

"What color are we painting the office?" I asked, hoping he'd have some answer that would satisfy our line of inquiry.

Hernandez handed us each one of the three paint cans that were labeled "Sky Fall Blue."

"Okay. It's Sky Fall Blue," I acknowledged, still confused. "And what color is the wall now?"

Hernandez snickered like a first grader who just farted. "Guys, the walls now are Quench Blue, and this one is Sky Fall Blue. This new one's slightly darker. It'll eat at him psychologically because he'll know…but he won't know, you know? The layers will eat at him. Maybe it'll take a week; maybe it'll be ten years from now, but he'll snap—all because his brain couldn't process why his office just felt darker to him one day."

Fonz nodded and scratched his chin, calculating.

"The day after he fucked me, his world goes dark," Weasel said, still drunk but satisfied. "I like that."

"Yeah. The day after he fucked Weasel out of walking at graduation, his work life got darker and never went back to how it was before. It's genius, right?" Hernandez looked so proud as he broke it down for us.

"It's something," Fonz said, still unsure.

"I think I get it," I said. "It's okay. I mean, I don't know about genius. It's no baby chickens in the teacher's lounge, but it's all right."

"Are you joking with me right now?" Hernandez couldn't believe what I'd said. "How is the baby chickens thing even in the same league here? This has *layers*."

"*Cabrón*," I said, cackling. "Just because you keep saying it has layers doesn't make it so, man. There's a difference between a plan and a pipe dream. Plus, I brought a camera for what? Do you want me to set it down and make a time lapse of paint drying? Still doesn't sound like a prank. Sounds like a few hours of physical labor for nobody's benefit. Baby chickens are cute, man. That at least made a bunch of people laugh."

"The prank is for us. There's nothing in the rules saying Mr. Trout or anyone else has to laugh. And I think this is hilarious. We're painting this office Sky Fall Blue tonight, and it's going to look perfect. Now help me take down the pictures and cover things up. I want this to look good, and we don't have much time."

"All right, we're in," Fonz said. "Chill out. But so you know, rule five does mention that the judging is partly based on how many people the prank makes laugh."

We loved poking holes in his idea, but at least we finally knew he had an idea. We all stepped up and started prepping the room. Weasel and I made a pile of all the picture frames from the walls on Mr. Trout's desk, and then we covered his desk, chairs, and filing cabinets with plastic tarps. We covered the rest of the floor with another tarp and taped it down. Fonz and Hernandez covered the sockets and molding with painter's tape to protect them from paint splash, and Fonz started sanding the walls. We were an efficient, free, evening labor crew. Once Weasel and I finished our tasks, we helped Fonz finish sanding down the walls while Hernandez prepped trays with paint and rollers.

"Don't we need to prime the walls if we want this to really look nice?" Fonz was reluctantly sanding a wall as he asked his question, obviously not done poking holes in the plan to further frustrate Hernandez.

"Just sand it, *pendejo*. We don't have time to let primer dry," Hernandez replied, looking at his watch as if he'd timed his shenanigans down to the minute.

"For real? Time to let the primer dry?" Weasel asked. "How about time to let this Sky Fall Blue dry in time to hang stuff back on the walls? This room is going to smell like fresh paint for the next week, dude. Are you sure you've thought this out at all? It sounds like you basically just bought the same paint he already had, and if this goes perfectly, then it's pointless."

Hernandez stopped what he was doing with the paint and stood in front of Weasel. "You know what? Y'all are a bunch of natural-born naysayers. Do you remember I got arrested last night on mushrooms and had to have my parents pick me up? Remember they watched me eat a dozen party burritos like I was out of my mind? I need a win. Let's paint fast and steady, boys. We don't have time for this. Please."

He had us there. Reasoning was never as good of an approach for convincing us as shaming was. Hernandez held out his hand, and we took turns slapping it in a series of slow high-fives to show our reverence. Then we went to work, doing our best to make the paint job look decent. The more I painted, the more I noticed how the new color was slightly darker. By 2:00 a.m., I'd started thinking maybe Hernandez was a genius after all and this would be the best prank of all time, but I think I was just exhausted. By three, we had pulled a large, metal, tilt-drum fan into the office from another part of the school, and we began slowly packing up our things and getting ready to leave while we let the fan do what it could. We turned off the light in the room and opened the window for about an hour. To his credit, Hernandez had planned it out all right. We finished on time, and it looked pretty good, but it was late. We'd all have to be in class again at 8:00 a.m., and I'd be furious about my lack of sleep.

By 3:30 p.m., we were all ready to leave, even if the walls weren't dry yet.

"All right, *cabrones*, let's get all *Sister Act* up in here. Clean this place up." Hernandez pulled a sage stick out of his jacket and lit it discretely, as if the magic bush would fend off our stupidity as well as the metallic pungency of the paint fumes. He shook it and danced around like an Aboriginal medicine man.

We hung the picture frames back on the walls, tidied the office, and returned the fan to its original location. Fonz climbed up the rope first and then grabbed two sides of the skylight opening and easily pulled himself to the roof. Weasel followed, making the climb look much more difficult. Hernandez and I found a large trash bag and stuffed it with all the plastic sheets, tarps, gobs of painter's tape, used rollers and paint trays, and paint cans. We handed the bag up to Fonz and Weasel, who set it on the roof. We figured we'd leave it there and hope someone would find it someday and piece together what had happened rather than deal with loading it all back into the car and finding a dumpster. I shot a few more seconds of the office on video, but it was too dark to make out anything. Then I climbed up. Fonz stuck his hand down and helped pull me up to the roof. Hernandez took another look around Mr. Trout's office and smiled contently, all his goals realized. That may have been the proudest I'd ever seen him. Then he climbed up, too, not saying a word to any of us. He just calmly walked over to the ladder and crouched down to untie the rope. He wound the rope back between his shoulder and his elbow and draped it on himself Rambo-style once again. Then he picked up and examined the baggie of skylight screws as if he were making sure they were all still there.

"I'm fucking tired," Fonz said, yawning.

"Yeah, you owe us for this one," Weasel said seriously. "We did everything you told us to and shit. You better do the same when it's time for my prank. I can damn well guarantee I won't make you guys paint a room all night. Maybe we should stop by Mr. Trout's house and clean all his gutters, though. Maybe wash his car too. That'll really get him."

As Hernandez bent down to grab the skylight, he said, "You know what? I'm proud of all you boys' efforts. Couldn't be prouder. Thank you for being real dawgs."

We were all ready to fall asleep, but we nodded to him as if to say, "Yeah, we just painted for three hours and have to come back here in a few more hours. This was hell."

Hernandez gripped the sixty-pound and rather long skylight by its sides and lifted it just enough to slowly slide it over the hole where it belonged. As the glass frame covered about half of the hole, Hernandez slipped and accidentally pushed the frame down instead of lifting it. There were maybe three or four seconds of the skylight sliding, falling, crashing on the desk, crashing again against a wall, and shattering everywhere, but it felt a lot longer, as if it was happening in slow motion. We all froze, stared, and watched. When the loud smashing finished, we peered into the hole to see that Mr. Trout's office was now decimated. Weasel smiled, and the rest of us shook our heads in disbelief, so I recorded a moment of it on video.

Just then, there was another terrible sound: a woop-woop from a police car. Looking down, we spotted the nighttime officer doing his rounds. He was still in his patrol car, but his lights were on, and he was using his spotlight to glance around the roof.

The light jumped to Fonz, who froze, looked at me, and yelled, "Run!"

CHAPTER 6

4:08 a.m.

Wednesday, May 17, 2006

The man in the police car trumpeted directives toward our vicinity. I don't know if the municipal vehicle had a PA system or a megaphone attached to it or what, but it was quiet outside otherwise, so when he started transmitting, we could hear him as clear as day. "You there. Stop what you're doing and come down. This is the police." We were not the smoothest of criminals. Doing something questionable and getting away with it was nothing short of an unattainable goal.

By the time the shock subsided and my muscles and jaw unlocked, I turned to discover that Weasel was already halfway back down the ladder and shouting instructions at us. "Leave my car! We'll go through the neighborhoods back to my house!" A wooden fence separated the athletic facility and football stadium from the closest neighborhood, and on the other side of that neighborhood were two more connecting neighborhoods, where Weasel lived. Luckily for us, the parking lot where the patrol car was had no direct entrance to the neighborhood streets, which would buy us at least a few minutes. These were nice, suburban neighborhoods with cul-de-sacs, trampolines, and portable basketball hoops parked in driveways. Real idyllic and all, like from some wholesome TV show. A neighborhood of families not expecting a police chase.

Weasel descended the ladder and started sprinting toward the fence. He didn't wait for us or even pretend to consider it. I climbed down next and started running after him, recording with my video camera to get footage that was sure to be shaky and unwatchable. Hernandez followed behind me, carrying the rope and power drill, and Fonz climbed down last. We weren't tired at all anymore; the adrenaline made us run like our lives depended on it. The four of us got to the fence and hopped over. Then we ran through someone's backyard, exited through the front gate to a street, and jogged down the sidewalk for a little more than a mile before we got to Weasel's house. We ran inside, sweating like crazy, and Weasel slammed and locked the door as though the cops were hot on our trail, but I honestly think the officer gave up on us by the time we left the school grounds. Trying to chase down four spry and motivated high school guys at four in the morning doesn't sound like something anyone would enjoy.

None of us could fathom driving home at that point and risking waking our parents by showing up late. So we decided that sleeping at Weasel's house was the only move. We took turns using Weasel's shower to wash the sweat and paint off ourselves and slid back into our sweaty boxers, ready for bed. We'd reached a tipping point of exhaustion and delirium by then but did our best to craft a text to send our parents to keep them from worrying. We each texted our parents a version of: "Sorry to send so late. Decided to sleep over at Weasel's and will go to school from here in the morning. Is senior day at school, no tests or anything." Weasel, predictably, slept in his own bed. I took Weasel's dad's bed since he was out of town. Fonz and Hernandez each took an area of the sectional leather couch in the living room since nobody felt they should sleep in Matt's empty room.

Hernandez was awake by 7:00 a.m. sharp. I do not know how he did it, given I was still asleep, but from what I heard, he sprung alive on time like he was trained to. No alarm or anything. Three hours of sleep, but you'd have thought he'd had ten. He brewed a pot of coffee and sat outside by himself, reading the paper as though he were an old man who'd always lived there. Weasel woke up next and had some coffee with Hernandez. I was briefly stirred awake by their laughter and story-sharing about the night before, but I put a pillow over my head and went back to sleep.

Since I remained asleep, I had to hear what happened next secondhand later that day. Hernandez reportedly found an apron and tied it on, and then he cooked some bacon and eggs he'd found in the fridge and made buttered toast smothered with avocado. As Hernandez and Weasel enjoyed breakfast and Fonz and I slept, Weasel's dad walked through the front door holding a suit jacket and briefcase. He was as surprised to see them as they were to see him. No one knew Weasel's dad's schedule, and we'd just assumed he was almost always gone. Weasel's dad's gaze went from Fonz asleep on the couch to Weasel sitting at the table eating toast, bacon, and eggs to Hernandez cooking at the stove. He turned back to Weasel. "Morning, son," he said and walked toward the kitchen.

"Morning, dad. The guys slept over last night."

"Yeah, I can see that." His dad looked puzzled at Hernandez wearing his apron and cooking up a storm.

"Morning, sir," Hernandez said brightly. "You hungry?"

"Sure, I'm hungry. Just let me put my things away. I'm sure you were all here late working on your studies, right?" His dad winked. He probably assumed we stayed the night to be responsible and not drink and drive.

"Yeah, Dad. Hernandez was showing us the line of work he wants to get into."

"Is that right? He was giving you all blowjobs for twenty bucks a pop?" His dad made a back-and-forth motion with his fist in front of his mouth—the international signal for a blowjob. He was in a good mood and was much cooler than my parents, who would never say something so coarse.

"Hey, *ese*, that's uncalled for. I was about to fix you *desayuno*, but now I don't know so much." Hernandez was acting like he was about to throw the plate of food in the trash, but he couldn't hide his grin.

Weasel and his dad both laughed like friends teaming up on a younger kid. His dad asked, "So Hernandez was showing you what he wants to do for a living. Are you going to explain what that means? Or is this some inside joke?"

"Nah, we can tell you. Hernandez wants to paint offices when he gets older. Maybe paint the exteriors of some business complexes, too, someday—if he's lucky. So last night we helped him paint a room almost the exact same color as it was before so no one will ever notice. It was pretty neat. Then, yeah, he gave us all blowjobs for twenty bucks."

"I did show them some finer techniques of interior design mixed with intense Freudian psychology, but it'd take a while to explain. It's boring," Hernandez retorted, flipping the bacon one last time before taking it out of the pan and starting the next batch.

"Yeah, it's boring. Exactly," Weasel said. His dad was confused and starting to get bored with the conversation. Weasel was still having fun, though, and made the blowjob signal again, making his dad laugh. To Hernandez, he teased, "You have to work your way up, pal, but I know you can do it. You want to paint an entire house a slightly different color someday? You work on that goal; that shit will happen, man." Weasel looked at his dad and laughed.

"Painting is a good profession, *ese*; I don't know what joke you think you're making right now. But in ten years, I'll have a high-powered job in finance. I've got straight A's." Suspecting where Hernandez was going, Weasel quickly straightened his face and transferred his gaze to Hernandez. "I'm already enrolled to go to TU in the fall and study economics. And I'm actually going to walk at graduation on Saturday."

The last part was an early morning jab too far. Weasel and his dad both felt the sting, and his dad shook his head and walked out of the room. Making fun of a friend for not getting to walk at graduation is unduly harsh, especially the day after it happened and just a few days before said graduation, but lines get crossed sometimes. That's how we find out where the lines are. Hernandez said what he said because he didn't like people assuming he was stupid just because he acted stupid all the time. When it came to books and tests and numbers, he was actually a very serious fellow.

Hernandez started fixing up another plate. "Sorry, man. Low blow."

"It's cool."

"Want to see if Fonz wants to get up and eat?"

Weasel's dad headed to his bedroom to take off his suit. When he opened the bedroom door, he let out a loud, "What the…?" and startled me awake from a sound sleep. And when I say startled, I mean *startled*. I'm not a morning person. I really hate being woken up in the morning, no matter who is doing the waking. Instinctively, I grabbed the pillow off my face and threw it at him, yelling, "Hey, give me ten minutes, man!" I was still too groggy to realize it was Weasel's dad I was yelling at.

He caught the pillow midair and threw it back at me, hitting my face as hard as a pillow possibly can. I was awake. Then he smiled and said in a mocking tone, "Time for school, *man*."

His dad took a step back into the hallway, shook his head, and yelled to Weasel, "Son, what the hell is going on here? This is my bed. Hernandez wasn't really giving you all blowjobs last night, was he?"

✳✳✳

8:01 a.m.
Wednesday, May 17, 2006

All our cars except Weasel's were at Weasel's house already, so we didn't have to go home before driving to school in the same clothes we'd worn the night before. As we headed out, Hernandez was so proud of his cooking that he asked us a dozen times if we liked it, fishing for a compliment or two. Fonz and Hernandez drove straight to school and made it to first period on time, which was good because their teachers were strict about attendance. Weasel's house was only about a mile from school, but somehow, I still managed to arrive late that day; I knew Ms. Allen probably wouldn't know or care. Weasel rode with me since his car was still parked across from the school. Even though I was satisfied with breakfast, I still wanted to go to the donut store. I hate to admit it, but I'm a creature of habit. I bought four sausage rolls and gave one to Weasel before I dropped him at his car, which he drove back home. Since he was suspended from class, he planned on watching tennis and brewing over ideas for his prank all day. According to the agreed-upon schedule, Fonz would pull his prank that night. Weasel would go Thursday, and I would go Friday.

When I got to first period, it was the same as always. No sign of my teacher. I gave Angelica one of the sausage rolls. She looked ready for conversation, but I must have looked like a junkie at the rough end of a binge, withdrawn and crabby. I went to my seat and surprised Cameron by giving him a pastry too. He happily scarfed it down in one bite instead of three, chewing with his mouth open while talking. I had never seen him eat before, and I never wanted to see it again. He said, chomping between words, "Thanks, man. I didn't think you'd actually bring me one, but that's pretty cool."

"No problem, buddy." I turned away from the sight of his disturbing open-mouthed chewing style and ate my snack. I wasn't as hungry as I usually was, so it didn't taste as good as I'd expected.

I regretted not having a conversation with Angelica, but I decided that I was too tired to feel regret, so I laid my head down and tried to fall asleep instead. Within what must have been only five minutes, Ms. Allen was in the room taking roll, and I felt Cameron shove my arm to wake me.

"Jon Ryan," Ms. Allen said exasperatedly, as if it were her third time saying it.

"Yes. Here." I lifted my head in acknowledgment and raised my hand, thinking she was calling my name for roll call.

"They want to see you in the office."

Most of the class instinctively sing-songed, "Oooohhhh," like we were still in grade school. But they were right. I was probably in trouble. We'd been sloppy the night before. Someone might've seen us, or maybe a camera caught us or Weasel's car parked across the street. Our fingerprints were on everything, not that my fingerprints were on file anywhere. We'd left Hernandez's paint supplies in a trash bag on the roof. There were a thousand ways we might've botched the secret paint job, and I was too tired to care anymore.

Ms. Allen waved the pink note from the office as I approached her and received the written summons. Then I left the lab while reading the message written in blue pen in perfect cursive: "Jon Ryan to principal's office." We'd felt so clever the night before, yet when I was handed the pink slip, I felt like a bank robber who'd finally been caught. I looked down as I walked and noticed flecks of paint on my pants. And the paint, I was confident, was a little something called Sky Fall Blue.

I figured I was screwed then and there. I walked, deflated, down the long hallway toward our principal's office. On my way, Fonz exited a classroom door and joined me for the walk, holding an identical pink note.

"Admit nothing. If they split us up, you claim ignorance on anything he asks. Trust me." Fonz wasn't using his normal jokey and silly tone of voice. He spoke in a genuinely grave, almost impressive tone that made me anxious.

When we arrived, Hernandez was already sitting and waiting in the outer office with his own pink note, and a receptionist told us to take seats next to him. Trout made us sweat for ten minutes before finally calling us into his office. Similar to our visit the day before, he sat in the chair behind his desk, and we all stood. Most of the glass and debris from the shattered skylight had already been cleaned up, and there was a plastic sheet taped to the hole above to keep rain from falling into the office. Carlos, the janitor, was on his hands and knees, looking for any hidden pieces of glass.

"*Hola*, Carlos," Hernandez said, and waved.

"*Hola*, boys," Carlos responded, briefly looking up at us and then getting back to business.

"Wow, sir," I said, as concerned as I could muster. "What happened to your office?"

Hernandez's lip started to curl, but he stopped himself before it came to a full smile.

"That's what I called the three of you in here to ask. What the hell happened in here?"

"I beg your pardon," Hernandez said. "I'm not sure I understand what you mean."

"What I mean," Mr. Trout responded, "is that I think the three of you and your Weasel friend all know what happened. This is federal property. Trespassing and vandalism are very serious charges. You might all be joining Weasel and not attending graduation." Why did he have such a hard-on about keeping us from walking at graduation? It was maniacal; there's no other explanation. "And you." Mr. Trout pointed at Fonz. "Since we weren't able to search your car yesterday, we're going to have Officer Dwayne go back out to the parking lot with us and see if you've been smoking on school grounds too."

"Um, no, I don't think so." Fonz shot an arrogant grin at Trout, who was unaccustomed to being rebuffed by students. I wasn't even aware that was an option.

"You're all on thin fucking ice. Don't test me." I had never heard Trout use profanity before. We had gotten to him. Maybe Hernandez did deserve some points after all. Even if he didn't intend to break the skylight, that was a big part of why that prank was remembered, as far as I see it. In fact, the broken skylight was the only part of the ordeal that even seemed like a prank. Obviously, the broken glass was the issue at hand, and I doubt our principal had even noticed that the color of his walls had changed. Somehow, the room didn't even smell like fresh paint. I guess the open skylight all night—or the sage—had miraculously aired out the room.

"I don't think you understand," Fonz said, cutting for a deal.

"Boy, I have thousands of other students and won't waste another whole day dealing with you punks. We're searching your car, or you will be expelled on the spot." Then Mr. Trout stood and walked to the doorway to holler at the receptionist. "Gladys, ask Officer Dwayne to join us!"

Officer Dwayne approached and stood at the door. There were now six of us trying to fit into the small office.

"I do not consent to this search," Fonz said soberly. "I have five witnesses that I do not consent to this search, and I have been threatened with expulsion if I don't comply. You got that, Carlos?" He pointed to Carlos, who was still sweeping up tiny shards of glass from the carpet.

"Okay, *amigo*. Good luck," Carlos said, without even turning his head or pausing from his task.

"Keys, Fonseca. It's either that or expulsion. Right now. You decide." Mr. Trout stuck out his hand, palm up, awaiting the keys.

Fonz reluctantly brought his keys from his pocket and, still holding them, said to Officer Dwayne, "This is illegal, and you know it." Then he handed the keys over to Dwayne. Cops never care if they're crossing lines when it's their word against some kid's since the chance of them being exposed is slim.

"All right, let's get this over with," Dwayne said, and we followed him and Mr. Trout back out to the parking lot, this time to watch Dwayne search Fonz's car. Fonz had a two-door, dark-blue BMW that he kept clean, so the search wasn't as time-consuming as the search of Weasel's filthy mess of a car. Fonz, Hernandez, and I stood a few feet from the car and watched, and I wondered why Hernandez and I were even there. Trout rested his hand on the roof of the car, leaning his head in as if he were somehow assisting Dwayne with the investigation.

"What's this?" Mr. Trout said, clutching a crumpled piece of paper from the backseat floorboard. He and Dwayne stared at it, and Dwayne looked perplexed. "The Official Top Secret Prank Rules," Trout read aloud, and then he smiled like he knew he'd won.

"Aw, fuck," Fonz muttered under his breath, but still loud enough for everyone to hear. Dwayne didn't find anything illegal in the car, so the incompetent dweeb returned the keys to Fonz and escorted us back to the principal's office. Mr. Trout took his seat behind his desk, and Officer Dwayne leaned against the door frame again, trying to be intimidating. I stood next to Fonz and Hernandez. Carlos had finished cleaning the room and moved on to mopping the cafeteria.

"So, obviously, this is incriminating evidence. With all your signatures. Planning to pull end-of-year pranks. Then there's this." Trout motioned to the taped plastic where a skylight once was. "This is grounds to suspend all of you, and that's exactly what is going to happen. None of you are going to walk at graduation. My next move is to call all of your parents."

Fonz stood like a solid oak tree and lit up with a confidence I had never before seen in him. "That would be a mistake. That piece of paper is a joke, and nothing about it relates to whatever happened here in your office last night. You have zero evidence tying us to the breaking of your skylight because there is none. As far as I know, it stormed, and some hail broke your window."

"You sound confident, but the school board will support me on this. They'll read this, and plus, I'll tell them all about you."

"An easy case can be made that you have some sort of sick vendetta against us. You've got, at best, some circumstantial evidence that proves nothing and that was obtained through an illegal search," Fonz proclaimed. "Even if your punishment stands over the next week and you really don't let us walk at graduation, you will get destroyed on the back end of this. I guarantee it. In fact, it may bite you on the ass even harder."

"Watch your tone when you speak to me. Now listen—"

"No, you listen. No judge would think you had any sort of reasonable suspicion to search my car today or their cars yesterday. That means that even if you had found hard evidence, like a skylight-breaking machine, in the backseat of my car, it would be inadmissible."

"Do you have a law degree, Mr. Fonseca?" Mr. Trout sneered. "You can afford a lawyer? Do you know how long I've been doing this? Do you have any idea how many snobbish, arrogant brats with no self-awareness I've seen come through here? You need to bring your tone back to respect really fast."

"My dad has a law degree and is a pretty damned good defense attorney; plus he plays golf with Mr. Raskind, the school board superintendent," Fonz retorted. "Do you play golf twice a month with Mr. Raskind? And I think my dad and Raskind were with Bob Sockolosky at his polo fields last weekend. I'm pretty sure Mr. Sockolosky has friends in low places, like the school board. And I'm sure my dad would be delighted to see you get fired and rain down on you with damages, especially if he doesn't get to watch his son walk at graduation because of some petty and illegal search that found—what exactly? A silly document that teenagers signed that literally says vandalism is against the rules of their pretend game. You won't have a job a year from now if you decide you need to flex on us right now. Two and a half more days of school, Mr. Trout, and then you never have to see us again. This doesn't have to lead to two years of lawsuits that'll ruin your life."

Mr. Trout's face was red by that point. Really red. Like a sunburnt baby with red-hot cheeks and forehead. He was steaming, clenching his jaw and trying to decide how to punish Fonz in front of us.

"Oh, look here." Inexplicably, Fonz pulled a business card out of his pocket and handed it to Mr. Trout. "If you're calling our parents about this, why don't you call my dad first? His cell number is on there. See if he doesn't sound twice as scary as me when he starts listing all the ways he will ruin you for these mistakes."

Mr. Trout accepted the business card out of reflex and briefly glanced at it before tossing it onto his desk. The vein in his forehead was about to pop.

"You know, I don't know what to make of all of this." Trout held the rules out in front of us again. "But I would have to be an idiot not to make something of it. I can't encourage the destruction of public property or trespassing. Or be seen to passively support these kinds of graduation antics."

"Except when they're done by the football players and their cute baby chickens," Hernandez pointed out.

"If I let you boys go—and I mean *if…*" It was obvious then and there that Fonz had won the battle. Anytime teachers or principals say something like that in the middle of a potential punishment discussion, you know they are trying to appear merciful, but really, they are just cowards trying to save face. Merciful cowards. "If I let you out of here right now, I don't want to see any of your faces again this week unless you're behaving yourselves. Not a peep. Don't give me a reason to call you in here again."

Hernandez, Fonz, and I looked at each other and nodded. It felt like the Three Stooges had just pulled a fast one on someone smarter than them.

"So we can go back to class now?" Hernandez asked.

"Yes. Go. Get out of here." Mr. Trout looked prepared to shut his door and blinds and cry for an hour. That's how bad I think Fonz broke him.

"My paper, from my car." Fonz pointed at the rules and then leaned over and scooped our document from Trout's desk as Trout looked at the opposite wall, presumably not noticing the darker color we had painted it the night before.

We walked out of the office, and Fonz looked as confident and happy as a young man can look. We all slapped each other's palms and shoulders, congratulating ourselves. "Man, I've got to tell you, Fonz," Hernandez said. "I really had no idea that your dad was a lawyer."

"Yeah, me neither," I said.

I never really thought about what any of my friends' parents did for work. Even though we played poker at Fonz's house once a week throughout sophomore year, I didn't know his parents very well. His dad joined our poker game two or three times, but he didn't talk about his job. The few other times I saw him, he was in his reclining chair in the living room watching football or napping with his enormous belly poking out from under his shirt, usually with his overfed, fat Rottweiler Lucy by his side. (Funny how some dogs and owners look alike.)

All I knew about Fonz's mom was that she was a sweet lady who liked to cook. She served us great bacon-wrapped snacks at poker—usually with little toothpicks in them so we could easily eat without greasing up our playing cards—and once, after a sleepover, she made us sausage balls for breakfast that were unlike anything I had eaten before. They were so delicious that I asked her for the recipe and gave it to my mom. Being the foodie that I am, I've gotta tell you the recipe is as simple as it gets: take a pound of Jimmy Dean ground pork breakfast sausage, a pound of shredded sharp cheddar cheese, and two cups of Bisquick, and mix them all together by hand. Form racquetball-sized balls of meat and then bake at 350 degrees for twenty-five minutes or so until golden brown. Trust me, they're like Christmas morning—they will make your whole day better.

CHAPTER 7

8:38 a.m.
Wednesday, May 17, 2006

After leaving Trout's office, I went back to my first period computer class. I didn't feel like playing video games, so I just sat and thought about what'd happened and how badass Fonz had acted when he emasculated our principal. Fonz didn't seem like some entitled rich kid. He'd never mentioned his dad's connections before. For a few moments there, I had been certain my parents were going to get a call from the principal saying I wouldn't be walking at graduation. I thought again about how Fonz had handled the situation, and I felt relieved and proud to have such an educated, arrogant friend with balls of steel.

Second period we started watching another movie, and I talked to Blake, the kid who had gotten me to chill out about the *Rear Window* remake, but I'd be lying if I claimed to remember anything we discussed. Maybe he filled me in on how bad the previous day's movie was. Third period that day is as much of a blur. All I remember is Mr. Derkatch playing another history documentary. I don't think he said anything to the class to attempt to engage us in conversation. After that was lunch—and lunch I remember because we had one of my all-time favorite meals. Instead of going to the cafeteria, I went straight to the parking lot and waited by Fonz's BMW. He and Hernandez showed up a few minutes later. After the Trout takedown, rewarding ourselves with an against-policy, off-campus lunch seemed reasonable. Not only did we want to eat lunch off school property one last time, but it was a chance to break bread with Weasel and see how he was doing. Plus, Fonz needed to fill us in on the plan for his upcoming prank that evening.

If you should ever fly into Tulsa, you'll find what seems to be an unassuming skyline filled with unassuming people. It's a city of folks who are generally friendly and are more likely to pull over and help you change a flat tire than people in most other places on earth. Okies do many things exceptionally well, and cooking and eating are right up there at the top. Their big guts and smiling faces tell it all. Most of the state's cookery involving meat is first-rate. Sure, the Mexican food is almost all Tex-Mex, and the BBQ isn't quite what it is in Texas, but if we're voting on what state has some of the most flavorful (and unhealthy) food overall, my vote goes to Oklahoma. You know a place has great steaks or burgers when in its backyard is a field filled with big, sturdy cows.

At the time of this writing, I haven't lived in Tulsa for some time, but when I go home to visit, I always make two necessary food stops: Coney I-Lander to get a chili-cheese hotdog or six and Ron's Burgers for a jumbo bacon cheeseburger, plain and dry. The patty is greasy and seasoned enough that you don't need any condiments—just crumbled bacon and gooey, melted cheese. Along with a side order of bacon-cheese fries, it's the kind of meal you could eat every day and gain a hundred pounds in six months. You'd have a heart attack, but damn is it good, and you'd enjoy a lot of those six months. If I'm home for as long as a week, I might go to Ron's and Coney's twice each. These local chains were my greasy staples growing up, and the quality hasn't changed a beat. I even get a box of Coney's heavenly miniature chili-cheese dogs delivered to me in dry ice about once a month.

Besides Ron's and Coney's, a third restaurant might make the cut: a spot out in Claremore called Hammett House. They make what is probably the best chicken-fried steak in the world, if you're into such things. They have a decent pecan pie, too, but the chicken-fried steak is outrageous. You can even buy a big bottle of their seasoning mix if you want to attempt the recipe when you get home.

Something like In-N-Out's animal-style burger is fine, sure, but nothing out west or out east can hold a candle to the Midwest when it comes to burgers. I love Ron's Burgers the way some people love snowboarding, birdwatching, or genealogy. They use quality beef seasoned with their special seasoning salt (which they also sell in bottles) to make ultra-wide, thin burger patties, charred to perfection. And they didn't just jump onto a passing smash-burger bandwagon; they've been cooking like this since 1975.

Semi-fancy big-city restaurants often sex up their menus by offering all sorts of ingredients on top of inch-thick Kobe medium-rare patties: blue cheese, portobello mushrooms, onion rings, barbecue sauce. You can get a California burger with avocado or a fried egg on top. I caught wind of a restaurant in New Mexico that touts burgers with feta cheese and cucumber aioli. In the Northeast, I hear rumors of coleslaw on burgers. In Latin America, they'll even put a slice of ham on top of a burger. The fancier restaurants in the US offer bourgeois overcompensation burgers that can cost more than $20. Like, sure, adding gold flakes and truffles makes you special. At those kinds of places, you're eating the burger for the novelty, not because it tastes great.

As far as I'm concerned, being creative when it comes to burger recipes is bullshit and unnecessary. It's not about the extravagant ingredients you stack on a burger; it's about doing the meat of the thing correctly. Thick-pattied, medium-rare burgers are bullshit too. Eat your steak medium rare, sure, but be a bit more judicious about what deserves to be rare and what doesn't. I want my burgers rail thin and charred, with American cheese or pepper jack, or a combination of both. Tomato, lettuce, and pickles if you want, but I don't need them, and I sure as hell don't need a fried egg on top—or, God forbid, blue cheese and truffles. Chili on a burger I can get behind, but at Ron's, I prefer them unembellished. They have the best burgers in the world, and they've been doing it right since before I was even alive.

***

11:14 a.m.

Wednesday, May 17, 2006

It's no surprise we chose Ron's Burgers for our off-campus lunch that day. We all piled into Fonz's BMW, and he drove us ten minutes to the Ron's location on 14th and Denver Avenue.

Weasel was waiting for us at a booth when we arrived, so we joined him. The place wasn't very busy, and we ordered as soon as we sat, already knowing what we wanted: burgers and fries and four root beers.

"Good to see you, boys. Feels weird being stuck at home," Weasel told us.

"Yeah, you too. I bet you got to sleep in today, you lucky bastard," I said.

"Hah! Yeah, I woke up about thirty minutes ago. Pretty nice, actually. I should've gotten myself suspended for seeds and an empty pipe a month ago."

The waitress brought over our root beers in ice cold mugs and then went off to help another customer. Hernandez leaned toward Weasel. "*Cabrón*, you missed the most epic role-reversal smiting today. Trout searched Fonz's car and then threatened to kick the three of us out like he did you. I was shitting my pants, but then our man, *the Fonz*, just starts spitting knowledge and put Trout in his place, man. He threatened to suspend all three of us for breaking his skylight when he found the prank rules in Fonz's car, and Fonz just laid into him, man. Starts citing legal words and shit. He said his dad would sue him and get him fired. It was radical."

"Your dad is a lawyer?" Weasel asked, surprised.

"Seriously. How did none of you know my dad is a lawyer? I've mentioned it, like, a hundred times."

"It was the coolest thing Fonz has ever done," I said, agreeing with Hernandez.

Fonz nodded. "Yeah, it probably was. I even made him give us the rules back." Fonz held up the sheet of rules, now weathered and worn like an eighteenth-century captain's log found in the wreckage of a sunken ship in some long-forgotten cove.

"Whoa, that's crazy." Weasel was chuckling, excited.

I turned to Weasel to give him a Fonz impression. "He said, 'No, *you* listen.'"

"What?" Weasel looked confused.

Hernandez laughed and provided the context. "Trout says, 'Listen to me,' and Fonz goes, 'No, *you* listen.' It was magical. Can't believe it worked. I thought we were done for."

The waitress returned and dropped off a large order of bacon-cheese fries. Not only was the food fresh and incredible, but they also served it quickly. We grabbed forks and small plates to scoop out our portions and added private piles of ketchup.

Hernandez took a bite of the fries and made a moaning sound, flabbergasted at how good they were. The way he closed his eyes and swallowed almost erotically reminded me of the way he described eating burritos while on mushrooms Monday night. Finally, he said, "All right, I've got a movie idea."

I turned to him and took a drink of my root beer. "Let's hear it."

"Okay, so this uptight dad finds out that he inherited an old yacht, but it's parked in Mexico, so he takes his whole family down and hires a captain to sail it up to Miami. When they get to Mexico, the captain is a sloppy, degenerate Mexican guy named Juan, and they proceed to run into a series of rollicking predicaments. I call it *Captain Juan*."

We laughed, and I said, "I'm not sure you can steal a plot and remake it in Mexico, man. But it's funny. *Captain Juan.*"

"I don't get it. Sounds like a pretty good idea," Weasel said.

"Like *Captain Ron*, but in Mexico," Hernandez explained angrily.

"Yeah, I still don't get it. Is that a movie?"

"Actually," I said. "I think *Captain Ron* is set in Mexico too. Your plot is exactly the same, except you swapped Kurt Russell for a Mexican dude. So maybe yours is actually more historically accurate."

"Whatever." Hernandez was over it. "Fonz, it's your turn at the prank tonight. Have you got an idea yet?"

"Yeah, yeah. I've got something figured out. Thought I should be cagey and secretive about it, like you were."

"Based on our limited success last night, maybe more collaboration could be helpful," I offered.

"Yeah, I need to know what we're getting into tonight. I'm going to be bored at home all day," Weasel begged eagerly.

"Okay, fine," Fonz said. "I won't keep mine secret like a total dumbass. Let's meet up at Weasel's around nine o'clock to prep. No drinking before tonight's heist. I think that fucked us last night."

"Yeah, Weasel was supposed to be the designated driver," Hernandez whined.

"*Cabrón*, we've been through this," Weasel said, annoyed.

"Can we still smoke before?" I asked, worried, because the answer might have been a deal-breaker for me and our friendship.

"Sure. We can smoke before. I'm not a monster," Fonz assured me.

We all breathed a sigh of relief.

"Hernandez, we need you to drive again tonight. The El Camino is key," Fonz continued.

Hernandez shook his head in disappointment. "Fine. The El Camino is clutch; I get it."

Fonz continued delivering his requests. "Jon Ryan, you bring your camera again. Hernandez, you bring your rope again and some wire cutters. And maybe some bolt cutters too. I'll buy the paint this time."

"We're painting something again? Oh boy." Weasel sighed in disbelief.

"Yes, Weasel. But it's a much simpler paint job. I promise."

"A rope? Paint?" Hernandez asked in a burst of jealousy, and I wondered why he brushed past the wire and bolt cutters, as if those two requests made sense to him but a rope was out of line. "Does it involve rappelling? Are you copying my prank, Fonz? Are we painting Trout's office back to Quench Blue? God, that'd be genius, actually. I'll fucking hate you if we do that tonight. But I'll also kind of love you for it too. Man, don't do it, please."

Fonz laughed and then shrugged. "Maybe."

"Fine. What do I need to bring?" Weasel asked, sounding resigned.

"Pick up, like, three or four magazines at the gas station. Something with articles in it that people who actually read like to buy. And a glue stick."

Weasel shook his head and then shrugged and nodded. "Sure. Stick glue and magazines. I can do that before nine."

"You're really not going to tell us what we're doing?" I asked. "At least give us the big picture. What are we painting? What're the rope and magazines for?"

Our burgers arrived, and Fonz waited until the waitress was gone before he responded while adding ketchup and mustard to his burger. "We're gonna steal a llama. A rich llama. But don't worry, Hernandez; it has layers."

"You don't know layers, Fonz. You wouldn't know a layer if it sat on your face."

Fonz just replied with a casual, "Nice. Look, we're going to fuck this llama, guys."

We all set our burgers down and looked at each other, a bit worried.

"I don't want to fuck a llama," Hernandez answered.

"Yeah, me neither," Weasel added.

"We're not literally going to fuck it," Fonz explained. "We're going to kidnap it and paint it blue and gold and leave a ransom note in a mailbox. That's what the magazines are for: so we can cut out letters to make one of those creepy ransom notes."

I smiled in confusion and demanded, "Say more."

"Aren't you mister animal lover, Fonz? How are you going to paint a llama?" Hernandez asked, and Weasel and I nodded, now also curious about this finer detail.

"We use water-based paint, guys. It's totally harmless."

I picked up my burger, took a big bite, and swallowed. Then I said, "Just tell it from the beginning like you're explaining the prank to five-year-olds. The way you'd imagine it all going if it worked perfectly. Because, really, it sounds as absurd as Hernandez's idea. Just coming up with a bizarre, illegal mission and calling it a prank doesn't necessarily make it a prank. I'm starting to wonder if we all have the same understanding of what a prank even is."

Fonz took a man-sized bite and then set his burger down and wiped his hands with a napkin. "Fine. You guys are like little kids that can't just wait for five minutes. All right, you all know who Bob Sockolosky is, right?"

"Obviously," Weasel answered. "Madison and Cole were both in our class before they transferred to some prep school."

"Yeah," I said. "You just told Trout that your dad plays golf with him and that they're friends and shit. Is that true?"

"My dad golfs with him sometimes, but I don't know if he likes him. I don't think they're friends or anything. But that's not the point. The point is: Bob Sockolosky has an estate, and one of the animals on that estate is a very important llama. The llama's name is Rudolfo."

"Rudolfo the llama," Weasel said sarcastically. "I'm falling asleep."

"So, anyway, Bob loves that llama. He treats it like a son. Or a mistress. My dad said sometimes Bob takes solo vacations on his private jet, and he takes that llama with him on the plane. On beach vacations to Miami and shit! This guy and his llama. He loves it. He probably fucks it."

"Yo, that's weird, *ese*," Hernandez sullenly admitted.

"So I figure we snag the llama, paint it blue and gold, leave a ransom note in Sockolosky's mailbox, and then drop

Rudolfo off at the practice soccer field. It gets at Sockolosky because he's a dick, and it's still a school-related prank since we're painting it with our school colors and detaining it on school property."

We all knew the soccer field to which Fonz was referring. In the spring, the girls' soccer team got the big high school stadium with a turf field to practice on, while the boys' team practiced on a field at the middle school, one that was fenced in and largely ignored by everyone but the gardeners. Now that athletic seasons were over and summer was approaching, only the landscapers would have reason to go to the middle school field, and they only mowed it once a week.

"How much?" Hernandez asked, talking through a mouthful of his last bite of burger.

"What?" Fonz asked, irritated at Hernandez for asking questions that way. "How much what?"

"How much is the ransom for? You said a ransom note, so what's the figure, sir?"

"Oh, uh, I don't know. A million dollars? We'll say we'll return Rudolfo for a million dollars. How's that?"

This made us all snicker and nod. A prank? Maybe. But a funny evening? Yes.

"Do you have any promising ways we can avoid getting caught this time?" I asked.

Fonz nodded and then pulled out a clipped-out newspaper article and handed it to me. "In fact, I do. Sockolosky is hosting some fundraiser tonight downtown. Meanwhile, we'll sneak onto his property, paint the llama, tie it up in the back of the El Camino, then drop it off at the middle school practice field. We're back at Weasel's in two hours, max. Then we have a few brewskis and a few laughs."

"We're going to be millionaires, *ese*. If that guy really loves his llama that much, I bet he'll pay. We'll have a pretty swanky summer vacation, fellas," Hernandez said excitedly.

"The ransom note is just a funny joke. We're not getting a million dollars, *jabroni*. When we drop the llama in the soccer field, the prank is over. They'll find the llama the next time they mow. Sockolosky will be calling around asking for a llama. It'll work itself out, but it'll be funny. It has layers."

"Fucking layers," Hernandez fumed.

"I like it," I said.

"Me too," Weasel agreed. "Hernandez, what's the first thing you'd buy if you had a million dollars?"

"Hmm. I'm not sure. First, I'd go get a mani-pedi. Then I'd get a pontoon boat. I think I could be a pontoon boat guy. What would you buy, Jon Ryan?"

"Aside from a mani-pedi?" I asked, and Hernandez nodded with a blink. "Probably a house. Real estate is an excellent investment. I'd buy a big place with an outdoor patio and my own huge brick pizza oven. I've always wanted my own pizza oven. But we're not getting a million dollars for a llama. That'd be insane."

"Oh, yeah," Fonz interrupted. "Hernandez, bring something to distract the dogs too. Hamburgers or something."

"Dogs? What dogs? Are they big dogs?"

"I don't know. They're regular dog size, I guess, like bull mastiffs or something."

Weasel and I looked confused, but Hernandez nodded at Fonz to let him know they were on the same page about the dogs and their sizes.

The rest of the school day passed quickly. I went through my routine. I went home and played with Stringer Bell. My family and I had dinner. I was on autopilot, and I remember very little of that afternoon. I couldn't even tell you what my mom made for dinner. All I could think about was the impending llama kidnapping, so I spent the afternoon getting myself into the right headspace for fake ransom tomfoolery. But that night I remember well, as if it just happened the other day.

Around 8:30 p.m., I drove to Weasel's house. Everyone in our small group was already there, including Naomi, Tera, and Alisha. Only the girls were drinking since Fonz insisted that we stay somewhat sober for his heist. Alisha, Tera, Weasel, and I sat on the couch watching a professional tennis match on TV while Hernandez, Fonz, and Naomi sat at the dining table helping Fonz craft his ransom note. Nobody used gloves, so if that note was ever actually taken seriously, detectives would find all three of their fingerprints on it. They cut and glued letters from the magazines, and eventually, they were pleased enough with their work to walk it around the room and present it to us. The paper read:

We have Rudolfo. He's fine but scared. Will return him for 1 million in small bills. Will call your cellphone tomorrow to arrange a meet. Do not call police. Call the police and Rudolfo is meat.

I thought it looked pretty hilarious, as I had never seen one of those kinds of collage ransom notes in person before. The plan was simple enough, though I still wasn't sure how we were going to keep the llama in the back of the El Camino. I assumed Fonz had a solution for that. By 10:00 p.m., the girls left, and we began loading up Hernandez's car. Unlike the previous night, when going to the school to paint Trout's office, I actually felt excited.

CHAPTER 8

11:02 p.m.
Wednesday, May 17, 2006

We took Highway 169 northbound, then took an exit and started making our way east down rural country roads. Hernandez was driving, and I was in the passenger seat, with Weasel and Fonz smushed into the uncomfortable back seat of the El Camino. Since Hernandez had the wheel, he was naturally in control of the music. When we exited the highway, he put on a nine-minute song by James Brown called "People Get Up And Drive Your Funky Soul," and he played it about as loud as the El Camino could manage. We had the windows down since Fonz and I were smoking American Spirits, and we were all nodding our heads to the funky tune. The song ended on cue as we approached Sockolosky Drive, and Hernandez killed the radio and headlights to make our final approach incognito. We drove past a maroon Jetta abandoned on the side of the road, drove past the main gate, and then made a classic five-point turn at the dead end, where Hernandez parked and shut off the El Camino.

We sat in silence for a moment to survey our surroundings. It was quiet, and everything was dark except for a few areas near the house lit with bright lights hanging from the roof. We stepped out of the car, and everything was still. We each closed our door carefully, except for Weasel, who slammed his door shut like a complete asshole. I shot him a scornful glance.

"What? You said the house was empty."

"Yeah, you're right. Be as loud as you can be, Weasel," I said.

Hernandez put two fingers between his lips and whistled loudly. Then he said, "Here, doggy doggy doggy."

Silence.

Hernandez let out another whistle. Reluctantly, two skinny dogs with droopy, red eyes drug themselves over to face us from the other side of the fence. They looked sleepy and non-threatening but curious about why we'd called for them. They were both greyhounds. Healthy and well-cared for, but as lean and trim as the breed gets. Hernandez pulled something out of his pocket and set it on top of the car: a wrapped fast-food burger.

"Don't worry, guys. I got this." Hernandez split the hamburger patty and then reached into another pocket to bring out a plastic baggie filled with weed shake. He jammed several grams of ground weed into each patty half and passed them through the fence. The dogs happily devoured them, wandering a few feet away to finish their patties in peace.

"So feeding the dogs our weed is supposed to be a part of the plan?" Weasel asked. "Don't edibles take like an hour to kick in? What are we supposed to do, just wait here?"

"Did you say our weed, *ese*? This was my weed. Fonz, by the way, you owe me $40."

"Were we supposed to keep receipts?" Weasel asked. "Fonz, those magazines for the ransom note were expensive, man."

The dogs walked away and found a comfortable spot in the grass to go back to sleep, and then they were both out cold.

"Holy shit," I said. "What kind of weed was that?"

"Indica. The best stuff that Pete had."

"I don't know. That didn't seem like a very normal reaction, Hernandez. Are you sure that shit isn't laced?" Fonz asked.

"Man, it's just weed. The same stuff we've been smoking. Oh, speaking of which." Hernandez produced a joint and lit it up. Our ritual before any ignorant endeavor.

"Those dogs don't look good, man. I thought weed usually takes longer to kick in. I think we're smoking the same poison that just killed them," Weasel said seriously.

"Hey, Hernandez," Fonz said. "How long do you think it'll take before you're a dog murderer?"

"*Cabrón*, you said they were bull mastiffs. I packed a lot of shake in the patties. How was I supposed to know they were dogs from Bulimia?"

"Brother," Weasel responded, laughing. "Bulimia isn't a place. You know that, right?"

"It's just weed. They'll be fine. Fonz, let's get this show on the road. I'm not getting any younger here," Hernandez said, forgetting about the dogs.

"Hand me the wire cutters," Fonz commanded, and Hernandez handed him a pair. Fonz went to work, cutting out a large enough portion of the fence for us to crawl through while we gathered the other prank supplies. Fonz handed me the ransom note, sealed inside an envelope, and said, "Jon Ryan, run down and put this into the mailbox."

"Can't we just drive back to it later?" I asked, feeling lazy after the previous night.

"We'll be hauling ass out of here. This is my plan, and you have to assist in any way I say, right? It goes into the mailbox now, please."

I didn't see any sense in arguing with Fonz, so I grabbed the envelope and took a shot of it with the video camera. Then I put the camera in the El Camino's back seat and jogged down to the gate. I opened the mailbox and put the letter inside. Only after did I look up to see two cameras on top of the gate. They were pointed right at me, filming my reaction as a dumbfounded nitwit. "Fuck," I said, shaking my head in disappointment. I would surely catch some heat for the evening's shenanigans. Still, I was excited and not smart enough to weigh any consequences, so I decided not to tell the boys the bad news about me being on camera. I jogged back to the dead end near the El Camino to rejoin the team.

By the time I returned, Fonz had crawled through his hole in the wire fence, and Weasel was putting the cans of blue and gold pet-safe spray paint on the ground next to the El Camino.

"The dogs are out cold, Hernandez. I don't know what you did, but I sure hope you didn't kill them. That'll disqualify me," Fonz said.

"They'll be fine, *cabrón*. We just smoked the exact same stuff. It's safe." Hernandez strapped his rope around his shoulders the same way he had the night before.

Weasel grabbed the bolt cutters and crawled through the fence, then went over to wait by Fonz, who was observing the landscape like a real man on a mission. I opened the car door and then grabbed my video camcorder and filmed a few seconds of Fonz saying hi and explaining the situation from the other side of the fence. I shut the camera back off and took it with me as I crawled through the fence, followed by Hernandez and his rope. We all crouched and moved quickly past the right side of the house toward the stables. A padlock hung from the stable door handle.

Fonz ordered an instrument like a doctor during surgery: "Bolt cutters."

Weasel passed him the instrument, and Fonz tackled the padlock. He squeezed and squeezed, but the steel didn't budge, so we all joined him and pushed on the device's handles together until finally, under the combined pressure, the lock violently snapped open. Fonz removed the lock and pushed the big, wooden stable door open. Three llamas and four horses looked at us. Luckily, each of the llamas wore a collar with a nametag so we knew which one was Rudolfo. He looked just like the others at first glance, until you noticed his eyes. He apparently had heterochromia because one eye was blue, and the other brown.

Hernandez made a leash of sorts with his rope, looped it around Rudolfo's neck, and tried leading the animal out of the stables. But Rudolfo didn't want to move. He dug in his heels and started humming. Seriously, the llama was humming at us and refusing to budge. Like he was taunting us.

Then I remembered I had something in my pocket that could save the day. I pulled out a Clif Bar and unwrapped it, sticking the wrapper back in my pocket and breaking the bar in half. I put half under Rudolfo's nose to get him interested. He stopped humming and sniffed the Clif Bar, and then he snorted and looked away from me. Then he went back to humming.

Fonz said, "Dude, even llamas don't want to eat that shit."

I shook my head. "It's delicious and nutritious. Full of berries, granola, and other bullshit I assume llamas love."

It may have been my confident voice, but just then, the llama snatched half the granola bar out of my hand and started chewing it.

"See," I said. "I told you guys."

The llama finished chewing and looked up for more. I held the other half of the bar in front of me, a few feet in front of Rudolfo's nose, and started walking backward out of the stables, so he'd have to walk toward me for his snack. Like a dope, he predictably fell in tow and followed me, while Hernandez held on to the end of his leash as if he could direct the beast in any direction if he so chose. Once outside, I fed Rudolfo the snack and started rifling through my pockets for more. Unbelievably, I had a second Clif Bar on my person. I used half of it to lure him toward the fence, stopping to let him eat it when we were halfway across the hill. I used the last half to get him the rest of the way to the fence, but then I put the treat in my pocket instead of feeding it to him. Instead, I started filming again.

"Okay, so this llama will not fit through that hole in the fence," Weasel said, pointing. I aimed the camera toward the three-foot-by-three-foot hole at the bottom of the fence.

Then I pointed the camera at Fonz, who addressed his audience. "So we are in possession now of Rudolfo. We just have to cross this fence and paint him and get him into Hernandez's El Camino. Then we should be all set." He nodded to let me know he was done and that I should stop recording. Next, Fonz got the wire cutters again and went to work making the hole big enough for a llama.

That gave the three of us a few minutes to chat, which is never helpful during a caper. "So we're painting the llama now and then putting him in my car?" Hernandez asked.

Fonz nodded and went back to cutting the fence. "Uh-huh."

"So won't it get paint all over the back of my El Camino then? Why don't we paint it on the school soccer field?"

"Because the soccer field is just a drop-off point. I have everything timed out to a T. The plan is what it is. You just have to trust it. It's what you agreed to."

"Fuck." Hernandez shook his head in acquiescence. "Fine."

Fonz finished clipping and removed a huge section of the fence, placing it on the grass nearby. I pulled out the last piece of Clif Bar and held it up to Rudolfo's nose again as I walked through the opening. The animal followed. Once we reached the car, I fed him the treat. Fonz began picking up the paint cans and handed us each one. "Let's get to work, boys."

"Are we doing any specific design here?" Weasel asked Fonz. Hernandez stopped himself from spraying at the last second and perked up for an answer. "Are we doing stripes or circles or anything special?"

"Hmm. Yeah, stripes, I guess."

That was enough direction for us. We quickly began spraying Rudolfo. He hated every minute of it, pulling around, moaning, and lightly bending away from us in various directions. Hernandez kept a tight grip on the rope, rubbed Rudolfo's unpainted skull, and talked sweetly to him while we worked. By the time we were done, it wasn't pretty, but he had a blue butt and tail, a gold torso, and a blue section covering his front legs and chest, along with a few spritzes of gold around his neck. Before we could properly admire our work, headlights pointed at us from the road, though a football field away. The oncoming vehicle stopped at the gate, turned in, and drove slowly up the brick road to the circular driveway in front of the house. It was a black SUV.

"Shit just got real," Weasel informed us, and I turned the video camera back on to document the hysteria.

"We need to wrap this up. Now," Fonz said seriously, in the same tone he'd used to put our principal in his place. "Hernandez, jump up in the back and pull Rudolfo up there. We gotta go."

Hernandez shook his head in a very this-is-never-going-to-work kind of way but crawled up in the back of the El

Camino anyway and pulled on the rope. Meanwhile, the SUV parked and turned off its lights, but it was too far away for us to hear the car doors shut. Hernandez pulled the rope, and Rudolfo jumped into the back of the El Camino. Hernandez kept petting him and talking to him calmly, and to my surprise, Rudolfo bent his legs and laid down, fitting perfectly into the back of the car. Hernandez was as shocked as any of us. Then he nodded and spoke softly to Weasel, as if trying not to wake a sleeping baby. "Psst. Take the rope; you sit back here and hold it."

"What? I have to sit in the back with the llama? It's, like, a thirty-minute drive, man."

"It's my car. I've got to drive. Jon Ryan has to film. And it's Fonz's night to be in charge. Just take the rope," he whispered.

Reluctantly, Weasel hopped in the back and cuddled up with Rudolfo while we piled into the car. Hernandez started the engine, and we cruised slowly with the lights off so we could remain cloaked in darkness. We rolled past the gate at a slow crawl, and everything was gravy. It felt like we were home free. Everything had gone off without a hitch. Once the house was out of sight, where the road got darker and more winding, Hernandez prepared to flip on his headlights when Rudolfo, spooked, jumped to his feet and violently spit in Weasel's face. Then Rudolfo leapt from the moving vehicle. Weasel, to his credit, did not let go of the rope so was immediately launched overboard. Weasel skidded on the pavement, which ground Rudolfo to a halt in the middle of the road and scratched up both of Weasel's elbows something good.

Hernandez screeched the El Camino to a halt on the right shoulder of the road a few feet away from the abandoned maroon Jetta we had passed earlier that evening. Hernandez shut off the engine, and we scrambled out, rushing toward Weasel to make sure he was okay. I turned on the camera and recorded all the action. Weasel was fine, aside from a few scratches and a wet face, and Rudolfo was okay but agitated. He was humming again. We all took a breath, and Hernandez scrutinized the back of his car for paint damage. Aside from some scratches on the bed, there wasn't much.

"Well, what do we do now?" Weasel asked sharply.

"We get him back up there," Fonz answered. "I don't know what you were trying to do to that llama, but you obviously freaked him out. It's a long ride back to the middle school. You need to control yourself."

"What? Are you kidding me? I'm not riding in the back with that thing again. Jon Ryan can do it. Or you can."

"It's fine," I said. "I'll ride in the back with the llama."

"Great," Weasel responded, walking away from us.

Hernandez grabbed the rope and tried to pull Rudolfo toward the car. Once again, Rudolfo dug in his heels and decided not to move.

Pop!

A gunshot rang out. Then another. Definitely gunshots, not a car backfire or fireworks. We all paused and looked around at each other in silent terror. Rudolfo was the only one who seemed unfazed, as he started humming again.

"What the fuck was that?" Hernandez asked.

"I don't know, man," Weasel replied. "Maybe someone is doing some night hunting. Or there's a night shooting range nearby. Or maybe someone is about to murder all of us."

"Yeah," I agreed. "Those were definitely gunshots. What should we do?"

"Aw, man," Hernandez answered. "If I get shot for stealing a llama, promise you'll tell everyone at school it was gang-related."

We spent another minute looking at each other, searching for leadership.

"Fonz, this is your prank. Are we getting out of here, or what?" Hernandez asked, terrified but trying to hide it.

"Oh, um…I guess. I guess let's get Rudolfo. We came all this way. I don't think anybody is shooting at us, but let's hurry anyway."

We all shrugged, and since the gunshots had stopped, the immediate sense of danger had passed. Hernandez tried again to tug the rope, and then Weasel took a turn. Rudolfo wouldn't budge. He was staying right where he was, in the middle of the road.

"Jon Ryan," Fonz said, using my entire name as usual, just in case there was another Jon around. "Use some of that shitty granola to lure him back in the car."

"I don't have any more. I used it all to get him to the car the first time."

Fonz didn't want that news and looked away, sighing.

"Rudolfo," Fonz wheedled, trying to bargain now. "We've got some good stuff in the car. Ice cream. We'll go on a little road trip. Come on. We'll take you to Big Splash. You'll be back home in those shitty stables by tomorrow." Fonz tugged the rope, and Rudolfo tugged back, not wanting to leave his home.

Less than the length of a football field away from us, the Sockolosky gate reopened, and the same SUV pulled back onto the road.

"Fuck the llama," I said. "We're out of here."

"Yeah," Fonz agreed. "Let's hide behind the car."

We all ran to the El Camino and took cover behind the passenger side in the ditch as we watched the SUV's headlights barrel toward us. The car was driving fast for the area, and Rudolfo still hadn't budged from the middle of the road.

"Rudolfo, move!" Hernandez kept yelling. Nevertheless, Rudolfo remained standing in place with his back to the SUV, staring ominously at us.

The SUV kept increasing its speed, and as the car got closer, Fonz said, "Oh, no. Please, no, Rudolfo."

Rudolfo wouldn't budge, but he kept looking at us, focused mostly on Fonz. The SUV came roaring over a hill and down a turn right toward us. It didn't even brake. The driver never even noticed Rudolfo standing on the road. The vehicle plowed through Rudolfo's plump body as the driver finally slammed on the brakes, and the SUV fishtailed, jumped into the left ditch, and slammed violently into a tree. An oak tree limb smashed through the driver's side front window. The llama was thrown fifteen feet forward into the ditch, spraying blood along its course. The hood of the car, covered in llama blood, crunched up like a contracted slinky, and airbags deployed. The car horn rang for a moment, and the emergency lights flashed. It was a few seconds of complete pandemonium, and then near silence.

"Jesus Christ," Weasel gasped, and we all shook our heads in disbelief. Minutes may have passed. Time stopped. We walked over to assess the damage and look for survivors.

A terrible moan emitted from the trunk of the SUV. We looked at each other briefly in trepidation, and then Fonz opened the trunk hatch. What we found was a disturbing shock: my third-period teacher, Mr. Derkatch, bloodied and splayed on a black, plastic tarp, barely alive.

"Mr. Derkatch," I said in disbelief.

"Whoa, Mr. Derkatch?" Fonz asked stupidly.

Earl Derkatch coughed, and blood came out of his mouth. He looked terrible. "Boys. It's nice to see you."

Weasel smiled, and the rest of us panicked. Then Hernandez and Fonz walked over to the driver's door to check on the driver while Weasel and I checked Mr. Derkatch, who sat up the best he could and coughed up blood again.

"Oh, he's dead," Fonz reported, walking back toward us. Hernandez nodded in agreement.

"Huh?" Weasel asked.

"The driver," Hernandez explained. "Tree branch right through his face. Guy's a goner. So is Rudolfo." He pointed to the ditch ahead of us, where llama bits and pieces lay scattered about in a gross impressionistic style. His expression didn't convey the least bit of surprise.

Weasel and I examined the crime scene for ourselves. Staring at what remained of the driver's face, we were both horrified and mortified.

"How's Mr. Derkatch doing?" Hernandez asked.

We all went back to the trunk to see if we could help him. "I don't know." I put a hand under my teacher's head to support him. "Sir, are you okay? We're going to get you an ambulance. Just hang on."

Mr. Derkatch tried to speak but could only manage another feeble cough.

"You know," Fonz said. "Bob Sockolosky isn't in this car."

"Well," Hernandez answered eerily, "maybe he was the one shooting the gun earlier. He's going to kill us for sure now. He would've heard that wreck. We've gotta get out of here. He's going to lose his mind when he sees Rudolfo all over the place."

"We can't leave, man," Fonz said. "We have to at least call 911. Look at him. We can't just leave. That's some evil shit. We'll get in trouble, but we can't just let one of our teachers die here like this. Can we?"

We all looked again at Mr. Derkatch, bleeding on the tarp and gasping for what sounded like his final breaths in the back of an SUV in front of a few of his students. Hernandez leaned in close to talk loudly to Mr. Derkatch, as if the crash had impaired his hearing. "Sir! Yo, do you know where you are right now?"

"Or what you are doing in Sockolosky's trunk?" Fonz added. We all waited for a response as Fonz pulled out his phone to dial for help.

Mr. Derkatch coughed lightly again and then spoke, painfully, "Aargh, I think the condom broke."

I looked at Weasel, then at Fonz, dumbfounded. Hernandez nodded like he'd seen this exact situation many times before.

"You're probably in shock, sir," Weasel said. "You were in a car accident. In some dude's trunk. We're going to get you an ambulance."

"For real, *ese*," Hernandez added. "You can worry about bitches later. We need to get you to a hospital right away."

Mr. Derkatch tried to push Hernandez away and grab me by my shirt collar, but he was too weak to do so. He grabbed his stomach, in clear pain, and then leaned forward and clutched the side of the trunk with his one hand to keep his balance. He looked like he was about to throw up or shit his pants. Then he groaned, "Mother. Fucking. Diamonds." He puked painfully into the tarp-covered trunk of the car and onto his chest. Not much came out, but what did was coated in deep, red blood.

"Whoa!" Hernandez shouted, jumping back to a safe distance. Mr. Derkatch lay on his back and closed his eyes for a moment before slowly wiping his mouth and looking over at us in embarrassment. On the trunk floor were four blood-covered globs with shiny specks peeking through the blood. I set aside my disgust and picked them up with my right hand. Then I gently wiped them clean with my t-shirt and held up four blue diamonds in the palm of my left hand. The guys and I studied them for a moment in awe.

"Motherfucking diamonds is right," Weasel said.

"I'd say that's what was upsetting your stomach, sir," Fonz added.

Being the only reasonable one there, I asked, "Where is all this blood coming from? It looks like he was shot."

"Apparently," Hernandez answered confidently, "someone shot him with diamond bullets. Maybe he's a werewolf."

When Hernandez finished speaking, Mr. Derkatch coughed one last time. His eyes rolled back, and he stopped breathing. Dead.

I hadn't ever seen even one person die, and now I had seen two, plus a spoiled llama that was more well-traveled than me. And it was all our fault. I moved Mr. Derkatch's jacket to the side, and that's when we saw the bullet wounds in his chest and stomach. Weasel felt for any sign of a pulse on Mr. Derkatch's neck while Fonz checked his wrist for the same. They both looked at each other and then at Hernandez and me, shaking their heads in disbelief. Fonz held up his phone again, about to dial for help.

"Yo, there's nothing we can do here, Fonz," Hernandez said. "They're both dead. The llama too. If they can prove we're the reason the llama was on the road, maybe we're on the hook for manslaughter."

Fonz nodded and then shut his flip phone and returned it to his pocket. "Fuck," he said sorrowfully. "I liked Mr. Derkatch. I wonder what the hell he was doing out here."

"Guys, I hate to break up the moment, but I think we should get moving," Weasel implored. "My guess is that Sockolosky shot Mr. Derkatch, and I'm pretty sure we just kidnapped and murdered a llama he really loves, so he'll probably shoot us too if we hang around in front of his house all night. Plus, the fucking diamonds?"

Weasel had a fair point that startled us all. "Okay, let's go. What about these diamonds?" I displayed them again, glittering with opportunity.

"What do you mean? Put them in your pocket or give them to me. Are you kidding? Make Rudolfo's death mean something," Hernandez answered. I shoved the four diamonds into the front pocket of my jeans, and we all ran to the El Camino.

***

1:21 a.m.
Thursday, May 18, 2006

We got back to Weasel's house and began drinking beers. We tried to drink them quickly enough to numb what had happened—what we'd seen and what trouble we'd caused. We sat around the table in Weasel's dining area, between the living room and the kitchen, voicing our surprise to each other multiple times, as if we were afraid of silence. As if we had to keep repeating ourselves to process the events of the night.

"What are we gonna do?" Fonz asked for the tenth time.

"Our part in this is over, *cabrón*. We don't do anything. We have a few beers and go home. We go to school tomorrow like nothing happened," Hernandez answered.

"Man, Mr. Derkatch is my third period, before lunch," I added, as if the situation affected only me in particular.

"I hate to say it," Weasel said, "but Hernandez is right. We weren't involved. We were never there. Tell the girls at lunch tomorrow that they're our alibis. We were here all night playing card games with them."

We were quiet for a moment, remembering the driver's demolished skull, the gunshot wounds in Mr. Derkatch's torso, and the pieces of Rudolfo lying in the ditch and splattered on the car hood. To this day, I've never seen a more disturbing sight.

"Hey, Fonz," I said, trying to lighten the mood. "I'm pretty sure you're disqualified now. Rules are pretty clear about hurting people or animals. You did both, so I think that's not very good."

Fonz was in serious panic mode. "Who gives a fuck about the game anymore? The game isn't important. People are dead. They're dead because of us. Hernandez, your dad is a preacher, and this doesn't bother you? Honestly?"

Hernandez shrugged. "I mean, it's pretty bad. Mr. Derkatch was shot, though. Something was going on tonight, and it wasn't all our fault. We're witnesses—victims, really. You had a silly prank laid out. We didn't plan to hurt anyone."

"Holy shit, man...we just killed two people," Fonz continued.

"Correction," I told him. "Two bullets and a llama just killed two people."

"Still," Fonz said, "shouldn't we have called 911? We have to. This isn't cool, man. We have to."

Hernandez sighed. "All right, *hermano*. You're right. But we can't use one of our cell phones. They'll trace it back to us."

Fonz calmed down once we agreed to report the accident. We went to a nearby gas station and used the payphone to call the police and provide an anonymous report about a car crash outside of Bob Sockolosky's house. And a dead teacher.

CHAPTER 9

1:05 a.m.
Thursday, May 18, 2006
(several minutes earlier)

While the four boys, Jon Ryan, Hernandez, Weasel, and Fonz, were staring in shock at the car wreck crime scene, four of their football-playing classmates were in a pickup truck, drinking beer and driving toward Mr. Trout's house on the other side of town, still intent on pulling their own incompetent versions of senior pranks. This time, there were no cute baby chickens. Jackson was driving, with Will in the passenger seat and Chase and James in the back. Jackson pulled over about three houses away from Mr. Trout's home to help shield their mission. They had just bought a shopping cart full of toilet paper and eggs. Surely the checkout clerk had had some idea what four drunk teenagers were doing with such a shopping list, but she exhibited no qualms as she scanned the items.

Jackson parked and shut off the engine, and they all exited the vehicle and started ripping open packs of toilet paper. Then they got to work. Mr. Trout's one-story, ranch-style brick home, surrounded by several large trees more than a hundred years old, was in a quiet neighborhood near the school. The football guys started launching rolls of TP up into the trees, making good use of their strong throwing arms. Once the trees were littered, they began tossing the remaining rolls over and across the roof of the house. Then, they got out the egg cartons. They'd bought six dozen eggs, and they made quick work out of painting the front of the house with them, as well as Mr. Trout's car. Like drunk, young, male idiots, they ran back to Jackson's truck, giggling as they piled inside and revved the loud engine.

Jackson started slowly driving toward the principal's home. Will rolled his window down, pulled a baseball bat off the floorboard, and leaned out the window of the slowly moving vehicle. Mr. Trout's cute, barn-shaped wooden mailbox was painted red with a brown roof and white trim. With one impressive swing, Will and his baseball bat splintered the mailbox in half, sending it flying into Mr. Trout's yard. The football players hooped and hollered, and Jackson sped off.

Lights came on inside three houses on the block, and window curtains were pulled back so neighbors with prying eyes could witness what mischief was occurring in their sanctuary. Mr. Trout was one of them. When he saw his toilet-paper-littered lawn, he ran out his front door to catch the hooligans responsible, not even stopping to shut it behind him. He slowed to a stop on his porch as he noticed all the broken eggs on his house and vehicle. Furious, Mr. Trout stood barefoot in his pajama pants and white t-shirt, shaking his head and wondering why he'd devoted his life to attempting to regulate adolescents. His relatable sense of humor and work ethic would have made him a good fit for an office job. As he unspooled his hose to wash off the eggs so it wouldn't cause any permanent damage to his paint, he noticed the mailbox was not where it should be. His eyes watered in disbelief. The eggs and toilet paper had been enough. Why on earth would they destroy his mailbox too?

Mr. Trout's personal life wasn't known to any of the students, or the football players might have had second thoughts about the prank. Mr. Trout was open with only a few teachers who had known him for years. Otherwise, he kept his genuine emotions close to his chest. He had been married for seventeen years and had no children of his own. Three years before, in 2003, his wife had passed away from leukemia. She had battled the disease for almost two years before finally succumbing to it. While his students often viewed him as a harsh ballbreaker of a tyrant, his wife knew his tenderness and was the only bona fide supporter he had most days. The two of them met in college when they were optimistic and fun, back when Mr. Trout still thought of education as a noble pursuit. Back before he became a jaded parody of himself. Pictures of his wife were displayed all over the house, but that mailbox was even more special to him. Before she died, she bought the wood, and they built the miniature barn together, and then she painted it. In the three years that she had been gone, seeing the mailbox when he came home from work every day was one thing that reminded him of her. It gave him a sense of joy to think about some of their final good days together.

Mr. Trout found the remnants of the splintered wood pieces and fell to his knees, crying harder than he had since she died. The two other neighbors who had been looking out their windows closed their curtains and shut off their lights, presumably to let him mourn in peace. He was an ugly crier, with snot running over his chin and a scrunched face full of angry tears. He shook his head in disbelief and stood, looking savage as he peered down the road in each direction. "Those sons of bitches. That fucking Weasel."

***

2:34 a.m.
Thursday, May 18, 2006

The scene on the road next to Bob Sockolosky's estate was a veritable circus, at least for those parts. An ambulance, a fire truck, and two police patrol cars were parked near the wrecked Lincoln Navigator when an unmarked police car, a Chevy Caprice with spotlights above the side mirrors identifying it as a municipal vehicle, pulled up behind the other cars, and out stepped detective Danny Finnerty. Danny was in his mid-forties and had been on the job since he was honorably discharged from the Marines. He was a nice guy but intimidating. He looked like the kind of guy who could win any bar fight.

"Detective." A uniformed officer approached him, and they shook hands like they'd known each other for years. "Sorry to have you come out so late."

"Officer Williams." Danny Finnerty looked tired, but that was his job. "What've we got?"

"One victim and a llama. Hell of a car crash. I've seen my share of deer accidents, but this is my first with a llama." The officer motioned toward the ditch scattered with furry pieces of animal. A few feet away, Bob Sockolosky was sitting on the ground, sobbing.

"Who's that?"

"That's Bob Sockolosky. This is his house, and that's his car, but he says he was in bed when the wreck occurred."

"Did he call 911?"

"No, sir. The 911 call was anonymous. It came in from a gas station in downtown Tulsa. But I guess he loved that llama. The vic worked for him. A forty-one-year-old male named Walter Murphy." Officer Williams handed Walter's wallet to Detective Finnerty, who opened it and studied Walter's license.

The two of them walked slowly toward the Navigator, where Detective Finnerty examined the driver, who was completely unrecognizable due to the tree limb that had crashed through the windshield. And his head.

"He's crying over the llama? Not this guy?"

"People deal in different ways, I guess." The officer pulled out his notepad and read from it. "Walter Murphy. Has a few priors for aggravated assault. The fire department was waiting for you before removing the tree branch."

They stared at Walter's body jammed in the driver's seat. It looked normal—his seatbelt was even on—but the branch was completely embedded in the center of his face.

"All right, let them know they can get him out of there. I was told the 911 call said there were two dead bodies?" Finnerty looked around at the dark scene.

"Yeah, I know. But they must have gotten it wrong. We've just got one dead person and one dead llama. We heard that report, too, so we looked all over the road for any signs of someone else. Haven't found much yet, but there is a 2002 Jetta parked right over here. That might have had something to do with all this. Plus, take a look over here."

The officer led Detective Finnerty to the back of the Navigator and peered into the trunk, which was empty. The officer used his flashlight to show two spots around the edges of the trunk that looked like drying remnants of bloody puke.

"Did the techs already get samples of all this?" Finnerty asked.

The officer shook his head. "No, sir. Wasn't sure if we were looking at just an accident here or something else. Thought this blood may be the driver's blood, thrown back here on impact. We were waiting for you before we do anything."

"Maybe it was from the second victim. What'd Sockolosky say?"

"Not much. He says the victim, Walter Murphy, drove him home from some political fundraiser downtown, dropped him off, and left."

Finnerty scrunched his chin like he was trying to compute the scene. Then he pointed to the gate. "Those security cameras work?"

"He says they do, but we haven't watched 'em yet. Was waitin' on you, and this guy hasn't stopped crying since we got here. There's something else, sir."

"What is it?"

The officer pulled out a clear evidence bag containing the ransom note and handed it to Detective Finnerty. "It's a little odd. We found this in the mailbox."

"Hmmm." Finnerty perused the note several times, then handed the evidence back to Officer Williams. "What did Sockolosky have to say about this? He hadn't seen it before you arrived?"

"No. One of ours found it. I don't know. He was just as confused about it as we are, I guess. It just made him cry harder."

"And I'm assuming Rudolfo is…?"

"The llama, sir." Officer Williams nodded toward the broken remains of Rudolfo.

"What the hell? So this was a llama knapping gone wrong?"

Officer Williams nodded, then shrugged and said, "Guess so. Not sure how common that is."

"Happens more often than you'd think. I'm not going with the accident theory just yet then. Let's get that blood in the trunk tested and find the address that the 911 call came in from. And run the plates on that Jetta, I want to know who was out here. I'll talk to Sockolosky, and then I want to pull the footage from those cameras."

Officer Williams walked back over to his cohorts, and Detective Finnerty started down the road in the other direction, where Sockolosky had planted himself on the pavement, looking at the ditch where most of Rudolfo's remains were. He'd stopped crying but still looked destroyed.

"Mr. Sockolosky, do you mind answering a few questions for me? I know it's a tough time, and I'm sorry for your loss." Finnerty nodded his head back to the car and a dead Walter.

"He was my pride and joy," Bob Sockolosky said somberly, then began tearing back up.

"He? Um…uh…the alpaca?"

"He was a llama. Rudolfo. He was fourteen years old. But he was still in his prime." Sockolosky spat out an embarrassing sob and then wiped his tears in an attempt to compose himself.

"Mm-hmm." Finnerty shook his head. "And that ransom note the officers found in your mailbox? What do you make of it? Did Rudolfo, um, have any enemies?"

Sockolosky cleared his throat and slowly got to his feet. "Are you fucking with me? Of course, he didn't have any enemies. He was a goddamned angel from heaven."

"Of course. I'm sorry. I don't mean to seem insensitive; this just doesn't seem like a ransom note from experienced criminals. Can you think of who might have left that note? Anyone you're having business issues with? Or someone who goes to school with your kids, maybe?"

"Nobody I know or my kids know would do something like this. You'd better figure out who did."

"What about the driver—uh, Walter? Did he have any enemies you know of?"

"Walter was always fucking everything up. He was bound to die in some tragic accident. I just didn't think my baby would be collateral damage from his terrible driving. This is his fault as much as anyone's."

"I beg your pardon? What do you mean by that? That this was his fault."

"He was driving my car, and it looks to me like the car hit my baby before it hit that tree."

The detective waited for more information, and when it didn't come, said, "I'm still struggling to see why it's Walter's fault."

"Rudolfo was deaf, ever since he was born. Couldn't hear a thing, so he wouldn't have heard a car coming if some asshole put him in the road. He may not have even seen it coming." Bob began crying again.

"Sir, we had a report on a 911 call about this, and the caller mentioned two dead bodies, though I only saw one. Can you explain why they would've said that? Or why you didn't call 911 yourself?"

Sockolosky looked genuinely shocked. He paused, as if trying to come up with a reasonable answer. "I have no idea who would have called or why they said that. When I heard the wreck, I ran outside. I was in shock. I was still sitting out here when the police arrived. I would've called it in; I just didn't get a chance."

"So no one else was here with you tonight? Or in the car, aside from Walter?"

"No."

"And do you know whose Jetta that is parked down the street from your gate?"

Sockolosky paused, surprised by that one question. "No. I think it's been there for a few days. I assumed someone broke down."

Finnerty nodded, wondering what his life had become. "I see you've got a couple of cameras at your security gate. Maybe they caught something. Can you take me inside and show me that footage, sir? Then we'll get out of your hair."

"Sure." Sockolosky took one last look at the pile of fur and blood and then turned toward his gate and plodded back to his house with Finnerty in tow.

***

2:50 a.m.

Thursday, May 18, 2006

Sockolosky turned on a few hanging monitors in what looked like an oversized walk-in closet outfitted with electronics and monitors above a long white melamine desk. Then he pushed a handful of buttons on the keyboard to rewind the video feeds from the gate. The screen showed images of a car rolling past, then a boy by the mailbox, then the same car approaching. Both men's eyes narrowed as they watched the events play fast in reverse.

When the video finished rewinding, Detective Finnerty took a seat in front of the monitors. Sockolosky pushed play and stood behind him. They could see more details as the footage played forward in real time: The edge of an El Camino rolling past the gate with its lights off, headed toward the dead end, but with no person or license plate visible. No movement for a few minutes. Then a slightly short and overweight teenage boy walking up to the mailbox, opening it, setting the ransom note inside, looking up directly at the camera, and saying something. The video had no sound, but it didn't take an expert lip reader to know the boy said, "Fuck." After that, the video showed the boy running toward the dead end, and a few minutes later, the El Camino drove past again, still with no person or license plate visible on the screen.

"Can you get me a copy of this video?" Finnerty asked.

"Yeah, I'll do it right now. You better catch these bastards before I do. My pride and joy is gone, officer. I don't know if it was some kid's prank, but someone is going to pay for taking my dear Rudolfo from me." Bob Sockolosky hit a few buttons to save the footage to a USB flash drive for Detective Finnerty.

"And Walter," reminded the detective.

"Huh?"

"The man driving your car? I was under the impression he worked for you. If someone is responsible for Rudolfo being in the middle of the road and causing this wreck before fleeing the scene, that person could be looking forward to manslaughter or negligent homicide for Walter."

"And for Rudolfo."

"Yes, sir. They could also be charged with animal cruelty or something, probably. You're sure you don't recognize that El Camino or the boy on the tape?"

Sockolosky shook his head and bit his lip.

Finnerty left to examine the crime scene again before heading to the gas station where the 911 call originated from. He needed a copy of its security footage.

***

11:02 a.m.
Monday, May 15, 2006
(two and a half days earlier)

Mondays were golf mornings for Bob Sockolosky. He would follow a round of golf with a late lunch and two martinis, and then he'd use the steam room in the club and get a massage before heading into the office. That Monday, he'd had an 8:30 a.m. tee time at the Forrest Ridge Golf Club in Broken Arrow for a grueling foursome. It was to be him and Walter Murphy, his company vice president, and two guys Walter had introduced him to a few years prior. Walter and Bob showed up early to warm up on the driving range. The other two men, Danny and Bear—Bear's given Cherokee name was Yona, but to anyone outside the tribe, he was simply Bear— showed up fifteen minutes late, which naturally irritated Bob.

Generally, when you think of Oklahoma, the mafia is not the first thing to come to mind. Likewise, you'd not expect to see Japanese yakuza gang members milling about. But statistics show that, on average, about 1 percent of the folks in any American city are gang members, and Tulsa is no different. The yakuza had a silent presence in the city, building relationships to procure firearms, which were then shipped to Japan. Bob Sockolosky seemed as square as they came, but, as they say, looks can be deceiving. Getting firearms in Japan was nearly impossible, so the yakuza struck up friendships with a few good ol' boys in Oklahoma, including Bob. Bob's golf partners weren't squeaky clean either. Walter had experience in the dirt; his past dealings connected them all to a few low-level money laundering schemes. Danny had ties to the local Irish mafia, and Bear was the manager of an Indian casino. Bob and Walter laundered the gun money for the yakuza enterprise through Bear's casino, which made Bear a third partner in their part of that laundering enterprise.

Bob, Walter, Danny, and Bear lingered at the eleventh hole, waiting for the slow group ahead of them to move on before teeing off. Bear was showing Danny an image on his phone. "Oh, she's adorable," Danny said.

"Let me see," Walter pleaded, reaching for the phone. Bear released his grip from the device, and Walter looked closely at the photo of Bear's two-month-old baby. "Oh, she's perfect. Congratulations, Bear. You'll make a good father."

Bob nodded at Walter to indicate he wanted to see the picture, too, so Walter panned the screen in his direction. Bob nodded and said, "Yes, congratulations." Then Bob took out his phone and pulled up a photo of his own. "Want to see *my* boy?" The others peered over Bob's shoulders to see a photo of a llama eating a blade of grass. The three guys scrunched their eyebrows and nodded blankly at the comparison. The group ahead of them finally left, so they went back to golfing.

"They'll pay for the shipment in cash, like always, but we owe them six months plus interest at the casino," Walter said to the group as Bob smashed his ball straight down the fairway. "Yuto and Hanzō are supposed to fly in from Hawaii on Friday, and I know both pieces of business are on the agenda. If we stiff them again, you can be sure they'll cut off some of our fingers, or maybe even an entire hand."

"No one is losing a finger," Bob said casually as Danny set his ball on the tee.

"No," Bear agreed. "No one will lose a finger. I'll put up the diamonds this time, four of them. That's more than six months, plus interest. But I take it out of all our shares equally."

Danny smacked his ball and sliced it into the trees. Then Bear walked up to the tee and arranged his ball.

"Great," Walter said. "That's great. We give them the diamonds Friday night and get the guns out by next week; then everything's good."

"Bob, you have to meet with them and give them the diamonds. Yuto and Hanzō can't be seen at the casino. It's too risky," Bear said solemnly. "Come by the casino tonight, and I'll give you the diamonds. You hold them until Friday, and make sure they get to Hanzō Friday night. Or you'll be the one losing a hand."

***

4:08 p.m.

Monday, May 15, 2006

If you have only one arm, golf is a tough sport. Tougher than most, even. Earl Derkatch never played the game, even before he lost his arm. But that Monday after school, he was sitting in his car listening to news radio at the Forrest Ridge Golf Club, eating the two cheeseburgers and the milkshake he had grabbed from Sonic on the way. Earl's obsession with Bob Sockolosky and his dirty deeds was motivated by convictions he kept to himself. He knew Sockolosky hung out at the club all day on Mondays, usually with his probably-also-corrupt VP Walter Murphy. As Earl waited for Sockolosky to appear, it began to rain. He slowly ate his meal, discarding burger and condiment wrappers in his passenger seat. No one would be waiting for him at home, aside from his three cats. Earl had never gotten married or had any kids. His only legacy would be the students he taught. He had a lot of time on his hands and DSL internet, which leant itself to lots of internet browsing. He'd go online and disappear into conspiracy-laden message boards, often posting his own theories, which were validated by other anonymous users. His obsession with the idea that Sockolosky was dirty, while correct, was motivated less by deductive reasoning than it was by boredom and a desperate inferiority complex.

Earl wasn't a professional at tailing anyone, but he was dead set on understanding what Sockolosky was hiding and, somehow, thought he was qualified to do so. So he sat in his car and ate, listened, and waited. Eventually, Bob Sockolosky and Walter Murphy walked quickly toward Sockolosky's Navigator, anxious to get out of the rain. Bob wasn't carrying any golf clubs, as he was a member and could leave them there, but Walter threw his clubs in the trunk while Sockolosky got into the passenger seat. When Walter climbed into the driver's seat and started the Navigator, Earl started his car and slowly followed them out of the parking lot and onto the Creek Turnpike. The dark skies and sheets of rain made it hard to see—making it less likely that Earl would be spotted. They drove fifteen minutes before pulling into the parking lot at the Hard Rock Hotel & Casino.

What the hell are we doing here? Earl asked himself as he found a parking spot fairly close to the Navigator. He followed Bob and Walter inside.

Earl walked past the slot machines and blackjack tables and spotted Sockolosky at the pit boss's station talking to a Native American man who managed the casino. The man nodded to a nearby bathroom, which he and Bob then entered while Walter stood guard. Earl moseyed slowly toward the restroom door, trying to be discreet while also pretending to be in a low-key rush to make it to the toilet. When Earl reached the bathroom door, Walter did not directly obstruct him, but he gave him a suspicious snarl as he entered.

Sockolosky and the Native American casino manager were standing at the sink counter when Earl entered the lavatory, and they both flinched like he'd caught them doing something wrong. The casino manager was holding a small velvet bag, which he pushed into Sockolosky's hand as inconspicuously as possible, and Sockolosky quickly shoved the bag into his coat pocket in turn.

They both eyed Earl to see if he'd noticed, but Earl glanced away from them, clutched his stomach, and acted as if he were in great pain. Then he went into a stall and locked the door. He sat on the toilet with his ears open for any information he could glean. The suspicious activity with the casino manager and the mysterious velvet bag gave Earl a certain confidence in his theories.

The two men at the sink looked at each other seriously, knowing the conversation couldn't continue around prying eyes or ears. The casino manager hit the timed water dispersal on the sink to drown out the end of their discussion. "Tell me you've got this covered," he begged.

"I've got it. Don't worry. Friday night at my place with the samurais."

The water turned off, and the casino manager opened the bathroom door to return to the floor. "Remember," he said before he left, in almost blind repetition, "you lose these, you're probably not the only one that'll lose a hand."

The bathroom door shut, and the casino manager was gone. Bob turned the water back on and splashed his face to compose himself. Then he used a paper towel to dry his face, and he exited the bathroom.

Once the bathroom was all his, Earl Derkatch scrunched his forehead and lipped to himself, *Samurais?*

Earl waited a few minutes and then flushed the toilet and went back to the casino floor. Sockolosky and Walter were long gone, but Earl had a lot of thinking to do. He was convinced that he was right about Sockolosky—that he was corrupt and needed to be stopped. Now, if he wanted to be a hero, he needed to sell himself on doing something even more courageous, like breaking and entering. Earl went to an ATM, took out two hundred bucks, and got comfortable in a seat at a slot machine.

***

9:13 p.m.
Monday, May 15, 2006

Hours had passed since Earl sat down at one of the Goblin's Cave slot machines. He poked the buttons in front of him and, when prompted, fed the machine more money. The machine didn't ask stupid questions or demand he learn complicated rules. Either the goblin gave him money or the goblin asked for money. End of story. He put money in, the wheels spun, and the money disappeared. Earl tuned out the whirring sounds, the other mostly elderly patrons, and the money at stake. In his trance-like state, Earl thought only about Sockolosky, Walter, the casino manager, and that velvet bag he'd witnessed in the bathroom. Once an hour, an older waitress with a raspy voice stopped by and brought him a scotch and soda. By 9:13 p.m., Earl had to pee. He had lost half of his two hundred bucks and had convinced himself to be brave.

Earl was walking toward the same bathroom where he'd been a halfwit spy earlier when he heard, "Earl. What are you doing here? Did you see the show too?"

Earl spun to find Mr. Trout emerging from an aging crowd coming from the direction of the concert hall, holding his hand out; they shook hands. Earl Derkatch and Mr. Trout had worked with each other for nearly twenty years and had become friends. Occasionally, they and two other teacher friends went to a bar that hosted trivia nights; together, they had won their share of competitions.

"Hey! No. What show?"

"Three Dog Night—they just played. You mean you're just here playing slot machines? Is everything okay?"

"Yeah, I was just clearing my head. Didn't spend much."

"Are you hungry? Want to grab a drink or anything?"

"No, I can't. I was just going to hit the bathroom and then head home."

"Oh, all right," Mr. Trout said, a little disappointed. He was there alone and had gone to the show because his wife used to like Three Dog Night.

"Hey, I saw a funny scene earlier." Earl laughed. "One of our seniors got arrested. Saw them take him away, and the cops said something about him smoking weed at a concert. He must have been at the same concert you were."

Mr. Trout looked very interested in this information. "Which student?"

"Um, David Hernandez. Poor guy."

"You're sure?"

"I'm positive. I saw the whole ordeal. They put him in cuffs and took him out to a police car."

CHAPTER 10

7:40 a.m.
Thursday, May 18, 2006
(three days later)

After all the nastiness endured at the Sockolosky estate the night before, I slept miserably. The oft-overquoted expression of "tossing and turning" comes to mind. But that's what it was. All I could think about was the llama, the guy driving the car with the brutal tree limb in his face, the four diamonds I had thrown into a cigar box I kept in my top desk drawer, and poor old Mr. Derkatch spitting out his final breaths in the trunk of the Navigator, coughing up four bloody blue diamonds like a twisted version of the goose that laid a golden egg. I felt like I had just finally fallen asleep when my alarm thrust me back into my tired and macabre reality. I looked at my alarm clock in disbelief, but it asserted it was already 7:40 a.m. I hit the button to stop the incessant buzzing and got out of bed. You could say going to school that morning like nothing had happened indicated that my friends and I were sociopaths; but I think shock was driving our frozen empathy.

I turned the shower on, made the water as piping hot as possible, stepped into the tub, and sat down cross-legged, or

"Indian style," as they said in elementary school. I was in no hurry; I needed the steaming water to awaken my miserable mind. It was my second-to-last day of school, and I knew that when I got to third period, Mr. Derkatch wouldn't be there anymore. I wondered if maybe they'd tell our class what happened, or maybe they wouldn't know any of the details yet. Homicide investigation procedures were a happy mystery to me. I got dressed and drove as fast as I could to school, estimating I'd arrive to first period about two minutes after the first bell—right on time for me.

The events of the previous night didn't feel real; part of my brain believed it was just a bad dream and none of it had actually happened. But it had happened, and I knew it. And I knew I had to keep the accident and those diamonds a secret between the four of us. Luckily, I had spent enough hours watching *Jackass* and insane reality TV shows that I was somewhat desensitized to violent and disgusting things. Therefore, I was more easily able to compartmentalize, to shove it way down and forget about it, as if everything was normal. None of it was normal, but it felt normal enough that morning driving to school. Like it was just another day.

When I arrived, every kid and teacher was in the parking lot, milling about in excited confusion. It was a congregation of joyous anarchy. I pulled my Bronco into my usual parking spot and joined the boys loitering and jabbering next to Hernandez's El Camino, along with Alisha, Tera, Naomi, and Elaine. Weasel was even there—despite the fact that he had been forbidden from the premises. Everything was out of sorts, and for a moment, I wondered whether whatever was going on might have something to do with the night before.

"What's going on out here? Is this a fire drill or something?" I asked, hopping out of my Bronco.

Each of the guys gave me a fist bump.

"Hey, what are you doing here?" I asked Weasel.

Weasel shrugged. "What are *you* doing here?"

"School's closed today," Naomi said while chewing gum with her mouth wide open. "Apparently there's a gas leak in the school." She rolled her eyes at the end of her statement, like we were all supposed to understand the implication.

"It's gonna be hard to pull off a prank when the school is closed," I said to Weasel. "You just felt like waking up early and showing up here even though you're suspended?"

"School being closed down today *is* my prank, you dimwit. They closed it because of a strange smell."

"So today's prank's already over?" Hernandez scowled at him, disappointed and confounded. "I didn't even get to use my rope. I thought it was becoming something of a tradition."

"What kind of smell?" Fonz asked.

"Yeah, you're all welcome that I didn't make you guys sacrifice a llama or stay up all night painting," Weasel said sarcastically.

"Why are we even still talking about pranks?" I asked, showing the only shred of human decency between us. "After what happened last night, I feel like I should convert to Catholicism and go to confession or something. I couldn't even sleep."

"Me neither," Fonz said.

"I slept like a bull mastiff on a quarter ounce of tropical kush shake," Hernandez declared.

"That's because you don't have a soul, Hernandez," Weasel answered. "I couldn't sleep either, honestly. So I got up and threw this plan together. Pretty good, right? Everyone gets out of school for the day. Top that, Jon Ryan."

"Did you get anything on video?" Hernandez asked him. "The rules say you have to get footage of the act in progress."

"I took these." Weasel fanned out over a dozen polaroids, and we each took a handful. The first few were close-ups of his hand holding small glass tubes of liquid. There were a few photos of him smiling, holding up a fist, and four photos of several bottles shattered on the floor. One shot was blurry, which, Weasel explained, was him trying to take a photo of himself sweeping up the broken glass. Finally, there was a photo of him smiling while holding a phone up to his ear.

"So how did it happen? I don't get it. Are those little glass containers stink bombs?" Fonz asked.

"Of course you don't get it, Fonz."

"Yeah, you left us out. That's not fair, and that's not what we discussed," Hernandez complained. "At least explain it to us."

"Fine. You know how natural gas doesn't really have a smell?"

We all looked at him blankly. Naomi nodded like she knew everything.

"Well, it doesn't, so gas companies add a chemical to it that makes it smell like rotten eggs. That way, people know if gas is leaking. I used a few stink bombs I had that smelled exactly like rotten eggs, smashed them around the school, and swept up the evidence. Then, while everyone was in the teacher's lounge, I snuck into the office and made a few calls using a deep voice. One call to the gas company, one to the police station, and one to the fire department, and I left a voicemail for the superintendent. After four calls about a suspicious odor, they had to close the place. It's protocol, I guess. They can't risk sweet little children's lives."

"Damn, dude," I said, impressed. "That sounds gnarly. You could probably get in some deep shit over this one, right?"

"This one? No one got hurt here today. This is silly. What are they going to do? Suspend me? If I get in trouble, I'll bet Fonz's ass it's about last night and those fucking homicides." The girls hadn't been paying close attention to us until Weasel said the word *homicides*.

"Did you say homicides?" Alisha asked.

"What the hell did you boys get up to last night?" Naomi followed.

"Nothing," Hernandez answered coldly, as if dismissing any further questioning. "Nothing happened."

The girls looked at each other, not believing us but not caring that much either. We were known to exaggerate, and as far as they were concerned, there was little chance of murder afoot.

"Gas leak day. Good on you, Weasel. I like it." Hernandez smiled. "So we can leave now? What should we do today? Is your dad home?"

"No, I think he's gone until Monday," Weasel answered. "We can pick up some beers and drink at my place. Ping-Pong tournament?"

***

10:14 a.m.
Thursday, May 18, 2006

We raised Weasel's garage door, set up his Ping-Pong table, and took turns playing a doubles tournament while drinking beers, smoking weed and cigarettes, and listening to old-school hip-hop music by Bone Thugs-n-Harmony and the Notorious BIG. Then Naomi took over the music and put some Shakira on her iPod. The girls all sang along to one song and mumbled the next few. That morning was a little sweet taste of what the freedom of college life might offer us. Even though classwork would have been nonexistent that day anyway, given it was the last week of school, we felt elated and unshackled to suddenly have the day off, with the added benefit of our parents not knowing about the school's closure. Gas leak day was like a snow day and a surprise party with underage day-drinking all rolled into one. The phrase *gas leak day* even sounded like it could be some sort of eastern European holiday.

In terms of tournament logistics, Hernandez and I paired together. Fonz and Weasel were another team, as well as Elaine and Naomi and Alisha and Tera. Weasel's tennis skills somehow transferred to Ping-Pong—he was unbeatable—so he and Fonz kept winning and holding court as the rest of us took turns trying to wear them down. I was decent at foosball throughout my early years but was never as great as I wanted to be at Ping-Pong.

"I'm still not sure how I come out on this one, Weez," I said. "I mean, I guess it's a prank, but I don't know. Is it really a prank? I mean, I think it's cool you managed to get us out of school for the day."

"But it's no baby chickens," Fonz interjected.

"Yeah," I answered, chuckling. "It's no baby chickens."

"Of course, it's a prank," Hernandez shouted at me, sticking up for Weasel's ingenuity. "Whole school got out today, not just the seniors. Could argue that out of the three so far, Weasel's prank made the most people smile."

"Oh, how many *smiles*, not just laughs, is in the rules now?" Fonz asked. "That's how you get points? Based on how many smiles you count? Last night was making us all smile until—" Fonz stopped himself, remembering we had agreed not to tell anyone else about the previous night's snafu, including the girls.

"What's Jon Ryan's prank gonna be tomorrow?" Hernandez asked, shifting topics.

"I still don't know, man. It's hard. I couldn't even sleep last night."

"Why are we even playing this stupid game at all anymore, guys?" Fonz asked rationally. We were in too deep to stop at that point, so we paid him no mind.

"What do you mean?" Alisha asked. "What are you guys talking about? What happened last night? Tell us."

"Nothing," Fonz answered angrily. "We were here playing drinking games with you girls all night."

"I know what you could do. You could frame Principal Trout, man," Weasel said to me, a little too eagerly and with a devilish grin on his face.

"Frame him? For what?" I asked.

"For last night. The whole enchilada. That'd be pretty hilarious. Get him convicted. Visit him in prison a few years from now and tell him how you did it. That would win our prank contest, hands down. Talk about layers."

"Convicted for what?" Alisha asked, not willing to let it go. "Are you guys just messing with us to piss us off or something?"

Weasel was already buzzed from the early beers and cocky from winning six games straight in Ping-Pong, so as usual, he didn't edit himself. "Fonz, sorry, bro. You're disqualified. Rules are rules. You lose the game, and you're probably going to hell too."

Naomi turned down the music.

"He's definitely going to hell," Hernandez confirmed.

"Okay, guys. What the hell happened last night?" Naomi implored.

"Nothing," Hernandez replied.

"Yeah, nothing," Weasel agreed, choking on a laugh.

That's when Elaine spoke up, slurring cutely. She was Fonz's girlfriend, so she hung out with us all the time, but she hardly ever drank. For the observance of Gas Leak Day, I guess, she'd decided to day-drink with us alcoholics—on an empty stomach to boot. "The boys saw Mr. Derkatch get murdered last night, and then they made off with a small treasure chest or something."

"Babe," Fonz scolded angrily. "We'll talk about this later!"

The interaction halted us in our tracks, and the Ping-Pong tournament was suspended. Evidently, on the drive from school to Weasel's house, Fonz had spilled the beans and told his girlfriend what happened the night before.

"What?" Tera looked like she didn't understand one word of what Elaine had said.

"Are you for real?" Naomi interjected, and Elaine nodded in the exaggerated way only a drunk can nod.

"Mr. Derkatch?" Tera shrieked. "I love him. He's such a great teacher. And he seems like such a good man. You guys are kidding, right?"

"Yeah, there's no way," Alisha said. "You guys are playing a joke on us. Right, Elaine?" Alisha didn't like the way Elaine was shaking her head no. Alisha turned to me for validation. "Jon Ryan, is Mr. Derkatch really dead?"

I looked down at my feet and bit my lip. Then I looked back up at Alisha. I wanted to lie to her, but I couldn't. "Yeah. Mr. Derkatch is dead. Someone shot him, we think."

Hernandez and Weasel both tossed their hands in the air in disdain, even though Fonz and Elaine were the ones who had spilled the beans.

"Someone definitely shot him," Hernandez clarified. "We're just not sure if he was shot with real bullets or— something else. The jury's out. There could be a whole werewolf scenario here that no one else is seeing."

Tera began crying, and Alisha tried to console her, wrapping her in her arms.

"You guys need to go to the police and tell them what you saw," Elaine demanded.

"Babe…later?" Fonz tried again, but she wasn't having it. She crossed her arms stubbornly.

"We don't know what we saw," Weasel answered.

"Yeah," Fonz agreed. "If we go to the cops now, we won't have anything helpful to tell them, and they'll get us on leaving the scene of an accident. Maybe manslaughter. It could be bad, babe."

The girls digested this information, knowing Fonz was serious and informed about the law because of his dad. Elaine appeared to loosen up again.

"What happened?" Alisha asked.

"It's a long story," Weasel murmured.

"Fonz tried to kidnap Bob Sockolosky's llama last night for his prank. We got it into the street, and then a huge SUV smashed into it and wrecked into a tree," Hernandez explained succinctly. "The driver died, and Mr. Derkatch was in the trunk puking up some fancy rubies or gold when we found him. Not a very long story, but it sounds bizarre when I say it out loud."

The girls all looked rightfully confused.

"Gold?" Tera stopped crying. "How much gold? He puked it up? Like, there was puke on the gold?"

"They were diamonds. Four diamonds. I still have them," I said.

Weasel burst into song about pirate treasure, singing an opening line from "Professor Booty" by the Beastie Boys.

"Oh my god. Can I see them?" Tera asked, and I shook my head. "What are you going to do with them? Are you sure they're real?"

"I doubt Mr. Derkatch got murdered over some fake diamonds, sweetheart," Weasel said with perfect drunken condescension.

"Elaine is right," Naomi insisted. "You boys should go talk to the police. Help them find who did this. If you have evidence and someone killed Mr. Derkatch for those diamonds, then don't you think someone might come after you guys too?"

Hernandez, Weasel, Fonz, and I all looked at each other, astounded none of us had considered the possibility that we were in danger.

"We should put them in a safe deposit box or something and leave 'em there for, like, five years, if we're smart," I said.

"You just want to sit on the diamonds, *ese*?" Hernandez asked, shocked by my suggestion to be patient. "Shit's evidence in a homicide, for all I know. Naomi's right. I want that shit as far away from me as possible—but I still want a taste of that moolah. You know what I'm saying? We should pawn them or find a fence like they do in those heist movies."

"You know a lot of fences in your criminal underworld, Hernandez?" Weasel asked, and I nodded along.

Hernandez puffed and crossed his arms. "Well, I'm sure I know someone. A friend of a friend, maybe. Diamonds are valuable. Who wouldn't want to buy them?"

"Maybe Pete would buy them. Or I bet he knows someone," Tera suggested.

"The drug dealer Pete?" I asked. "Is he really the most connected person we know? I mean, we don't really know him that well."

"Well, he's best friends with Jake," she replied.

Weasel nodded. "Right, and you're fucking Jake, so you think we could trust Pete with this? I heard they tried to break into Captain D's one night last year and couldn't even open the safe, so they just left empty-handed. Those guys are a joke."

"Those two are as far from gangsters as you can get," Hernandez said, still pretending like he might know some real gangsters.

"He has real money, and he knows people," Tera said confidently, which caused the other girls to raise their eyebrows. "Plus, do you know anyone else who deals drugs or associates with criminals?"

The boys and I looked at each other and shrugged, then shook our heads.

"Okay," I said. "I bet these things are worth, like, a million dollars or something. They're really fancy. We'd be happy if he gave us, like, five or ten grand. He could turn around and sell them for a huge profit. It could be the biggest deal of his life."

Hernandez and Weasel nodded approvingly. Fonz wasn't so sure. "You really think they're worth that much, Jon Ryan? Maybe we should sit on them. I don't want to just make Jake and Pete rich."

"You don't want to split five grand four ways this week, Fonz?" Weasel asked. "You could quit your job at Fuddruckers early, before college. Plus, it's not like we can just take these things to a pawn shop. They'd trace them back to us. Whoever *they* are."

Fonz considered this, seemingly swayed. Then he smacked himself in the face. "Fuck. I have to work a shift tonight."

"Me too, buddy. We're both closing." Hernandez stretched out his arm and gave Fonz a fist bump.

"Split *five* ways," Tera said. "If I'm helping you get the money for it, I deserve some."

"No way," Weasel countered. "We all have Pete's number. We all buy weed and mushrooms from him. We don't need you just because you're fucking his friend. Plus, you didn't almost get killed finding the treasure."

Tera was so blown away by the statement that she jolted her head backward, as if a gust of wind had struck her face. She even fixed her hair before answering. "Excuse me? It was my idea."

"Yeah, we want a piece too," Alisha said, and Naomi nodded. Then Elaine followed suit.

"Girls. No one is after you and trying to kill you. We deserve the money. We put in the effort," I said.

"I don't know about that," Tera continued, pouting. "But I know if Pete pays you, I deserve at least part of it. It was my idea, after all."

I looked at the guys, and we shrugged. Then I said, "Fine, you can have 10 percent if you make it happen by tonight."

"Jake gets home at five. Then we can all go to Pete's house." Tera seemed fine ending the negotiations with the proposed 10 percent.

"Okay." I nodded, as did Weasel.

"Fonz and I are working from four to ten tonight. Can we do it after that?" Hernandez begged.

"Maybe. I don't know. This is our first time trying to fence stolen diamonds," I said. "Maybe Tera should talk with Jake at five and then text us if there's a reason to meet up."

"That sounds good," Fonz agreed, and Hernandez nodded.

"Can we come to watch you guys sell the diamonds?" Alisha asked on behalf of herself, Elaine, and Naomi. "We know Pete and Jake too. Plus, maybe someday we'll have to testify about all of this or something."

I shook my head and grimaced. "We can't show up like it's a party. How about we tell you what happened tomorrow?"

"No, I don't—" Elaine started, but Fonz raised an eyebrow.

"Babe." He glared, and she acquiesced.

"All right," I recapped. "So, Tera, you'll talk to Jake when he's off work?"

She nodded, and we all sat in silence.

By noon, everyone had left Weasel's house. Naomi and Alisha decided to go home and take a nap before going to work that afternoon, as did Fonz and Hernandez. Weasel said he was going to watch tennis on his TV and take a nap, so he invited me to stay and hang out, but I headed home instead. On my way, to soak up the beers we'd had all morning with a magical lunch, I picked up a sandwich from Giant Subs, a local spot with a fifty-square-foot area for customers to order inside. I ordered my usual: the cracked peppermill turkey and capicola, along with too much mayonnaise, chopped lettuce, onions, jalapenos, and the most incredible cheese there is, the bold three-pepper Colby Jack cheese from Boar's Head, all on untoasted white bread—as this is a sandwich meant to be eaten cold. Giant Subs was, and still is, my favorite sandwich shop in the entire world. They bake their own fresh, fluffy bread daily and use fresh produce and quality Boar's Head meats and cheeses to create the ultimate meal. Even imagining having one right now brings a tear to my eye. I hope you will try it one day. I ate the entire sub in my car before I even entered my neighborhood.

When I got home, I was full and tipsy, and I had the abode all to myself. Heather was still in middle school, so she didn't get the privilege of Gas Leak Day. I made a jug of sweet tea and filled it with ice, and then I poured some into a thermos to drink while I took Stringer Bell on a long walk. When we got back, I was feeling better from the tea and food, and Stringer Bell was in a great mood, as always.

The weather was nice, and the grass in our yard was getting too long, so I changed into shorts and made my way to the riding lawn mower. Mowing was one of my two main chores growing up. The first, taking the trash bins to the curb Tuesday mornings and bringing them back to the house Tuesday afternoons, was mindless and didn't bother me, but mowing the grass, including weed-eating around the curb and mailbox, was a responsibility I actually enjoyed. I had a lot on my mind between the diamonds still resting in my cigar box, my dead teacher, and starting college in the months ahead. I couldn't imagine being able to focus enough to watch television or read a book, but mowing always relaxed me. I popped *The Marshall Mathers LP* by Eminem into my colorful portable CD player, put on my headphones, cranked the volume, and powered up the mower. For about two hours, I zoned out, lost in another dimension while I made our yard look pretty. Actually, it must have been more than two hours because I listened to the whole CD twice and even started it a third time. It wasn't the newest album by Eminem, but it was his peak album, as far as anyone my age was concerned. I listened to that CD so many times that I could probably sing along to just about any of those songs to this day.

By the time I finished with the lawn, a school bus appeared, and Heather deboarded. The sandwich, iced tea, walk, and mowing had sobered me up. I waved at Heather as she went inside the house to make herself a snack. She barely responded with a half-hearted wave to me—like she was a busy suit making deals on Wall Street. I parked the riding lawn mower back in the garage, went inside, took a shower, and then lay down in my snug bed. I tried to read a few pages of the philosophy book Mr. Derkatch had given me, but it was dense, and I had just seen the man die the night before, so my focus was absent. I do remember liking one particular passage, though. It explained the philosophy that some people are thoughtful but irrelevant because they don't force their wills onto the world or change anything about the present or the future. The book explained how those people have no relevance to the actual act of creation itself because they just sit back in passive indifference. It reminded me of what Karl Marx said: philosophers may interpret the world, but the point is to change it.

Then I fell asleep.

It was the best three-hour nap of all time.

***

5:02 p.m.
Thursday, May 18, 2006

My phone kept chirping, alerting me to a series of new text messages, until I stirred awake from my afternoon nap. The sun was in the midst of setting, and an orange hue streaked across the cloudy sky outside my bedroom window. I stayed in my comfy bed and snatched the phone off my nightstand. It was a 2004 Motorola Razr, and I felt like a big-shot, high-tech badass with a phone so cutting edge in my possession. I was the first in my friend group to have a cell phone equipped with a camera: a 2.0-megapixel camera with an LED flash. The photos taken with it were pixelated and objectively horrible, but at the time, we thought they were incredible. The rest of my friends had gotten cell phones the year before me, but my parents didn't sign off on getting me one until I was almost seventeen. That being the case, technology had graced me with the latest and greatest. When Heather turned fifteen the year after I graduated, my parents bought her a brand-new iPhone, and the youth have only gotten more plugged in ever since.

I flipped open my shiny silver cell phone and read three new texts, all from Tera. The first: "Jake says Pete is interested." Then another: "Meet me at Pete's house at 6 pm with the rocks." And the last, most promising one: "He'll buy them from you, and then he'll sell them." Group texts didn't yet exist, so I assumed Tera had sent identical messages to Fonz, Weasel, and Hernandez. I sent Weasel a message asking if he wanted to pester Hernandez and Fonz at work and grab some grub while there. He obliged, and I informed him I'd scoop him up from his house. I got dressed in less than a minute (in track pants and a hoodie as usual—didn't have a lot of variation in my wardrobe) and snatched the four dangerous blue diamonds from the cigar box. Diamonds that probably still had traces of blood on them despite the mediocre cleaning I'd attempted. I stuffed them into a sock and shoved the sock in my pocket.

My mom was home early from work, so I told her I was going to grab dinner with the boys and would be home before it got too late. She asked me if I would drive Heather to school the next morning, and I responded, "Sure," in an annoyed tone of voice, conveying I was in a desperate hurry. I fired up the ignition on my trusty Bronco and steered to Weasel's house. We smoked a fatty at his place, and then I navigated us to Fuddruckers and parked in between Fonz's BMW and Hernandez's El Camino behind the restaurant, by the dumpsters, where all the employees parked.

The parking lot was a vast waste of land, an area that had once been home to grass and trees but was razed for its commercial real estate value. The parking lot connected to a shopping center that sported a Kohl's, a Home Depot, a spa, a pharmacy, and stores that sold random expensive wares like cell phones and reading glasses. In addition to Fuddruckers, there were a handful of other chain restaurants, including Chili's, Hideaway Pizza, Panera Bread, and Cracker Barrel.

It was a real suburban middle-class haven, and people were slowly swarming for shopping and dinner for their after-work capitalistic respites, desperate to spend the money they'd worked all day to earn.

The Fuddruckers dinner rush was just starting to pick up, so we took a seat at the bar in front of the dessert area, where Hernandez was stationed for the night. His duties included making cookies and pies, but mostly he was busy creating milkshakes. We sat across from him to chat while Fonz worked as a line cook in the kitchen behind us, grilling a never-ending stream of way-too-thick burger patties. They both wore their Fuddruckers aprons and hats.

"Any chance you guys can get off early tonight?" I asked.

Hernandez finished making two chocolate milkshakes and set them on the counter for a waitress to grab. "I doubt it, man. Dennis is working our shift tonight. The dude is a complete asshole. He already yelled at me for showing up ten minutes late today." Dennis was the general manager of the location. From what I understood, Dennis didn't work a lot of shifts, but when he did, he was an egotistical tyrant.

"Tera texted us and said we can meet with Jake and Pete around six tonight. They agreed to buy the diamonds off us," Weasel added.

"Shit, man. I doubt Fonz and I can make it. Do you guys want to get a burger, and I'll ask Fonz what he wants to do?"

"Sure, but it's nearly six now, so chop-chop."

Weasel and I ordered burgers, and Hernandez typed our request into the restaurant's point-of-sale system. Sometimes we could get the employee discount, but not while Dennis was working.

The shtick that made Fuddruckers unique was cooking burgers to order and allowing customers to take their plates around the extensive horse-track-shaped salad and condiment bar to add all the fixings themselves. It was like paying them so you could make your own burger, which I guess some people enjoyed, but I wasn't a huge fan.

Hernandez finished placing our order and slowly began prepping cookie dough on a tray. He was placing the tray in the oven when Fonz came over and shook our hands.

"What's up, guys?" Fonz pulled his hat off, wiped beads of sweat from his forehead, and then replaced the cap and sat next to us.

"What's up, Fonz?" Weasel asked. "You on break?"

"I can take, like, five minutes, but we've only been here for two hours, and Dennis is a jackass."

"Did Tera text you?" I asked Fonz.

"I don't know. I haven't looked at my phone. What'd that slut say now? Does she want 30 percent?"

"She said Pete is down to buy the diamonds off us, and then he'll find someone to sell them to. Wants us to bring them to Pete's at six o'clock," I said.

Fonz looked at his watch and said, "Nice."

"Fuck this place, man. What are you getting, like $8 an hour? We'll split five grand, and each have a grand to play with," I spewed.

"It's $7.25 an hour," Hernandez corrected him, dejected.

"Me and Weasel can handle it," I assured them. "We just ordered, so we'll eat our burgers real quick and then head over to Pete's."

"Well," Hernandez said, checking on his cookies in the oven, "make sure he doesn't screw us. Remember, 5K is our bottom line."

Just then, Dennis walked over and tried to sound intimidating. "What's going on here? Is it already your break, Fonz?"

Fonz looked at his watch. "I've got three minutes, Dennis. I'm just saying hi to my friends."

"We've got four tables waiting for chocolate chip cookies, Hernandez."

Hernandez nodded. "They're two minutes out, Dennis. They're in the oven now."

Dinner time was approaching, and customers kept streaming in through the front entrance of the establishment.

"Okay, well, we're getting a dinner rush. What have I told you guys about this not just being a hangout for you and your friends? This is a job, and you need to act like it."

"Hey, buddy," Weasel chimed in. "We're paying customers here. Just waiting for our burgers."

"I'm literally taking a two-minute break to say hi, Dennis," Fonz said. "It's not like we're throwing a party."

Dennis had a bad case of little-man complex and didn't appreciate back talking. "Break's over, Fonz. And we need those cookies ASAP, Hernandez. You can catch up with your friends when you're off the clock."

Hernandez exhaled deeply. "You know what, Dennis? Why don't you make your own damn cookies?"

Dennis was appalled. "What did you just say to me?"

Hernandez took off his Fuddruckers hat and handed it to Dennis, who accepted it reluctantly. "I quit, big guy. And you're a terrible boss." Hernandez undid his apron and set it on the counter, and then he went around the bar to join us on the customer's side. Dennis still looked shocked and unsure of what to do. The rest of us were reeling from the performance.

"Yeah, we've got an emergency we've got to go deal with." Fonz joined the mutiny.

"So you quit too, Fonz? If so, I'm not going to include today on your last paycheck."

"All right, Dennis, we've got to go, so you can call it quitting if you want. Here's your hat." Fonz took off his hat and handed it to Dennis, who was now awkwardly holding two hats. Fonz placed his apron on the counter next to Hernandez's. "Let's go, guys."

"I mean," Weasel said, "we're still waiting on our burgers."

"We kind of just made a big exit, guys," Hernandez pointed out. "We need to go."

"Yeah, you all need to go right now," Dennis agreed.

"Can we get them to go, at least?" I asked hungrily.

"Get out of here!" Dennis yelled, and a few customers looked over their shoulders in concern.

CHAPTER 11

5:52 p.m.
Thursday, May 18, 2006

"Man, guys, what the hell did I just do?" Hernandez questioned every choice he'd made in his entire life as we stood by our cars in the Fuddruckers parking lot.

"You acted like a man for once, Hernandez." Weasel congratulated him like a proud father. "I've never been more impressed with you. That was awesome, man."

"Yeah, dude," I said, patting Hernandez on the shoulder. "'Why don't you make your own damn cookies?' That was classic. You even convinced Fonz to quit too."

"All right," Fonz said. "What's done is done. Let's smoke a joint and go sell these diamonds, yeah?"

"For sure," I answered. "But I'm starving. Can we stop for some food on the way? I'll text Tera that we'll be there by 6:30."

I texted Tera, and we all piled into my Bronco and moved across town toward our drug dealer Pete's house. I stopped at a sandwich place called Bill & Ruth's on the way. I ordered a Philly cheesesteak, and the boys ordered their sandwiches, and then we piled back into the car.

The cheesesteak was all right but could have been better. The meat, onions, and peppers were properly cooked and seasoned, but the cheese slices were frugally applied. Now, maybe I'm alone in my opinion about cheesesteak sandwiches, but two slices of melted provolone on top of an inch of meat and peppers just doesn't cut it for me. Cheese is literally half the name of the dish, so I'm convinced that cheese should be nearly half the recipe, or at the very least more than two thin slices. Throw some American cheese on top, or even some hot Cheez Whiz, for Christ's sake. I keep hoping, but I have yet to find a cheesesteak establishment that subscribes to my meat-and-cheese proportion ideology.

Despite these dairy concerns, I scarfed my sub down in record time while driving. The boys and I finished our meals before we got to Pete's driveway. On the road, we ate in silence, and I played the Geto Boys song "G-Code" to help get us in a ruthless-criminal mindset and ditch the sheltered-middle-class-suburban-juveniles-who-buy-pot-and-mushrooms-now-and-then vibe.

I parked by Pete's driveway, turned off the car, and called Tera. She answered quickly, and I informed her we were outside. She opened the front door of the small home and instructed us to come in.

Pete's home was not well cared for. The grass was growing wildly and should have been cut a week before. The inside of the house was just as dirty and messy, in the kind of way a sloppy college kid's first home might be. Pete lived there alone. He and Jake had not gone to college. They worked together in a warehouse that printed signage for companies, like the big vinyl displays at gas stations that list how much a case of beer costs. Tera was standing by the front door when we entered, smiling and happy. She gave us each a slight hug, and then we migrated to the living room. Jake and Pete were playing the newest NCAA football game on a PlayStation 2 while sitting in matching brown La-Z-Boy recliners, and their other friend, Obie, who also worked with them in the warehouse, was sitting on the couch watching them play.

"What's up, boys?" Pete asked. We all found room around the long sectional couch, and Tera plopped into Jake's La-Z-Boy, squeezing in closely on top of him.

"Hey, what's up, guys?" Obie asked, while Jake just gave us a quick nod and kept his focus on the game.

The room smelled like they'd just finished smoking a blunt, and they were all sedated. A large black safe with a keypad sat on the floor next to the TV. In front of the couch, a glass coffee table was strewn with a pile of ground-up weed on one side and three lighters, three thick green pill bottles filled with nugs, and two full ashtrays on the other side.

Jake's team won the virtual game, so Tera planted a kiss on his lips. Both La-Z-Boys spun around to face us as Jake and Pete set their controllers down. Then they took turns leaning forward to slap each of our palms, as tradition necessitated.

"What's up, boys? I heard you had a crazy night last night." Pete offered this as he lit a cigarette. It was the kind of house where smoking cigarettes inside was fine with the owner, if that gives you a sense of how grungy the place was. I thought smoking inside was trashy but lit a yellow American Spirit and joined anyway, as did Fonz.

Pete, Jake, and Obie were all about five years older than us, and we were all familiar with each other. Pete was short, but he was built like a wrestler or boxer. He had a thick neck and a fat face that would be intimidating if I didn't know him. He'd been selling weed for years, and as his operation grew, he kept taking bigger risks. At that point, he had upgraded to having weed FedExed to him from California and had just started buying pills and coke in substantial quantities.

Obie was tall and skinny and got his nickname from his last name, O'Brien. He helped Pete with the pills and powder side of the business. Unfortunately, neither of them could follow the well-known rule of not getting high on your own supply. They were both crushing and snorting two 80-milligram OxyContin pills a day. Jake took pills, too, but not nearly as much or as often as Pete and Obie, possibly because he couldn't afford it. Jake had been a star baseball player in high school, and by then he had accepted that he'd already peaked in life.

"So can we see the diamonds?" Tera asked excitedly.

Pete looked at Jake, and Jake looked at Tera. Then Jake said, "Babe, why don't you grab us some beers?"

She looked ready to scoff but instead stood, relented to his request, and headed into the kitchen like a servant.

"Yeah, let's see them," Obie said.

I looked at the guys to make sure we all still felt good about it, and then I reached into my pocket, pulled out the sock, and rolled the diamonds onto the glass coffee table.

"Holy shit," Pete said, visibly shaken. Obie, Jake, and Pete leaned over the coffee table, and each picked up a diamond to examine.

Tera returned with beers for the three of them and then turned to us four. "Do you guys want beers too?"

"Yeah, that'd be great, sweetheart," Weasel answered for us all, and she sighed and returned to the kitchen. She hurried back this time and passed us all beers before joining us in gawking at the precious gems.

"Wow, I thought you guys were full of shit," Obie said, impressed. He used a small circular magnifying glass to inspect the merchandise. "These do look valuable, and they're definitely real. How did you guys get these?"

"Tera didn't say? That's a first," Hernandez chimed in.

"She said something about your teacher puking them up and then dying? And you got them off his body?" Pete suggested.

We all nodded, and I responded, "Yeah, that's pretty much what happened. Like we told Tera, you can probably get a lot for these. We just want five grand and maybe some weed, and we'll get rid of them today."

Pete and Obie set the diamonds back down on the table while Jake and Tera kept fondling them in awe.

"Five grand and some weed, huh?" Pete asked. "What do you think, Obie?"

"I think it sounds like a good deal, man. You should take it."

"Yeah, so do I," Pete decided. Tera and Jake set the diamonds back on the table, and Tera sat on Jake's lap. "How about half a pound and 5K?"

We were stunned. We'd seen half a pound of weed before but had never owned one.

"Yeah, perfect," Fonz blurted out.

"Deal," I said, sticking my hand toward Pete until he shook it, meaning our transaction was official.

"You guys are all good with that?" Pete asked Weasel and Hernandez. "Anything else?"

"Do you have the Beatles' *White Album*?" Hernandez asked.

Pete didn't get the reference. "Huh?"

"Nothing. Ignore him," Weasel advised, and Pete gave a stoned confident nod and went to open his safe. The boys and I were all excited. Back then, four teenagers sharing five grand was beyond anyone's wildest dreams. I was already thinking about buying flights to Cancun. Plus, half a pound of weed? It was like Christmas and Gas Leak Day all rolled into one.

Pete unlatched his safe and reached inside. I could see big vacuum-sealed bags of weed, pill bottles, and stacks of rubber-banded cash.

Pete pulled out one of the vacuum-sealed bags of weed and set it on the coffee table. "Half a pound," he said casually and then turned to crouch next to the safe again. Obie and Jake gave each other a look that gave me a queasy feeling. Pete pulled something out of the safe: a short, black stick made of metal. He stood and extended the bar into a baton. "How about instead of five grand and a half a pound, I just give you five seconds to get the fuck out of my house? I'll hold on to the diamonds for you."

"*Cabrón*, I think five grand is more than fair. It doesn't have to be this way," Hernandez sputtered.

"Yeah, man," Fonz said. "There's four of us and three of you, and Obie is lanky and malnourished. You think a stick is going to scare us? Let's talk this out."

Fonz stood, and Pete swung the baton, striking Fonz's face and cracking his jaw. Fonz fell back onto the couch, holding his face. "Holy fuck!" His voice was thick and jumbled, like he'd dislocated something in his mouth and bit his tongue.

"Aw, hell no," Hernandez said, getting to his feet. I stood, too, while Weasel sat frozen.

Obie stood and pulled out a taser and hit me in the neck with it, which jolted me to the floor, where Pete started kicking me in my face and ribs. Hernandez turned to Obie and immediately got tased in the balls with 5,000 volts. Hernandez screamed, fell to the floor, and immediately started pissing himself and crying.

Jake pulled Weasel to his feet by grabbing his shirt collar and then punched Weasel hard in the nose. Weasel fell like a twig and didn't even try to get back up.

I got to my knees. Pete punched me in the face, which sent me back to the floor. Obie was hitting and tasing Fonz, and Jake was beating Hernandez. It was the sort of tragedy I'd only seen in slow motion in war movies, where one side is getting demolished and you empathize with the losers because you just spent the last hour getting to know them. It was a proper slaughter.

"Okay, okay, okay," Weasel yelled. "We'll go! Fuck this. Truce."

"What have women accomplished now, Weasel?" Tera asked menacingly.

"Still nothing?" Weasel answered.

The beatings stopped, and we were all whimpering. Tera was in the recliner still, covering her mouth with her hands but not-so-secretly enjoying the show.

"Fine. Get the fuck out," Obie screamed as we stumbled to our feet.

"And don't ever fucking come back here," Pete added.

Bloodied and broken, we started out of the room. We looked like we'd gone to hell and back. I had a swollen eye and a bloody nose, and one of my ribs felt broken, but it turned out to be just bruised. Weasel was scuffed up but didn't get the brunt of it. Hernandez and Fonz both looked the worst, with their faces covered in blood and Hernandez groping his balls in agony.

"How could you do this to us, Tera?" I asked, rubbing my face in disbelief. "We were friends."

"Listen, guys, I didn't know this was going to happen."

"Yeah, right," Obie said, laughing at us. "It was all her idea. She set you guys up. Said she wanted 20 percent."

"I don't doubt it," Hernandez exhaled in a high-pitched squeal.

"I do wonder," Tera said to Jake, "how much do you think we'll get for these?" She put an arm around Jake's arm, and he pushed her away.

"We? Listen, Tera, it's been fun, but I think we should see other people."

"You're joking."

"No, I'm not. You should leave with your friends, and we'll take it from here."

She gasped and immediately began to cry. He pushed her away again.

"All right, you fucking assholes," Pete said, "get the fuck out of my house."

Pete and Obie brandished their weapons at us again, and we hurried out the front door. Tera tried to convince Jake to let her stay, but he forced her outside with us.

I walked to the driver's side door of my Bronco and stepped inside. Hernandez hopped into the passenger seat, and the other boys got in back.

"You're going to hate me," Tera said, standing by my car.

"I'm pretty sure we already do," Hernandez answered.

"Jake drove me here. Can you drop me at my house, please?"

"Jesus," I said. "Fine. Get in."

"Guys, I was just playing. I didn't know they were going to beat you all up. Honestly."

"They said this was all your idea, Tera," Fonz snapped. "Good going, you selfish bitch."

"Those fucking jerks," she said, sliding into the middle of the backseat between Fonz and Weasel.

Weasel told her, "Yeah, you were bested by a man. Who would've guessed?"

"Will you shut up, Weasel?" She was crying again. "I'm sorry, all right? I didn't know they were going to beat you up. Really."

I drove each of them home and dropped them off, and then I went home and caught my parents and little sister finishing the stew my mom had made for dinner.

"Are you hungry?" my mom asked as I came in through the garage door. I had hoped to sneak upstairs unseen.

"No, thanks. I already ate."

"What'd you do tonight?" my dad asked. "I heard they had to close the high school down because of a gas leak."

Knowing I couldn't make the break upstairs, I entered the kitchen and approached the table. The overhead lights made my beaten face and body look worse than they really were, as I hadn't had time to wash off any of the blood.

"What the hell happened to you?" my dad asked, shocked.

My mom turned to see me and then shot up from her chair to touch my face and examine me. "Oh my god! What happened?" my mom shrieked.

"Some older kids jumped me and the guys. I'm fine. I just want to shower and go to bed."

"It's almost like you're always getting into trouble," Heather said slyly, "and I'm never getting into trouble. It's weird."

"Shut up, brat."

"Don't tell me to shut up."

"Both of you shut up," my mom interrupted. "Go clean yourself up, and I'll bring you an ice pack. Are you sure you're okay? Maybe we should go to the hospital. You look terrible, Jon."

"He'll be fine," my dad assured her. Then he set his spoon down, which meant he was done eating. "Did you and your friends at least get any hits in? Or did you just get pummeled like wimps?"

"We just got pummeled like wimps, Dad. No, I don't think we got any hits in."

"That's a shame."

***

11:21 p.m.
Wednesday, May 17, 2006
(the night before)

Wednesday night, Bob Sockolosky showed up early to the Mayo hotel where he was hosting a benefit for a local politician. He had a series of rough phone calls, the first one from his ex-wife, who rightfully claimed he was behind on alimony payments and was late in sending tuition payments to their kids' school. He assured her that everything would be handled and got off the phone as quickly as he could. Then he got a call from Bear, the casino manager. Bear said the yakuza members were flying in a day early and wanted to get the diamonds on Thursday instead of Friday, along with a status update on the guns Bob was procuring for them to ship to Japan. He was on edge the rest of the night, doing his best to smile and shake hands with the Tulsa political machine while dosing himself with a cloudy scotch.

Then he asked Walter to drive him home.

The Sockolosky property was an immense, remote, and woodsy respite outside of town, allowing its owner to do what he pleased in total privacy. An eight-foot fence topped with sharp barbed wire surrounded the property. There was only one way in and one way out: a gaudy, golden, motorized gate that opened by entering the correct digits on a keypad or using a remote clicker. The gate was armed with security cameras and a sign that half-jokingly warned, "Trespassers Will Be Shot…Survivors Will Be Shot Again." A winding brick road led from the entrance gate to the house. The estate had no alarm system; its only security features were the barbed wire fence, the locked gate, the two gate cameras, two greyhound dogs, and an old revolver in Bob's nightstand.

The estate had been passed down through three generations and, in its glory days, was maintained by a large staff. The grounds were composed of more than sixty acres and included polo fields and horse stables, though only four horses remained on the estate, and hardly anyone ever rode them. The horses and other animals roamed freely on the compound, including llamas, goats, sheep, chickens, and peacocks. An elderly groundskeeper, Frank, and an elderly housekeeper, Louise, were the sole remaining staff, both originally hired by the home's previous owner, Bob's father. Frank lived down the street and came by a few hours every morning to feed the animals and cut the grass. Louise came by once a week to dust, mop the floors, do some dishes, and change the sheets on Bob's bed; not much cleaning was required since Bob's wife and kids moved out. There was no traffic at the estate aside from dwindling family visits and the meager staff's infrequent visits. On increasingly rare occasions, Bob hosted a banquet on the property, celebrating a birthday or a holiday, replete with polo a competition and caterers, but most days, it was a barren homage to what their family had once meant, which few remembered.

The home had deteriorated such that one cleaning lady could hardly make a noticeable impact, no matter how often she came. It would have taken an entire construction crew to restore the place to the unique charm it had proudly exuded in years prior. Ivy crawled up once-immaculate marble columns. The exterior paint was chipping off. When it rained, several spots in the ceiling leaked. The home needed a total renovation. The house was set back three blocks from the entrance gate, so while the mansion was visible from the road, it was too far away to see how dilapidated it was or what was happening inside.

The road leading to the property was so remote that it was named Sockolosky Drive after the family who had lived there for generations. From town, the road curved through hills for miles before passing two gated neighborhoods of fancy homes. About a mile further, it passed the Sockolosky entrance gate on the left and, a few blocks further, dead-ended. The only other significant landowners on the Sockolosky side of the dead-end road were wealthy people like the grandson of "father of the atomic bomb" Robert Oppenheimer and country music legend Garth Brooks, who each owned hundreds of acres on either end of the road on that side of the dead end. Kids sometimes raced their cars on that road because of its remoteness, inevitably leading to terrible crashes—sometimes from hitting a deer, or occasionally from spinning out and crashing into the ditch on the side of the road. At least once or twice a year, a tragic accident involving a car full of drunk teenagers occurred. To make things worse, if someone managed to call 911, an ambulance would take at least thirty minutes to find its way to the victims.

Bob Sockolosky was the grandson of a long-deceased oil magnate and the son of a prominent real estate mogul who died a decade before the events of this story, so Bob was his family's sole patriarch. He ran for mayor of Tulsa once in his early forties but lost by 10 percent of the vote. Then he ran for and—just barely—won a seat in the state senate. After six years, he retired from public office to run the real estate empire his father had bequeathed him, which accounted for his legitimate income. Bob worked little but sure acted like a busy man. He was a wealthy, reclusive eccentric that no one truly knew, with the exception of his ex-wife and one or two close advisors.

Bob suffered from various addictions, not the least of which was gambling. He owed more than he made, and he kept placing bets until he no longer could. Bear and Walter covering his losses was the only thing keeping him afloat.

When he got home from the benefit that night, his day became progressively worse. He and Walter walked into his office and found a painting on the floor next to his unlocked safe. He rummaged through the safe and discovered the diamonds in the velvet bag Bear had given him earlier that week had been replaced with rocks from his bonsai. Just then, the light coming from under the crack of the bathroom door turned off. Bob motioned for Walter to ready himself with a weapon, and they both hid in a corner and waited. When the intruder finally left the bathroom, Walter cracked him in the back of the head, tied him up, and searched his body and clothing for the diamonds. The man, who was missing an arm, just like the man he had seen in the casino bathroom Monday night, awoke but refused to give up any information about the missing diamonds, which was not an acceptable conclusion. Bob asked Walter to handle things, and then he retired to his bedroom to try to get some much-needed sleep.

Keeping the man's hand tied behind his back, Walter pulled him to his feet and led him into the backyard, close to the driveway where the Navigator was parked, but still in the grass. Walter didn't say a word or ask the man if he had any last remarks. He simply cocked his revolver, aimed, and fired two bullets. The first shot hit the man in the stomach. The second went through his left lung.

Bob heard the two gunshots that signaled half of his instructions had been followed, and then a few minutes later, he heard a car crash. He looked out his bedroom window to the sight of a crashed SUV north of the front gate.

"Oh, that stupid son of a bitch."

Bob put on his robe and slippers, powered on his golf cart, and drove toward the car wreck. He found a dead Walter in the driver's seat and a dead one-armed man in the trunk, which was wide open.

"Oh, man," he said. He didn't look as concerned as he should have been.

Then he noticed what looked like an animal's bloody body parts on the front of the vehicle and in the ditch. He walked closer and leaned down, realizing the animal that had been struck was a llama. He reached down and picked up a battered name tag that read, "Rudolfo." Bob fell to his knees, sobbing, wondering why such an ugly ending had to befall such a beautiful creature—his prized possession. He thought about the day Rudolfo was born, when he first glimpsed the llama's blue and brown eyes. About how he had chosen the name *Rudolfo* on the spot as an homage to novelist Rudolfo Anaya, one of the founders of Chicano literature. The animal's innocence and kind eyes reminded Bob of his favorite character in one of the author's books.

Bob wept for a long while before deciding to clean up the scene enough to stay out of prison. With great strain, he dragged the one-armed man and his plastic tarp bed out of the trunk of his SUV and onto his golf cart. Then he drove to the far side of his property. Bob had neither the time nor inclination to dig a proper grave, but he figured animals would take care of the evidence for him if he left the body deep enough in the woods. So he simply dumped the body on the ground and covered it with tree branches, leaves, and dirt the best he could in the dark, intending to spend the next day doing a better job of hiding it and Earl's Jetta.

Next, he went home to pull up his security footage. He wound it backward, pausing it when he saw a young teenager looking up at the camera. Bob scowled at the kid's face in anger. Then he fast-forwarded until he saw himself exiting the gate on the golf cart and returning with the dead body. He deleted that entire twenty minutes' worth of footage.

He knew he should call emergency services about the accident now that the evidence was handled, but instead, he allowed himself to grieve once again. He walked back to the accident site, found a spot on the road near Rudolfo's remains, and sat and cried.

CHAPTER 12

7:12 a.m.

Friday, May 19, 2006

(two days later)

After Thursday night's horror of being jacked and getting my ass kicked by Pete, Jake, and Obie, I fell asleep by 9:00 p.m., utterly broken, bruised, and exhausted. At 7:12 the next morning, I woke up to Heather poking my chest and saying, "Jon, Jon, Jon, Jon, Jon," in the most annoying way imaginable.

"I'm up! Stop it," I pleaded with her. I hated being woken up but, actually, didn't mind as much as usual since I had been having a nightmare—a horrific reenactment of the beating from the evening before but even gorier.

"You said you'd drive me to school today, and you're always late. I can't be late. Get up."

"Can't you just take the bus?"

"It's the last day of school. Nobody'll be on the bus today. Pleeeease. You said you would."

Our parents were already gone for the day, and I did have a slight recollection of agreeing to take her to school. And of the hundreds of early mornings I had endured in public school, at least this one would be my last.

I sat up and looked at Heather, rubbing my eyes gently due to my bruising and swelling. "Yeah, I'll take you, squirt." I had never called her squirt before a day in my life, so I'm not sure why I said it that day. She smiled and walked out of the room. Her hair was wet, but otherwise she looked completely ready for the day. There was no telling what time she'd woken up. I've never understood morning people—not even my little sister.

Heather went downstairs to eat some cereal and dry her hair. I took a hot shower, got dressed, and spent a few minutes looking at my disfigured face in the bathroom mirror. In a way, I thought I looked tough and rugged, but the truth of the story was like my dad had said. We didn't even fight back. We were pummeled like helpless, worthless losers. I was tying my shoes when Heather started yelling my name again from downstairs.

"Okay, I'm coming!"

We got in my Bronco, and I drove to the donut shop.

"Do we even have time to stop for donuts? I don't want to be late again, Jon. Please."

"We'll be fine. It's 7:40. This is the earliest I've been on the road all year. Trust me."

Heather smiled. She was still trusting of anything promised to her by an elder, and my confidence eased her young, worried soul. "Hey, Jon," she said as I pulled into the drive-thru lane at the donut shop. There were five cars ahead of us.

"Yeah? What?"

"What's your favorite color?" The cars were moving, and now we were fourth in line from the small take-out window.

"My favorite color? I don't have a favorite color."

"Why not? I thought everyone had a favorite color."

"Maybe I had one when I was, like, eight years old. I don't have a favorite color anymore because I'm not a little kid anymore."

She looked disappointed in my answer and frowned.

"What's your favorite color, Heather?" The line of cars moved up again, and I tried not to be as grumpy as I usually was first thing in the morning.

"Blue. I *love* blue." She smiled and showed off her blue backpack, blue shoes, and blue scrunchy holding up her ponytail.

"Blue's good. I like blue too."

We got to the order window, and I asked for five sausage rolls and a cinnamon roll. Heather asked for a dozen donut holes. I paid and pulled out of the line and back onto the main street.

"Man, the donut place was sure busy today. Must be because it's Friday," I commented.

"Yeah," she responded without a thought. "Imagine how busy it'll be tonight."

"You idiot," I scolded. "People don't eat donuts for dinner. This place closes at, like, noon."

She was a smart kid in many ways, and she had read a lot of books, but her understanding of reality was still all fairytales and garbage. The workings of the real world were elusive to her, and I wondered how in the hell she imagined donut shops would have a busy dinner rush.

She nodded, and I felt like a complete asshole for reprimanding her and questioning her intelligence. She was too young to know how restaurants operated or that people ate donuts mostly for breakfast.

"Hey. I've had a rough week. I'm being an asshole. I'm sorry, Heather." I said it with as much compassion as I could muster in my bruised, cynical body.

She frowned again and then looked up at me and gave me a gentle pat on my arm. "It's okay. I'm sorry you're having a bad week. I hope it gets better."

I don't know what I expected her to say, but it wasn't that. Her calm, supportive tone made me feel even worse about being so mean to her, and not just that morning. I thought about every time I had been rude to her and regretted them all at once. It was her last day of seventh grade. Maybe she had a rough week too. I hadn't been a fair or good enough big brother. I was out chasing diamonds and getting in trouble like an idiot instead of enjoying the final moments of my family all living together. I offered her one of the sausage rolls. She finished it quickly and put the donut holes in her backpack to save for later. I dropped Heather off at her school, drove to Will Rogers High School while swallowing the center of the cinnamon roll, and, for the very last time, parked in my usual spot by Hernandez's El Camino.

For the first time in ages, I showed up to my computer class before the bell rang, and also for the first time in ages, Ms. Allen was already at her desk, smiling and talking to a few students about graduation. I gave a sausage roll to Angelica, gave one to Cameron, and then I set down my backpack at my station. Then I approached Ms. Allen's desk and offered her a sausage roll as well, which left one for me.

Ms. Allen was surprised that I got her something, and she replied, "That's so sweet of you, Jon Ryan. Oh, my gosh. What happened to your face, sweet child?"

"I was playing backyard football and got hit. It's nothing."

"Doesn't look like nothing. Are you sure you're okay?"

"Yeah, I'm fine. Thank you."

"Where is your gown? Graduation rehearsal is in the auditorium in fifteen minutes."

I looked around the class and noticed nearly everyone putting on their dark maroon graduation cap and gowns over their school clothes, preparing for rehearsal. "Oh, it's in my car. I forgot."

"Go grab it. We'll be dismissing class soon."

I started toward the door, and Angelica stopped me. "Are you okay, Jon Ryan? You weren't really playing football, were you?"

"It's a long story. Everything's okay. Thank you." I waved off Angelica, went back to my car, and grabbed my cap and gown.

***

8:23 a.m.

Friday, May 19, 2006

Our entire class lined up in the cafeteria and down the connecting hallways to practice formations and learn how to enter a large room and sit down. I figured we'd need to be in alphabetical order or arranged by height or something, but we weren't told what order to stand in, so I just went with the flow. We were the longest line of giddy teenagers you've ever seen. We practiced walking to and sitting down in the gymnasium as a handful of teachers and our assistant principal herded us and explained the process. It was simple enough, but I could see why we had to rehearse for things to go smoothly at our actual graduation. Our ceremony the next day was at the Memorial High School stadium, and our auditorium wasn't an exact replica for rehearsal purposes, but it was apparently close enough. I don't understand who schedules graduation venues or how they decide on them, but I thought it was odd that ours was held in the stadium of a nearby high school instead of our own.

None of my friends were in line next to me. Weasel was home, prohibited from entering the school grounds or from attending his own graduation because of a dirty pipe, a few seeds, and a petty, prickly, middle-aged man named Mr. Trout. Fonz was likely somewhere with Elaine, and I had no idea where Hernandez was. Jackson and Chase were in front of me in line. Jackson turned to me and asked, "What's up, Jon Ryan? Did you hear about Blake?"

Blake was the Puka-shell-wearing guy with gelled-out hair in my speech class. "No. What happened?"

Jackson shook his head slowly and wearily, like he had bad news to deliver and had been handing out the same bad news to people all morning. "He overdosed, man. He's dead."

"What? For real?" I was shocked.

"Yeah, man. Was coke and Xanax, I think. You mix enough of those two, and your heart stops. His mom found him this morning."

Jackson looked like he'd been crying earlier and had since put on a strong face. Jackson and Blake had been good friends for years, and I knew that he and Chase were closer to Blake than just about anyone.

"I'm so sorry, bro. I loved Blake. He's a great guy. Man…I just had a really deep conversation with him at Alex's party, like, two weeks ago. Holy shit."

I shook my head, and Jackson nodded and then turned back to talk with Chase. I couldn't remember a lot about Alex's party, but nearly the whole school had been there, and I'd hung out with Blake in a corner outside for at least an hour, smoking weed and cigarettes and talking about life. The exact conversation is muddy now, but we had a moment. We talked about graduation and college and all the stuff we wanted to do when we moved out to start lives of our own. I wasn't close enough to him to cry, but the news still stung like a dagger. He was about to graduate and had his entire life ahead of him. The previous evening, I had been getting my ass kicked, thinking I might be killed, but Blake actually did die. I wondered if he felt scared when it happened. Then I imagined his mom finding his body, seeing his stiff face with drool leaking from his mouth. It really shifted my perspective for the day, and that moment of aching in line with my classmates, all in our gowns, is a moment that has stuck with me in a way that will likely never dissipate. Blake was always a nice guy to everyone. I had never seen him act hostile or insolent. It was a tragedy, and yet life just went on for everyone else.

The procession moved, and teachers kept shelling out positive affirmations as we all took our seats in the auditorium. The assistant principal got on the stage with a microphone and described how the next day would unfold. Everyone was happy and nervous, but I just kept thinking about Blake. When the second-period bell rang, we were released to change out of our gowns and return to class. I went to my speech class, and the seat next to me was empty. Everyone in the class was whispering about the sad news of Blake's demise. Some of the girls, along with Mrs. Woolery, were crying. A student came into the class and delivered one of those pink notes from the office to Mrs. Woolery, and she called me to her desk while blowing her nose with a tissue. The note was familiar, as it requested my presence once again in the principal's office.

From prior experience, I knew such a summons was never good news, but I was happy to leave speech class so I could try getting Blake's overdose off my mind. Fonz exited his classroom and joined me in the hallway with his own pink slip. When we got to Mr. Trout's office, Hernandez was already seated in the reception area, and we were told to silently sit next to him.

The door to the office opened, and Mr. Trout stood in the frame, looking like a desolate, shipwrecked, frail, old man. Behind him stood another grizzly man in a suit with a badge that asserted his name as Detective Daniel Finnerty.

"Boys, this is Detective Finnerty. He wants to talk to you each, one on one. Fonz, since you're the resident counsel, I figured maybe you'd want to go first."

Fonz stood and looked at us with a confident I've-got-this sort of nod. Then he went into the office, where he remained for more than twenty minutes. By the time the office door reopened, Fonz's face was grave, and he was uncharacteristically silent, as if they'd instructed him not to talk to us.

"What's going on?" Hernandez whispered to him.

"It's all good, guys. Just tell them the truth," Fonz said, and then he walked out of the office and back to his second period. It was my turn.

I entered the office and closed the door behind me. The three chairs in the room had been rearranged for more hospitable conversing. Detective Finnerty sat in Mr. Trout's desk chair, and Mr. Trout was in a chair turned around to face the middle of the room. I took the remaining chair and felt my hands get clammy.

"Jon Ryan, this shouldn't take long. Detective Finnerty has some questions. It's about Mr. Derkatch."

"Hi, Jon. Do you go by Jon? Or Jonathan?"

"Oh, no, sir. Please. Just call me Jon Ryan."

Detective Finnerty looked stumped by my request but continued.

"Okay, Jon Ryan. You're still a minor, so you have the right to have your parents present. You're not under arrest or anything, but you are a person of interest in this investigation, so I do need to talk with you and your friends. Is it okay if we just talk now and Mr. Trout stays in here as your parental figure?"

"If you boys want, I can call Fonz's dad. I have his business card here somewhere. But Fonz was smart and didn't ask for that," interjected Mr. Trout.

I nodded. "It's fine. We should have gone to the police right away. I'm sorry, sir."

"Good. So, your friend, Fonseca? Fonz? He spent a few minutes playing dumb, but eventually, he opened up when he realized that I'm not after him. I'm after whoever shot your teacher, Earl Derkatch."

I nodded.

"We found Mr. Derkatch's body yesterday evening, about half a mile from the car accident that you were a witness to. You do realize that leaving the scene of a crime is also a crime, right?"

I nodded again.

"You don't say much, do you, kid?"

I nodded and then asked, "Is there a question, sir?"

Detective Finnerty produced a manila folder and pulled two large, printed photos out. Both were in black and white. He slid them across the desk and spun them around so I could view them in their all their glory. The first photo was a screengrab from Sockolosky's gate security camera. It showed me looking up at the camera right after putting the ransom note in the mailbox. The second image was from the gas station security camera where we placed the 911 call. The image showed all four of us: Fonz using the payphone by the parking lot, and us all standing around him, right in front of Weasel's car.

"I see. Yes, that's me in both of these. I'm sorry again. We know we should have gone to the police, but we did at least call 911."

Detective Finnerty nodded disarmingly and then admitted, "You know, that 911 call was actually helpful. It's good that you boys made that call. It shows you at least care. The ransom note and the llama are another story, but I don't think you had anything to do with Mr. Derkatch getting shot."

"We didn't. I promise. We heard the gunshots. But we didn't see who did it. Mr. Derkatch died before we could even call for an ambulance."

"Okay. I understand. Relax. This is a murder case, and I've got you on camera at the scene. I could have had you held for questioning at the station last night if I thought I needed to."

"So do you know who did it, then?"

The detective looked offended by my question, as if I had just asked a woman how much she weighed. Then he said, "We've got a suspect, yes. Now, when you left the accident last night, are you sure Mr. Derkatch was still in the trunk of that SUV?"

I nodded, "Yes, sir."

Detective Finnerty nodded back agreeably. "Good. Okay. And the plan with the llama was to do what exactly?"

"We painted it, and we were going to leave it at the boys' soccer field. The ransom note was just a joke."

"So you didn't mean to cause that car accident?"

"No, sir. The llama jumped out of the car and stood in the road. We tried to make it move, but it was almost like it wanted to die."

Mr. Trout's face looked sad and angry, but not at me. He was distraught over his friend being murdered under bizarre circumstances.

"It's a strange coincidence," Detective Finnerty said, "that the same night you boys try pulling a prank at Bob Sockolosky's house, your history teacher was there doing something too. Do you have any idea why Earl Derkatch was there that night?"

I paused and considered. "Um, no. I don't think so." I wavered and was nervous about the situation, but cops always made me nervous. "I think it might have had something to do with the diamonds."

Mr. Trout and the detective both sighed, and I was reassured that Fonz had already told them about the diamonds. We'd been beaten to pulps the night before over them, so we didn't have much else to lose by being honest.

"Your friend Fonseca mentioned the diamonds too. And I visited your other friend—what is it you call him, the badger? Weasel? Well, I visited Weasel's home last night, and he told me everything then. Tell me about the diamonds."

"There were four of them. Blue. Fancy looking. Mr. Derkatch spit them up. We panicked. I grabbed the diamonds, and we left. Then we called 911 to report the accident after we calmed down."

"I know, Jon Ryan. And what happened next? Where are the diamonds now?"

"You probably noticed we all got the shit beat out of us. A couple of older kids, Pete, Obie, and Jake—they took them from us yesterday. I don't know their last names, but I know where Pete lives. I can give you their phone numbers."

The detective looked like he had what he needed. He flipped through his notepad to see if there was anything else to cover and then tore out a page to hand to me, along with his pen. "Yeah, why don't you write down everything you know about them? Names. Addresses. Phone numbers. Where they work."

I did as instructed and copied the information from the contacts on my phone.

"Just one more thing; then you can go." Detective Finnerty sighed as I handed the paper and pen back to him.

"What time did you leave the scene of the accident on Wednesday night?"

"Oh, um. Let me think. It must have been around 1:00 a.m., I guess. We got back to Weasel's house around 1:30, and then Fonz must have called 911 by 2:00?"

The detective looked at his notes and nodded. "Thank you. This is helpful. Might have been more helpful if you hadn't fled the scene of an accident, but we'll assume you boys were scared by the gunshots you heard."

"So you boys really didn't break my mailbox? It would've been around that same time." Mr. Trout looked at once relieved and disappointed.

"What mailbox? You think I watched my history teacher bleed out and then went smashing mailboxes? Is that what this is about?"

The detective shook his head. "No, that's not what this is about. All right. Well, that's all for now. Thank you, Jon Ryan."

The bell rang, signaling the end of second period.

"You can go back to class," Mr. Trout said to me in a kind voice. "It's almost third period. At lunch, you can try and enjoy Senior Day."

"Sorry for whatever happened to your mailbox, but I had Mr. Derkatch for third period."

"Yes, I know." Mr. Trout acted like we'd both lost a great friend, and I wondered if he also already knew about Blake. "You have a substitute, obviously. It's probably best if you don't tell your class what happened. Just let them think he's out sick so some of them can enjoy their last day." Mr. Trout began to cry, and that made my gut wrench. I had never felt so sorry for him before, and I didn't know what to do about it. Patting him on the back felt trite, so I just slowly stood and left the room. Hernandez was still seated in the reception area and looked to me for guidance, but I just ignored him and walked back to second period to get my backpack.

They called Hernandez into the office, closed the door, and continued their morbid investigation.

Third period was rough. The substitute didn't have a movie for us to watch, so the class just talked among themselves all hour, except for me. I kept my head down on my desk, mad and sad that no one else in the room knew our teacher was dead and replaced by some temporary wannabe. I felt like the only grown-up in a room of oblivious children. After third period, the seniors were released to go outside, where carnival and fair-like attractions had been set up. There were food trucks, games, and activities, like tug-of-war. The football coach sat in a dunk tank, and kids lined up to shoot him down. I found the boys, and we bought some food-truck tacos. The whole class seemed happy, but I was despondent. Fonz and Hernandez tried cheering me up for a while, but I had no interest in being happy. We finished our tacos, and Hernandez crept out of my eye line to sneak behind me.

Fonz said, "Hey, Jon Ryan."

I pivoted to my right to look directly at him. "What's up?"

"You know, something about what that cop said to me earlier…" Fonz started, like he was going to say something important, but then Hernandez knelt behind me on his hands and knees and Fonz pushed my chest. I toppled over backward, slipping over Hernandez and flailing onto the ground. A few people nearby laughed. Fonz and Hernandez totally lost it, both laughing so hard they were crying from the prank, which we called "table-topping." As in, they table-topped me. It was a completely stupid prank, but we thought it was hilarious at the time.

I stood and collected myself. "You bastards. I'll get you back."

"You're too slow, Jon Ryan. You even fell slow. It was like, whoa!" Fonz waved his hands around, imitating my awkward tumble, then he and Hernandez started busting up again.

"Fuck you guys."

"Man, you need to snap out of it. You gotta learn to make lemonade, *ese*," Hernandez advised.

"Yeah, buddy," Fonz agreed. "Snap out of it. What's your prank going to be tonight?"

"Literally, why are we even talking about pranks anymore? After all the shit that's happened. Plus, did you hear about Blake?"

"Yeah, that's a sad deal. You shouldn't mix coke and Xanax. I thought everyone knew that," Fonz said unempathetically.

"I really don't want to participate in the prank thing anymore, boys. I'm sorry. It's not right. We saw people die, man. How can we even think about it?"

"*Cabrón*," Hernandez said. "Is there a dense moral quandary hanging above us lately? Sure. But you signed the document, *hermano*. Do your words and signature not mean anything anymore? This is our last stand. Our Alamo."

"Why the fuck is it so important to you?"

"For the same reason we decided to do this in the first place. So we'll be remembered. You know that, man. Plus, after everything that happened this week, there's even more reason to finish the game. It'll help get your mind off all that shit."

"Fine," I lamented. "I'll come up with something. I guess we'll go to the party tonight, and I'll have something planned by then." A kid on the football team had invited the entire school to a party at his house that night, so we were naturally planning to stop by.

"Good boy," Fonz said and patted me on the head like a dog. "Who's driving tonight? Should we meet at Weasel's around, like, eight or nine?"

CHAPTER 13

9:34 a.m.
Thursday, May 18, 2006
(the day before)

The plane landed at 9:27 a.m. at the Tulsa International Airport. By 9:34, two ruthless Japanese gang members of a merciless yakuza faction stepped off flight 452, a commercial Boeing 737 operated by American Airlines, and sauntered onto the thin, blue terminal carpets. A sign announced they were now on Tulsa Time, which did not concern them, as Yuto and Hanzō hadn't slept a wink on their overnight journey from Hawaii.

Hanzō was almost fifty and had been relegated to virtual exile in Hawaii six years prior to oversee low-level gambling and gun-running deals. He'd made a mistake in Osaka that cost him more than his honor. In order to appease the head of his family, known as his *Oyabun*, he'd cut off his own right pinky finger and delivered it to his superiors personally as a sign of respect and as a sacred apology. The practice was symbolic, as it originated back when the Japanese fought with katanas, and one cannot properly wield a katana sword without a pinky finger. Even though katanas are rarely used anymore, the bloody gesture saved Hanzō's life by proving his commitment to the family. His subsequent overseas appointment was his punishment, as well as the higher-ups' rationale for letting him keep his role of *shateigashira* (regional boss).

Yuto was in his early thirties and was still earning his chops in the organization. As an assistant to Hanzō—a *shateigashira-hosa*, a typical appointment for a regional boss—he deferred to Hanzō with reverence.

Being in Hawaii was torture for Hanzō because his wife, Himari, died while giving birth to their only child, his daughter, and he was sent away from Japan when she was only three years old. From then on, she lived in Osaka with Hanzō's brother-in-law. But Yuto embraced the new lands and responsibilities as exciting. He hadn't been back to Japan in years and grew comfortable on the white sands of Hawaii. Yuto was learning from Hanzō and viewed him as one would view a father or a mentor. Together they oversaw numerous small casino and gun-running deals in multiple states in the US, but neither of them left the big island very often. The bosses they reported to were based in Osaka, and though their group did not have many members, they did exert a considerable amount of power.

Japan's strict prohibition of guns led to crucial black-market trade, and compromised Texas oilmen had been Hanzō's main suppliers of guns. However, they'd recently found dirt on an oilman in Oklahoma named Bob Sockolosky, and when you have adequate dirt on someone, you can command that person's loyalty. Sockolosky embezzled millions from the company his father gave him in order to cover his compounding gambling debts, and he had not obfuscated the paper trail as adequately as he'd believed. He'd built a house of cards through skimming and lying, hoping that one wrong would fix another. Since Texas and Oklahoma both had similarly lax requirements for acquiring weapons from gun shows back then, and since New Orleans (where the guns were shipped from) was about the same distance from either state, Hanzō had taken the initiative to move operations to Oklahoma the year before. He'd worked through intermediaries and had never once had to show his face in the Sooner State until that point.

Hanzō and Yuto, both relatively short and thin men, were sporting smart, slim suits as they exited the airplane. Hidden beneath their suits were tattoos—mostly involving dragon images—that covered their entire arms, chests, backs, and lower necks. The tattoos had been applied using an ancient and painful *tebori* technique that loosely translates to English as "hand engraved" and involves using the tip of a piece of bamboo to pierce the skin slowly and repeatedly. Getting covered in ink in such an old-school, excruciating fashion made the gangsters seem like even badder badasses. The two violent men looked quite unassuming as they walked through the bright, fluorescent terminal early that morning and found their way to the baggage carousel to collect their belongings, reflecting on their eleven-hour journey to Tulsa.

"Sir. How did you like that last movie?" Yuto asked with great veneration as they watched bags spill out onto the slippery carousel.

"Yuto, once again, your taste in cinema is admirable. *Agent Cody Banks 2* is a modern masterpiece. You would never guess a sixteen-year-old CIA agent could be so competent, but that Cody. He is something else." Hanzō smiled as the two men's bags approached, and Yuto smiled, too, relieved that his elder appreciated his discernment.

The small terminal and airport were relatively empty. After they collected their belongings, they found their way to a nearby Budget Rent a Car window with no line. A sweet, middle-aged lady was working that day, and her name tag identified her as Patty.

"Good morning, Ms. Patty," Hanzō greeted her.

"Good morning, gentlemen. How may I help you today? Do you have a reservation with us?"

"Yes, we do." Hanzō handed her a piece of paper on which he'd printed his confirmation numbers. She entered the data into her computer, performing a series of keystrokes.

"Hmmm." Patty kept clicking for what felt like a very long time.

"Is everything okay?" Yuto asked.

"Oh, sure. I am just looking through your reservation now. It should only take a minute. Is this y'all's first time in Tulsa?"

"Yes," Yuto answered.

"We have been to Texas before," Hanzō clarified.

"Aw, hun. I won't hold that against ya." Patty clicked the keys a few more times and then stared at her screen. She said, "So it looks like we have a complimentary upgrade for you today. Instead of a two-door sedan, we can get you a four-door SUV with a GPS for the same price."

Yuto and Hanzō looked at each other, perplexed. Then Yuto said, "We only paid for a two-door sedan."

Patty smiled at them. "Aw, sugar, it's no extra cost. Don't worry. It's a complimentary upgrade based on what we have available. It's a much better car; trust me. And you'll love the GPS system, especially if you don't know your way around Tulsa."

"That is very kind of you," Yuto said.

"Yes. Ms. Patty, your kindness will not be forgotten. We will repay our debt to you," Hanzō explained seriously.

"Oh, hun, don't you even worry about it. We solve problems creatively and take action on behalf of our customers."

"That is lovely fealty to your customers, ma'am," Hanzō replied.

She blushed. "It's from the Budget Rent a Car vision statement."

"Even still. We will not forget this, and we will repay our debt to you. You have my word, on my honor. Thank you, Ms. Patty." Yuto bowed as he spoke. Hanzō and Patty watched the bow, feeling embarrassed and flattered, respectively.

A credit card was presented. Insurance was purchased. Forms were signed, and keys were handed over. The men went outside to find the Budget-branded customer van that took them to the next phase of the rental process, where the rental cars were kept about a mile down the road. They were the only customers in the van and the only customers at the next rental car location. It was a ghost town filled with midsized sedans. Keys were exchanged, and the two men took charge of their SUV, with Yuto in the driver's seat and Hanzō in the passenger seat.

Yuto looked at his phone before starting the car. "Bear says there's a problem with the interest payment. He says he gave four diamonds to Sockolosky to hold onto for us, but someone stole them from Sockolosky."

"These amateurs. No way do I believe someone stole them. He probably lost another bet. That man has no respect. Yoshio is expecting us to have that payment on the Big Island by Sunday. You know he's not going to accept any excuses."

For Hanzō, it was a matter of course to strongarm and extort men he was blackmailing, but sometimes a blackmailed partner could be the least reliable. Moving operations to Oklahoma was a risk in itself, let alone relying on a gambling-addict real estate tycoon he'd never even met. Hanzō put the operation in place after meeting Bear in Hawaii the previous winter and developing trust in the Tulsa Indian casino manager.

"What should we do?" Yuto was less than fifteen years younger than Hanzō, but he looked up to the man with deep reverence. Hanzō rarely demonstrated mutual respect. In matters of basic decency and honor, Hanzō seemed to have strayed, even in the common formality of bowing to show respect. Only Yuto followed the courtesy; Hanzō bowed only to his superiors.

"Remember what Ms. Patty from Budget said, Yuto. We solve problems creatively and take action on behalf of our customers. We just have to be creative."

Yuto smiled, knowing he'd just received an important lesson.

"Let's get breakfast. I'm hungry. We'll check into the hotel and go to the museum you wanted to visit. Then we'll find Bear and then Sockolosky."

"What about the gun shipment?" Yuto asked.

"I don't trust these people anymore. Let's cut off their hands and then cut ties. We'll go back to dealing with the rednecks in Texas next week."

"You need a nap. You're being grouchy, sir." Hanzō shot a nasty glance at Yuto. "But I agree with you, sir. We just need food and rest before we solve this problem—creatively."

"No, you're right. Text Bear that we'll come in and see him tomorrow evening. We need a good night's rest to consider how we'll proceed."

***

8:10 p.m.
Friday, May 19, 2006
(the next day)

Obie and Pete took bong rips, snorted OxyContin, and played video games at Pete's house all afternoon and into the evening. Jake had left the evening before after they beat up the boys and stole their booty, and they hadn't heard from him since. Obie and Pete both liked Jake and didn't mind working with him, but they didn't really care about him all that much. Obie and Pete had been close friends since middle school, whereas Jake had been popular in high school and hardly spoke to them at all until after graduation, once he lost his local fame as a star athlete. Jake didn't start hanging out and smoking weed with Pete and Obie until he was out of better options.

"What do you think Jake's problem is?" Pete asked.

"I think he just doesn't want to get mixed up in the diamonds and shit. He's a pussy."

"Yeah," Pete agreed. "That was hilarious how he ditched Tera like that, though."

"That chick's hot, man."

"I know, bro. You think she'd hook up with me? I should text her."

"Probably. I heard she's a slut. Might make Jake mad, if that matters," Obie said.

"He's being a little bitch, anyway. Did you text him?"

"He hasn't answered. Tell ya, the guy is scared. We'll see him at work on Monday."

Pete pointed to the diamonds, still on the glass coffee table. "If we don't become millionaires and quit our jobs by then. I can't believe we scored these so easily. Those high school kids were weak. I figured they'd at least try to put up a fight."

"They never even saw it coming. I think that Hernandez kid pissed his pants."

"I bet we make a killing off them," crowed Pete.

"Yeah, for sure," Obie replied. "Once we sell those diamonds, we'll have boatloads of money. I'm gonna buy myself a fedora and a cane and wear a monocle and shit."

Pete laughed and nodded. "I'm going to get a bigger TV for us to play NCAA on."

"Oh, that'll be dope. I'll be here playing with my fedora on and shit, and you'll be with that chick."

"You got any ideas for how we sell these things?"

"You know what we could do?" Obie asked.

"Order a pizza and watch *Black Hawk Down* again?"

"Obie laughed. "Yeah, for sure. We should do that later. But with the diamonds. That manager at the casino. Bear-something. I've heard he's got ties with some real gangsters. I bet he'd buy these things off us. He's the only guy in town I know of who's plugged in."

"You really think so?"

"Yeah, for sure. We should try to get rid of the diamonds before someone comes looking for us. Let's stop by the casino tonight and see if Bear's interested. Who knows if those douchebags will tell on us or something."

"Or Tera will. That chick's a snake. Cool. Let's order the pizza, and then we'll head over to the casino to see what's what."

"Cool."

Obie dialed a number and ordered a large supreme pizza for delivery, while Pete put on the movie.

***

10:21 p.m.
Friday, May 19, 2006

Hanzō and Yuto entered the casino through a service entrance behind the building. Bear had asked them to come in through the back so nobody could place yakuza members at his establishment. Bear greeted them, along with a beefy security guard with a ponytail, and led them to a nondescript room used for storage. It had no security cameras, nor did the connecting hallway. Just fluorescent lights and concrete walls. The room contained three folding chairs and about one hundred sealed cardboard boxes. Bear, Hanzō, and Yuto took a seat, and the security guard left the three men to argue in privacy.

Bear was on the defensive. "Listen, I'm sorry. Sockolosky fucked up. He says some high school kids made off with the diamonds and murdered his pet llama."

"How did he let that happen?" Hanzō's face was stern. He did not accept excuses, just as his superiors wouldn't accept them from him.

"I don't know. Honestly."

"Let's talk to Sockolosky, then," Yuto suggested. "Have him come meet us right now. He must know something about these kids. We're not leaving Tulsa without those diamonds and a few fingers, at the very least."

"That's the thing," Bear sighed. "I just heard. Sockolosky got arrested. He's in jail right now. For murder."

Yuto and Hanzō looked more upset than confused.

"Murder? Who did he kill?" Hanzō asked nonchalantly.

"I don't know. Some high school teacher or something."

"Why the hell would he do that? What the hell kind of operation are you running here?"

"I don't know. But remember, I reached out to you first. I gave Bob the diamonds to make things right, and I was hoping he wouldn't screw things up further. I'm going to do everything I can to help make you whole. Please just consider giving me some time and mercy."

Hanzō nodded. "Sure. We'll give you twenty-four hours to identify these kids for us. You reached out and got ahead of this. We appreciate that. It sounds like Sockolosky's the one who should pay the price."

Someone knocked on the door to the storage room. The door opened, and the security guard stepped back inside.

"Boss, you're not going to believe this." The beefy man in the ponytail was as jovial as a teenage girl loaded with hot gossip.

"What is it?" Bear asked the man.

"Two redneck junkies just came in asking for you. Said they have some diamonds they want to sell. Four of them. They look desperate and stoned."

Hanzō and Yuto looked at each other in disbelief.

"Bring them back here," Bear said.

***

11:01 p.m.
Friday, May 19, 2006

Pete and Obie were tied with thin rope to the folding chairs in the storage room, whimpering and sobering up. The security guard punched Obie on the side of his neck. Obie screamed. Pete cried. No one outside the room could hear a thing.

"We're sorry!" Pete yelled.

"We didn't know who they belonged to," Obie insisted. "They're in my jacket pocket. Please, just take them. We'll forget we ever even saw the diamonds. We're sorry."

Yuto reached into Obie's jacket pocket and seized the diamonds, holding them in his palm for a moment. Then he handed them to Hanzō, who secured them in his own pocket. Bear exhaled a sigh of relief.

"So can you let us out of here now?" Pete asked. "We're really sorry, but we just got these a few hours ago. It was a total mix-up. We took them from these dumb high school kids. We had no idea they were yours. They stole them from you. You should punish them instead of us."

"You don't tell me who to punish," Hanzō warned, raising his hand to show them his missing pinky finger.

"You disrespected our family," Yuto added. "The fact you didn't realize it just means you are ignorant. We'll give you something to remember this by. Or take something, to be more precise."

Yuto pulled a sharp Tori Tanto blade from its sheath that had been concealed in his pants. Pete and Obie wept. The blade shimmered terrifyingly as Yuto held its tan stingray-skin handle with a tight fist.

"Please, sir, don't do this," Obie implored.

"You are right, though," Yuto said. "Tell us the names of the kids you got these from, and we'll deal with them next."

Pete nodded. "Of course. Whatever you want. I can tell you their names and what kind of cars they drive. Anything. There's a high school graduation party tonight. They'll probably be there. I can tell you where it is."

Yuto used the blade to cut through the part of the rope that was holding Pete's right arm down and took a step back. Bear pulled a pen and a small notebook from the jetted pocket in his jacket and set them on Pete's left knee. Pete scribbled all the information he knew about the boys onto the notepad and then handed it and the pen back to Bear. Bear skimmed the confession, tore the paper from the notebook, and handed the sheet to Hanzō, who nodded approvingly to Yuto.

"Good. I assume you are right-handed?" Yuto asked Pete.

"Huh?"

Bear and his security guard turned their gazes to the door while Yuto held Pete's right hand over a cardboard box and sliced off his index finger. Pete screamed and bled. The security guard used a first aid kit to patch him up while Yuto moved to do the same to Obie.

CHAPTER 14

10:30 p.m.
Friday, May 19, 2006

Fonz ferried us to the party in his BMW, and I rode shotgun so he'd let me control the music. I put on "Car Thief" by the Beastie Boys for our final approach, and we showed up at the scene of our last high school shindig around 10:30 p.m. I rode with a cardboard box on my lap that was about the right size for a toaster, but I refused to tell the boys what was in it. I left the box in the car when we arrived. By the time we parked, there were countless other cars already lined along the road and driveway leading to Austin's house. Hernandez helped me carry the cooler we'd brought, filled with beers and a bottle of rum, to the front porch, where we set up shop, while Weasel and Fonz carried another case of beers inside to put in the refrigerator.

Austin was a tall, fit football player who hung out with both football and baseball players, so I assumed he played on the baseball team, too, but I couldn't say for sure. His parents let him throw parties sometimes, the kind of fun, outlandish gatherings where someone might jump off the roof of the shed and into the pool. The kind of unforgettable parties that you can hardly remember. Austin's parents were both at the graduation party that night. It felt strange when parents tried to act like they were still young and cool by allowing a party and then attempted to mingle while they lightly chaperoned. It would have been better if they were gone, as we could govern ourselves. The only bit I felt bad about was that nobody seemed to use trash cans or ashtrays and opted instead to lazily toss empty cans and cigarette butts on the ground. I imagined Austin and his parents would have to spend the next several days cleaning up the mess.

The house was nice, a stained-wood, two-story property with an outdoorsy feel—not as rustic as a log cabin, but close. It had a big backyard, wooden paneled front and back porches, and a path that led to a large pool, all lined with tiki torches. Inside, teenagers gathered around the island in the large kitchen, taking Jell-O shots, doing beer bongs, and celebrating the end of an era. A state-of-the-art sound system in the living room connected to outdoor speakers and an indoor surround sound system. Girls took turns plugging their iPods into an auxiliary cord to play DJ.

The property was on three or four acres with a lot of large red maple trees, and since no neighbors lived in close proximity, we felt free to be as loud as we wanted to be. A tournament of beer pong was in full swing on the back porch near the pool. A handful of our classmates took turns being lifted upside down to do keg stands. There was a break in the rain, and the air felt fresh with a slight breeze. The atmosphere was electric in a way that occurs only when everyone around you is feeling free and light, unburdened by any responsibilities.

After depositing the beer in the fridge, Weasel continued to make his rounds inside and Fonz joined Hernandez and me on the front porch to drink some beer. Remember, the beer sold at Oklahoma gas stations was only 3.2 percent ABV, which meant drinking it was like drinking water for drunks like us. By the time we were seventeen, we were splitting thirty-packs of beer between two of us most nights, as we could easily manage fifteen each of the watery stuff. Weasel often binged twenty in a night, but then he'd usually be belligerent and rude. To supplement the weak beer, we'd often smoke weed or take pills, or sometimes we'd split a bottle of Robitussin, which we decided to do that night. Drinking cough syrup made the end of the night rough, causing a particular kind of nauseous spinning when lying down that accelerated when you closed your eyes. But while you were upright, you felt like you were floating around in the midst of a fun blackout. I popped the cap from a bottle of Robitussin and drank half of it in one gulp, and then I handed it to Hernandez to finish. After chugging it, he went inside to find Weasel. That night, since Fonz was driving, I bought a case of beer and let him have a couple for free. He and I each opened ice-cold cans and lit up American Spirits.

The song "Crazy" by Gnarls Barkley was playing, and the crowd was already raucous. Fonz and I tapped our beer cans together and then took long swigs. A stoner, hippie dude in our grade wandered up to us and spent a few minutes trying to convince and warn us of a few vague conspiracy theories. Fonz and I were stoned, too, but never as stoned as he was. The guy had never been quite the same after watching *The*

Matrix. He asked us questions like, "Do you even know what year they started the Federal Reserve, man?" There was no way to get him to stop aside from silently nodding like he'd cracked the code until he finished his tirade. Finally, he went inside to harass other people, and Fonz and I were alone for a minute.

"So what's in that box in my car? I can just go look if you don't tell me."

"Where's Elaine at? Is she coming?"

"She's working until twelve, and then she'll stop by. Figured if we got too wasted, she could drive us all home. But don't change the subject. What's in the box?"

"Easy, Brad Pitt," I said, referencing the detective the actor played in *Se7en*. "Hernandez kept his prank a secret. Why can't I?"

"I guess I want to know if we're painting something again. I'm not really dressed for it." Fonz pulled his shirt from his chest with his thumbs and index fingers to show off the vintage De La Soul t-shirt he was sporting.

"No painting, but maybe a rope. We'll have to break into Trout's office again."

"Exciting," Fonz said dully. "Real original."

"Listen, man, I've got a good one. And it'll only take a few minutes, so it's nothing like repainting the whole office or killing a llama."

A kid named Paul from my English class came outside and joined Fonz and me.

"What's up, guys?" He was smiling and holding a beer and acting drunk already. He shook my hand, then Fonz's, then mine again, and I braced myself for another active hand-shaker situation.

"Not much, Paul. Good to see you, man. Excited about graduation?" I asked.

"Aw, hell no. That shit's stupid. I'm excited to finally be done with all the bullshit, though. Say, can I bum a smoke?"

"Sure." I pulled out my yellow pack of American Spirits and offered him one. Paul put the stogie in his mouth, then motioned for a lighter, so I provided one of those too. He didn't thank me. He just lit the cigarette and handed my lighter back.

"Hey," Paul said, annoyingly drunk. "How do you get a dog to stop humping your leg?"

Fonz and I shrugged our shoulders.

"You pick him up and blow him."

Fonz and I squinted and nodded, and then we turned to each other.

"That's wonderful," I said. "Fonz, should we go in and check out the party?"

We left Paul alone and went into the house with our cooler to begin making the rounds, greeting people. Everyone was jubilant. It was a big day, and we all had reason to celebrate.

Outside, the rain began again, extinguishing all the tiki torches. Most of the crowd in the backyard fled inside for cover, though a few stragglers stayed in the pool to enjoy the rain—until they heard the sounds of thunder.

We found Weasel and Hernandez playing flip cup on the kitchen counter with six other people, including Austin's mom. It looked like their team was losing, but then, in an incredible come-from-behind win, Austin's mom flipped her cup in one try and won the game for her team, which caused a mini explosion of cheers in the kitchen. When Austin's mom saw me, she asked if I'd brought a piñata. She looked disappointed when I told her I hadn't.

Austin hosted a huge Halloween party every year, and the boys and I had proudly been on piñata duty for the last three of them. That was partly what inspired the idea for the prank I'd enact later that evening. I was the one who'd perfected the piñatas, though Weasel, Hernandez, and Fonz always contributed. We would get a bunch of kids to pitch in money to purchase an ounce of weed shake, put about half a gram each into individual plastic baggies, and stuff them in the piñata so that when the paper-mâché popped, fifty little weed presents rained down. We'd also stuff the piñata with a hundred condoms, fifty of those little plastic bottles of booze you get on airplanes, and more traditional items like glow sticks and confetti—but no candy. I played a big part in making the piñata such a smashing success each Halloween, not that anyone cared to congratulate me. The graduation party didn't call for a piñata, but being at that house made me think of piñatas, and apparently seeing me did the same for Austin's mom.

After winning flip cup, she excused herself, and a new group of kids started setting up for the next game, so the four of us guys formed a huddle. Presumably, the benefit to a large gathering was being able to hang out with people you didn't already see every night, but we couldn't help but group together like a herd of hapless dogs. Weasel nudged my chest and said, "Hey, look who it is, Jon Ryan. It's your last chance to make a move."

I turned around and there she was: Angelica, smiling and beautiful as always. She was talking to two other senior girls, radiating charm and happiness and innocence.

"Brother, she's still dating Jackson. I've got no shot."

"Speaking of shots…" Fonz grabbed three solo cups and a bottle of vodka and poured us each a shot, which we downed with squinting grimaces. Fonz abstained from the vodka due to his obligation as our responsible driver.

"You've got no shot if you take no shot," Weasel insisted.

"Truth, *ese*. Be a man," Hernandez added. "What's the worst that can happen? She says no? Then you're back where you are now."

"Yeah, I mean, she could say she's not interested. That would suck and be embarrassing. Or she could say some shit like how she sees me more like a brother to her or something."

Weasel leveled off and stared me directly in the eyes. "Jon Ryan, what would Magnum P.I. do? Do you think Magnum would be a little bitch? Or do you think he'd walk over to her and take his shot?"

Hernandez and Fonz nodded in agreement with Weasel, so I shrugged. They were right about having nothing to lose, and they were right about Magnum. The cough syrup, vodka, and beers had given me a dose of confidence. I threw away my empty in a trash can, opened a fresh beer, and strode toward Angelica like I had something to prove.

"Hey, how's it going?" I asked her.

"Oh, Jon Ryan! I'm so glad you're here!" She flung herself at me and hugged me like a long-lost friend, letting me lift her off the ground for a moment. She slurred in a familiarly drunken way as I set her down. Her two friends moved away to give us privacy.

"Me too. I'm glad you're here, I mean." I had always been nervous and shy about romantic endeavors, which was why I had never been successful in them.

"Do you have anything exciting planned for this summer? The girls and I are talking about taking a trip to South Padre next month. You boys should come."

"I like the idea of it." I took a lengthy swig of my beer. "Are you and Jackson going to keep seeing each other until college starts, or what? Honestly…I've always had a crush on you, and I'd hate to lose the chance to find out if there could be something between us." I could hardly believe I'd said it, but once it was said, I felt unburdened.

Angelica blushed, took a drink from the curly straw sticking out of her cup, and flashed her mesmerizing brown eyes up at me. It looked like she was drinking a sugary mixture of fruit punch and rum.

"To be honest, I've kind of always had a crush on you too, Jon."

Half my lip curled, and we looked at each other in a way we hadn't ever before. Or if we had, I hadn't noticed. I didn't realize the song that had been playing on the stereo system was ending and fading out when I blurted, "Plus, Jackson's a nice guy, but he's kind of a douchebag."

Enough chuckles and hushed whispers made their way around our section of the living room to inform me I'd spoken too loudly. I turned, and Jackson was standing right next to me. I mean, right there, as if he'd snuck up to surprise me with a million handshakes but stopped short as I verbally shit all over him. He looked upset, but his eyes were twinkling like he didn't want to have any enemies. Real charming and all. He just wanted to enjoy the evening and would have been perfectly fine with a rote, if perfunctory, apology.

"Homie. Did you just tell my girl that I'm a douchebag?"

"Well…yeah. I was saying she should date me instead. You being a douchebag was just one of the reasons." I had never had that much courage in my entire life, but I thought, *What the hell. You have to give love a shot, right?*

"You want to go? Is that what's happening right now?" He stretched both his arms from his sides, palms facing up, like he had just seen someone trying to parallel park his car and instead had run over an old lady. Like he wanted to shake me and reason with me and say, "What the fuck are you thinking, Jon Ryan?" But a good portion of our class had just heard me insult him twice in a row, so solely in response to peer pressure, he had to make the sacrifice to consider kicking my ass.

"Guys, if you've got to do this, do it outside, please!" Austin shouted from the corner, sitting on a couch full of people, with a girl on his lap, and in no position to regulate.

The girl on Austin's lap asked him, "Is anyone going to stop this? Where's your dad?" Austin pointed to the recliner, where his dad was already passed out and had a sombrero resting over his face.

By that time, half the room was watching us. The other half hadn't noticed a fight breaking out, or they would've been watching too. The girl on Austin's lap tapped the iPod hooked to the auxiliary cord, and "Wanna Be a Baller" by Lil' Troy started on all the speakers on the property. She turned it up loud.

Jackson and I took stock of the situation, glanced at Austin, who was still motioning for us to go outside, and then faced each other again, now only inches apart like we were in a spaghetti western. Looking back, I can only think that the cough syrup and stress from that week had taken their toll. I didn't realize it at the time, but I was moving like I was underwater when I gave a hard, slow push with both my palms into Jackson's chest.

Jackson almost tripped over backward but caught and steadied himself. "You just made a big mistake, Jon Ryan. I've always liked you, but you just crossed a line."

I gulped the rest of my beer and dropped the empty can on the floor as confidently as possible. The thing with chugging beers on cough syrup is that everything is moving at regular speed, but in your mind, you feel like an elegant motherfucker moving with the grace and speed of a cheetah.

"You know what, Jackson?"

Almost everyone in the packed living room was watching us now, ready either for the fight to start or for us to shut up. I inched closer, and we were eye to eye.

"What?" he said, just as cocky as he deserved to be.

"You're a fuckin' slut."

"You sure you want to do this, bro?"

I swung.

Act first; think later. Be the man in the arena. That's what they all say. So I did it. I took my best shot and made the first move. My fist was perfectly clenched and flying in what seemed to be a demonstrative path toward Jackson's perfect jawline. He easily dodged me like he was Ali in his prime and then returned almost instantly with his left fist in two swift jabs—the first to my ribcage, and the second to my right eye. He popped me good, and I fell to the ground in front of my entire class, defeated. The worst part was that my right eye wasn't the eye already black and bruised from the beating the day before, so I'd have to explain a fresh black eye to my parents the next day while taking tragic graduation photos with them. Of course, he had to be left-handed.

I was stunned, and when I looked up, Jackson had already walked off with Angelica and a few of his friends. Apparently, he'd decided that he'd won. I thought I even heard him say to one of them, "I pity the fool," but I was loopy and could have imagined that part. An old-school hip-hop classic was playing loudly in the background like it was his goddamned theme song, after all.

I sat cross-legged for a minute on the carpet and shook my head like a wet dog, and then I rubbed the fresh battle wound on my right eye. Someone tapped my shoulder, and I turned to find Fonz. He handed me a gorgeous, unopened can of beer, then stuck out his hand to help me up, though it would've been easier if he'd helped me up and then handed me the beer. After I struggled back to my feet, Hernandez and Weasel appeared behind Fonz and diligently brushed off my shoulders as though I'd fallen into a mound of dirt.

"I'm proud of you, buddy," Weasel said.

"What the hell are you talking about? I got my ass kicked." I opened the cold beer and drank half of it in one fell swoop.

"But you made a stand. That's righteous. Plus, he didn't whoop you nearly as bad as Pete did yesterday."

Fonz laughed and then patted my shoulder again and said, "For real, man. That was bold. Really nice. It took guts. Maybe it'll make her mad at him, and she'll run over to you for a revenge affair or something. You know, summer lovin' and all that."

Hernandez desperately wanted to contribute, so he added, "Sometimes you just gotta put your dick on the table and play the cards you're dealt. You know? Like Bill Murray in *Groundhog Day*."

"Huh?" I tried to embrace the compassion and ignore Hernandez's nonsense. "Every time there's a fight, it seems like Weasel's just in the audience. He never helps anyone out."

"Hey, man. That's not fair. Nobody helped. It was a simple difference between two men."

"And yesterday? It seemed like you were on the sidelines, man," I reminded him.

"Yesterday? I got punched, kicked, and tazed. We all did. What else do you want from me?"

"Eh, yeah, sorry. I'm just pissed at Jackson, I guess. You're right. Sorry."

"*Cabrón*. Head up. You took a shot, and that's what counts," Hernandez pep-talked me. "I know it's not going to ruin us having a fun time at this party or keep us from pulling the final prank tonight. Whatever you got in your secret cardboard box, we're gonna have fun, yeah? God, I hope it's a doozy."

"Yeah, thanks, guys. Maybe we leave around one to do the prank, then? I've got something planned. I think it's cute."

Fonz looked stumped like I'd used the wrong word by accident. "Did you say *cute*?"

The boys agreed to leave at 1:00 a.m., and I went into the downstairs bathroom, closing and locking the door behind me. I put my hands on the sink counter and looked down, closing my eyes. It'd been the most stressful week of my life. I hadn't ever had the shit kicked out of me before, let alone twice in two days. I opened my eyes, turned on the faucet, and splashed water onto my face. Then I shut the faucet off and used a towel to dry my face and hands. I sighed, shook my head, and then moved to the toilet. I didn't raise up the seat and instead opted for pissing all over the floor around the toilet before flushing and leaving the bathroom. I'm not sure why I decided to do that knowing either Austin or his parents would have to deal with cleaning it up, but I made my puddle and felt proud over it.

I grabbed an extra beer and went onto the front porch by myself to have a cigarette and ponder. On one side of the porch, a couple sat on a wooden porch swing, but they were enamored with each other, making out and oblivious to me. They hadn't even noticed my ten-second fight inside, what with the music and heated groping and all. I sat in a wooden rocking chair on the other side of the porch to light my smoke. Then I ruminated and thought about the image of Jackson walking off with Angelica. I reimagined him saying, "I pity the fool." An hour passed. Then two, and I didn't move from my seat. People flowed in and out. On the patio, off the patio. Coming and going from the party. The rain slowed for a while and then returned a few minutes later with even more ferocity and with even louder cracks of thunder and lightning. People came out front to smoke or hang out, but I didn't move once. If my beating had been in slow motion, everything right after sped up, and I couldn't depict any of it for you now with any sort of confident clarity. Fonz came out and joined me occasionally, and each time he brought me a fresh brew. I don't remember what we discussed, if anything. Sometimes a friend just needs to be there; it doesn't matter if anything is said. Mostly what I remember is that the rain and thunder kept getting louder and more intense after each lightning strike.

At one point, I remember Paul coming out and being sort of an asshole. He approached me and asked if he could bum another cigarette. He didn't even bring up my bruises or my confrontation with Jackson. I was already irritated and in pain, so I snapped at him, "Man, why don't you buy your own cigs?" Every time I ran into that prick, he always pulled the same shit. I knew I probably wouldn't ever see him again after the party, and I was tired of fake smiling for his emotional benefit. Plus, I had just been publicly humiliated in two quick jabs.

"I only smoke cigs at parties, bro. I don't buy them, so I'm not addicted."

"I'm not a bodega that's handing out free shit all night, man. Here's one more, but it's your last one from me."

Paul was obviously uncomfortable with my aggressive attitude and did his best to lighten the mood. "Hey, why are fat girls so good at giving head?"

"Paul, I am not in the mood to hear you recite old fucking jokes."

He indicated that he obviously needed my lighter again, too, and he looked miserable and offended as he lit the smoke. Then he handed my lighter back to me and walked to the other side of the patio to enjoy my American Spirit, standing in front of the couple who were still vigorously making out. If anyone had reason to be offended, it was me. The leech.

It was silent. Paul looked at his phone, coughed out a laugh, and then put his cigarette out and went back inside. He didn't even smoke half of it. He got a free cigarette and wasted it in front of me.

Right after he left, the power on the entire block went out. Thunder was shaking the ground, and lightning flashes were striking around the property, but I felt safe, drunk, and unphased in my throne on that sturdy wooden porch. I remember looking around a few seconds after the power went out and realizing I was alone; the amorous couple had fled inside. When the music stopped, I could hear girls' muffled shrieking and some boys' laughter, and through the front windows, I saw people lighting candles. The vibe still sounded festive in the dark home filled with young people, but their conversations were garbled; none of their words were clear through the wall separating us.

For a few minutes, the thunder stopped, the rain slowed to a mist, and an unusual quiet descended. I didn't care for that one bit. I detest silence in the evening; it's uncomfortable and unnerving to me. Silence in the morning is fine, possibly even good. I like silence in the morning. Silence at night, though, is scary. I've never liked it. When I go to sleep, I want some sort of racket in the background. Some white noise. Rain, waves, crickets. You name it. Maybe a flowing waterfall, but never just silence. I'd rather the beeping of a semi-truck in reverse for an hour over silence at night.

In the midst of that dark calm, Chase, a kid on the football team, came outside with a cheerleader on each arm. Then the rain picked back up, and the thunder and lightning continued, though further off in the distance. I looked at Chase and his two female companions enviously as he winked at me.

"You heading out?" I asked.

"Yeah, bro, my parents are out of town, and we have a generator, so there'll be power there. Plus, I have an indoor jacuzzi." He winked again, and I thought about telling him that was enough winking.

The cheerleaders hanging on his arms seemed excited about the mention of a jacuzzi. I tried to whisper so the girls wouldn't hear, asking him, "How do you do it, man?"

"Simple, bro. Fifty push-ups a day. That's all you need to do. Trust me." Then, as if on cue, the three of them jogged through the storm together to find his car, and I shook my head like a totally dumbfounded loser.

Fonz, Weasel, and Hernandez appeared on the dark patio in search of yours truly.

"Are you ready to do your prank, *cabrón*? Power's out. Is as good a time as any."

"Sounds like a tornado's coming. Should we really drive around right now?" I asked, responsibly and drunkenly.

"Is your prank an indoor or outdoor affair?" Hernandez asked.

"It's indoor."

"Okay, then," Hernandez replied.

"I hope I die in a tornado," Weasel alarmingly admitted.

"Let's go, guys," Fonz said. "I'm driving. You said we're going to the high school again, yeah?"

"Yeah, exactly."

CHAPTER 15

1:32 a.m.

Saturday, May 20, 2006

We piled back into Fonz's BMW, and honestly, I'll go on the record as saying that Fonz wasn't too drunk to drive that night. He knew he'd be piloting us around, so he cut himself off after a couple beers and then drank only water the rest of the evening, like a sensible adult. While his car was warming up, Fonz put the windshield wipers on their fastest speed to combat the fierce rainstorm. All at once, the lights around Austin's house and down the road came back on. The storm still raged on, but having power was always better than no power. I had my secretive cardboard box back on my lap in the front passenger seat, and Fonz insisted we buckle our seatbelts before he put his car into gear.

Austin's house was pretty far from where the rest of us lived. In fact, I'm not sure why he was even in our school district. We were about fifteen minutes from the school when the rain started to test the windshield wipers. Fonz slowed the car, but the wipers couldn't swing back and forth fast enough to allow visibility more than a dozen feet ahead. The huge raindrops looked like a never-ending stream of clear water balloons bursting on the windshield. Fonz slowed the beamer even more, and then something bolted across the street, stood in front of us, and turned its head to reveal its shimmering eyes glowing like a spooky green alien: a deer, and it must have been a ten-pointer. It was a big boy, and it was right in our path. Fonz did all he could. He stepped on the brake, and we skidded on the rain-soaked roads, immediately hydroplaning despite our slow speed. The car first spun in one direction and then, when Fonz tapped lightly on the brakes again, sort of corrected and started to slide in the other direction. If it hadn't been raining, I think Fonz could have handled it. The car jutted off the road and pitched into a ditch head-on. His front bumper was smashed, but we were all okay. Even the cardboard box I'd been holding was still intact, though it had flown out of my hands and come to a rest on the dashboard.

After we composed ourselves and checked in on each other to make sure we were all good, Fonz muttered sarcastically, "Nice." Then he then turned his car off, hiked his jacket over his head, and opened his door to quickly pop out and assess the damage in the pouring rain. He jumped back into his seat and slammed the door shut with a grim face, punching his steering wheel in frustration. "Dammit! Boys, I don't think the car is gonna move." He tried turning the key in the ignition, but the engine didn't turn over. Plus, we were deep in a ditch that was becoming a fast-flowing creek.

"Shit, man, that fucking deer. Animals just got it out for you, huh, Fonz?" We all chuckled at Weasel's bit. Even Fonz laughed.

"I guess I have to call triple A and get a tow truck?" Fonz asked in a defeated tone. "Does that mean Jon Ryan does his prank on a different night or what?"

"Sssss," Hernandez hissed in audible contempt. "It was the last day of class today. It's the last night of high school. There's no rescheduling this, *ese*."

"Uh, I mean…" Fonz struggled. He really loved his car. "I guess I can call a tow truck later on tonight. They're twenty-four hours and all. I could call Elaine, and maybe she'll drive us to the school, I guess? I just really don't want to leave my car here in this ditch, man."

"It's Jon Ryan's prank night," Weasel said. "We signed oaths to assist him in his endeavor this evening, not to get in car wrecks and screw things up. The way I see it, we are bound by law to make this happen. Whatever he's doing with that stupid cardboard box, I want to be involved. I hope it's not a bomb, though."

This was a convincing enough speech for our drunk teenage minds.

"Fuck," Fonz said and then looked at me. "Weasel's right. It's your prank tonight. You decide what the next move is."

"Well, what would Magnum P.I. do?" I asked.

"Hell fucking yes!" Weasel nearly jumped in his seat with excitement. "Magnum would finish the mission. Call Elaine, Fonz. Have her pick us up and take us to the school."

Fonz followed our self-imposed code of honor solely because he'd signed a handwritten list of ridiculous rules. He called his girlfriend as Weasel instructed, and she came to rescue our evening.

***

9:06 a.m.
Thursday, May 18, 2006
(two days earlier)

On Thursday morning, Detective Finnerty drove to Will Rogers High School after staying up most of the night reviewing evidence, including the security footage from Sockolosky's gate and the gas station where the 911 call had been placed. The gas station footage showed four boys' faces, as well as the license plate on one of their cars. The car registration led him to Weasel's name and address, as well as to Will Rogers High School, where he planned to show the faces to the principal to learn the names of the other three kids. By the time the detective arrived that morning, the parking lot was nearly empty, and gas company employees were inspecting various pipes while a man with thinning gray hair watched.

"Can I help you?" the man asked Detective Finnerty.

The detective flashed his badge and said, "I hope so. What's going on here?"

"Report of a gas leak. I'm the principal here. Stan Trout. We had to close for the day while they check on the leak."

"I see. Do you know an Earl Derkatch, sir?"

"Of course. He teaches here. What's the problem, detective?"

"I'm sorry to have to tell you this, but, though we haven't found the body yet, we believe Earl Derkatch may have been murdered."

Mr. Trout stepped back in shock. "What? Are you serious?"

"I'm afraid so, sir. We have some DNA evidence that supports that theory, plus a 911 call. The caller reported that he was shot—twice. We found his car and some blood, but he hasn't turned up. We have a suspect we're planning on taking into custody, but we need help tying up a few loose ends."

Mr. Trout teared up. "Of course. What can I do to help?"

"If you could take a look at this photo and tell me if you recognize any of their faces." Detective Finnerty handed over a printed screengrab from the gas station security camera depicting the boys placing a 911 call.

"Yes. They're students here. That's Jon Ryan, Weasel, Fonseca, and Hernandez. And that car? It's Weasel's, all right. They're real troublemakers. You think these boys had something to do with shooting Earl?"

"No. No, sir. I don't. But they might have information about who did. I think they might have witnessed it."

"Gosh almighty. What a day. Earl Derkatch has been my friend for nearly twenty years. This is a crying shame."

"I was hoping to talk to the boys here, but since school is closed, I guess I'll go to their homes. Or they might be more willing to talk if I come back tomorrow morning. You could call them into your office and I could question them, if that's okay with you?"

"Of course."

The detective drove back to the station and updated his captain, confident that Bob Sockolosky was the culprit. The captain obtained a search warrant for the estate grounds and ordered a few uniformed officers to help sweep the estate in case the boys' 911 report of a second body was accurate. Detective Finnerty returned to the Sockolosky estate and poked around, trying to envision what possibly could have happened there the night before. Soon four officers arrived, along with two K9s, and together they trudged the rain-soaked property, all the way out into the woods. By early evening, the officers found Earl Derkatch's body under a small pile of leaves and twigs. The cavalry was called back to the scene, and Bob Sockolosky was placed under arrest for suspicion of murder.

Finnerty wanted to let Bob sweat in his cell for a while, so he decided to make use of his time by questioning one of the boys that night. He pulled Weasel's license plate number again, traced the registration address, and went to Weasel's home.

****

11:08 p.m.
Friday, May 19, 2006
(the next day)

With their finger-chopping business complete, Hanzō and Yuto drove toward the house party that Obie and Pete told them about. It was rather a long drive. They spotted the BMW they knew belonged to a boy named Fonz—again thanks to Obie and Pete—and found a place to park with a good view of the car. They sat in their SUV in the pouring rain with their headlights off, watching and waiting.

"Hanzō, please forgive me for asking, but do you think our bad luck is just God's way of punishing us?" Yuto asked.

Hanzō scoffed. "We already recovered the diamonds. Not such bad luck. But this whole scenario happened because of my decision to move guns out of Oklahoma instead of Texas. It was my mistake, not yours. When we leave here, we will stop in Dallas to make new arrangements."

"You don't think it is karma for what you did in Osaka?" Yuto looked terrified to ask, but he had to.

"It is not karma. It is fate. Only what was meant to happen will happen, Yuto."

"If fate is real, sir, then what is the purpose of living each day? If everything that happens is out of our hands?"

"Even if you don't control the world around you, you can control your attitude about it. That is all that matters."

They continued their surveillance until four boys left the party and scrambled into the BMW—it had to be Fonz and his three friends Pete and Obie had ratted out. Yuto started the engine and began to follow the car, keeping a safe distance behind. When a deer bounded into the road and the BMW landed in a ditch, Yuto quickly slowed down, parked the SUV a safe distance back, and turned off the headlights to watch what would happen. He and his boss discussed whether they should ambush the boys on the road.

Before they had come to a decision, a small car pulled up to the accident and picked up the boys. Yuto followed the new car until it stopped in a high school parking lot. He parked a discreet distance away and watched the boys get out in the pouring rain, run to the school, and climb up a ladder that went to the roof. The driver remained in the car.

The two yakuza members waited with the intent of jumping the boys in the parking lot when they returned. But when, after ten minutes, the boys still hadn't emerged, Hanzō and Yuto began to lose patience.

"Should we wait for them, sir? Or go inside?" Yuto asked.

"What would Agent Cody Banks do?"

Yuto laughed, and they both opened their car doors and jogged to the main entrance of the school, where they picked the padlock that chained the two large front doors shut.

***

11:13 a.m.

Friday, May 19, 2006

(earlier that day)

After talking to the other three boys at the school Friday morning, Detective Finnerty spent a few hours interrogating Bob Sockolosky at the station. He was being held based on the evidence but still hadn't been formally charged and still hadn't asked for his lawyer. He maintained only guilty people needed lawyers and was adamant that he was innocent. For the first half of the interview, Bob was stoic and refused to admit any knowledge of any wrongdoing. By the end of the day, he was hungry, and Detective Finnerty had worn him down.

"I've got information on certain people. I'll tell you what you want to know, but you have to guarantee witness protection or something for me. We can cut a deal, but these are bad people."

"I can't promise you anything, Mr. Sockolosky, until I have a better idea of what is going on here. Why was a high school history teacher with one arm dead in the trunk of your wrecked SUV, and why was he later hidden in the woods behind your house?"

"Maybe I am being framed."

Finnerty laughed. "If you think that's going to work for a jury, then fine, we can go ahead and charge you, and you can call in your lawyer. We don't need your confession based on the sheer amount of evidence. I'm talking with you right now for your own benefit."

Bob took a deep breath and then said, "I'll tell you whatever you want to know, and I hope you'll be understanding enough to cut me a deal in exchange for my testimony against people much worse than me. For now, can you at least agree to let me out for an afternoon this weekend so I can attend the funeral?"

"What funeral?"

"Rudolfo's. My llama. He has to be buried; he needs a proper ceremony. For a number of reasons, this has been the worst forty-eight hours of my life, but I won't be able to forgive myself if I don't give Rudolfo the send-off he deserves."

"Sir, I don't think you understand the gravity of this situation. Two people are dead, and you're being charged in the murder of at least one of them. I don't care what weird freak shit you and that llama were up to, but if you sign a confession and tell me what's going on here, I'll allow you to be escorted to the llama's funeral and back here to jail. How's that sound? And I will tell the DA about your cooperation in case it helps them look favorably on you enough to reduce the charges or consider some sort of deal or protection. That's the best I can do."

It took only a moment for Bob to consider. "All right. Let me call my lawyer so he can help me draft something."

Within an hour, Bob's lawyer arrived. An hour after that, a confession was written and signed. Bob denied pulling the trigger himself; he claimed that Earl Derkatch had broken into his property and that Walter had shot in self-defense. He denied knowledge of any diamonds. He denied hiding the body and suggested that Walter had probably done so. He did name names. Sockolosky was ultimately a weak man and offered up specific details of corruption, money laundering, and gun running. He gave up Bear and the yakuza and claimed he was merely a pawn in their operation. He said he was being used because of his mounting gambling debts. If anything, he was the victim, really. He claimed he had been forced to help transfer guns to these guys, that it wasn't his idea, and all that sort of garbage. And the detective played along and nodded until he had enough information and a signed confession admitting some culpability. He then took a late-night drive over to the casino to put more of the pieces together.

By 11:00 p.m., Detective Finnerty was pulling into a parking spot in a dark corner behind the casino. He shut off his car to stake the place out.

A service door in the back of the casino opened, and a security guard with a ponytail pushed two young men out of the building, each with a bloody towel wrapped around his right hand. The young men scurried around the building to find a taxi and vacate the area. The detective wasn't sure what was going on with those two, but he had a hunch something was amiss. He kept watching the same door, and after a few more minutes, two Japanese men exited the building and got into a four-door SUV rental car. Keeping enough distance to hide his presence from them, Detective Finnerty started his car and tailed the two men, whom he assumed were Hanzō and Yuto, the yakuza members Sockolosky had told him about.

Eventually, the SUV parked near a house where a party was obviously underway, given all the cars parked outside and the dancing, laughing teens Finnerty glimpsed through the windows. The detective parked a short distance behind the SUV to watch what Hanzō and Yuto would do. The rain was steady enough that he could linger in anonymity. The yakuza members stayed in the SUV. While he watched and waited, Finnerty called in the license plate on the yakuza rental car to try getting some information on the driver.

A big bolt of lightning struck in the distance, and the lights on the entire block went out. Then a high school kid left the party with two girls on his arms, and they dove into a car and drove off with reckless abandon. A few minutes later, four boys, who Finnerty recognized as Jon Ryan, Fonz, Weasel, and Hernandez, left the house and piled into a BMW. Then the streetlights came back on. As the BMW took off in the rain, Hanzō and Yuto followed behind in the SUV. Then Finnerty noticed another car switch on its headlights, pull out, and follow the SUV; he could not see who was driving and did not recognize the vehicle. Detective Finnerty followed behind the whole bunch as the only witness to all parties involved.

A few miles down the road, a deer jumped into the street, causing the BMW to swerve, hydroplane, and plow into a ditch. Yuto and Hanzō parked their SUV a safe distance back and turned off their headlights, and the car behind them turned off its lights and parked as well. Detective Finnerty, at the end of the caravan, also parked and shut his lights off. The heavy rain kept the passengers in the other cars unaware of the parked cars around them.

Fifteen minutes passed, and a Dodge Neon arrived and picked up the boys, who deserted the damaged BMW and drove off. Once again, the SUV and the other car followed sneakily, as did Detective Finnerty.

Finally, the caravan arrived at the high school, rain still spilling down with intermittent cracks of thunder and lightning. Finnerty watched the boys scurry to the administrative building and climb the outside ladder while the driver of the Neon remained in the car, head down, staring at her glowing phone screen. As Finnerty waited, trying to decide whether to follow the boys or wait for them to return to the car, he called a tow truck to haul the BMW to the police station parking lot. About ten minutes later, he saw Hanzō and Yuto leave their SUV, run through the pouring rain to the school's front doors, and, within a few minutes of fiddling with the lock, enter the school. Just then, a man with a baseball bat emerged from the mystery car and ran into the school as well. The detective, sensing something bad was happening, called for backup before entering the same door the yakuza guys and the man with the bat had entered.

***

10:34 p.m.
Friday, May 19, 2006
(a few hours earlier)

Stan Trout, high school principal, devastated widower, and well-regarded member of his community, had a few extra glasses of whiskey while sitting on his couch at home looking through photo albums, remembering all he'd lost and pondering what he had discovered. He had spent the past two days asking several of his most brown-nosed, tattletale students about the pranks and vandalism to his house earlier in the week. In the course of his investigation, he gathered four names of students who were suspected of smashing his mailbox: Chase, Jackson, Austin, and Will. Finally, something snapped in him. He had never been a violent man, but the broken mailbox had stirred up emotions that Earl Derkatch's death only amplified. In one athletic swing of a baseball bat, those boys had wreaked havoc on his emotional state more than they would ever know.

Trout looked up the addresses of the four students, scribbled them onto his notepad, and decided to take matters into his own hands. He opened the closet by his front door and pulled out a wooden baseball bat of his own, feeling a surge of desire for vengeance. Then he hurried to his car and drove to the first address scribbled on his paper, Jackson's house. The lights were off when he arrived, and it was pouring rain. The family was asleep, and Jackson's pickup truck was absent. Trout parked his car, grabbed his baseball bat from the backseat, walked casually—despite the rain—to Jackson's family's mailbox, and began hitting it repeatedly. Trout had real brute, old-man type of strength, but the mailbox wouldn't dislodge from its stand. He struck it a dozen times, but the aluminum just folded into itself. The mailbox was damaged, but not as destroyed as he had hoped.

Fearing being caught, Trout jumped into his car and drove directly to the next address on his list: Austin's home. He was already starting to feel better. He needed to get his pain and anger out by inflicting it on those who'd hurt him. To him, this violence was the therapeutic breakthrough he'd been denying himself.

When Trout arrived on Austin's block, he discovered a huge party, so he shifted his plans from mailbox bashing, at least temporarily, to staking out the comings and goings of his most recent class of seniors while he sipped from a flask and congratulated himself for finally taking a stand.

It was just after 1:30 in the morning when he saw Jon Ryan, Hernandez, Fonz, and Weasel appear through the rain and get in Fonz's BMW. Trout knew they'd had nothing to do with desecrating his mailbox, but he suspected that they might be in trouble, especially after he detected two men in an SUV following them while they pulled away from the party. Trout put away the flask, put his car into gear, and followed the SUV, unwittingly joining a secret caravan that would lead him back to the school he administered. He did not even notice Detective Finnerty following behind him.

CHAPTER 16

1:51 a.m.

Saturday, May 20, 2006

Elaine picked us up from the ditch where Fonz's wrecked BMW was lodged and drove us the rest of the way to school. She arrived at Austin's party a little after midnight, but as usual, she hadn't been drinking. Fonz had, for the most part, blown Elaine off during most of our boys' prank week, so she was happy to be around him and didn't mind chauffeuring us, even though Fonz kept whining and worrying about his car the whole time. I had my prank supplies in the beamer and the storm outside was no joke, so I quickly transferred the cardboard box into Elaine's car and instructed Hernandez to retrieve his rope from the trunk. Weasel, Hernandez, and I all squeezed into the backseat of her Dodge Neon, while Fonz sat up front in the passenger seat.

It was Elaine's car, and she was doing us a huge favor by rescuing us and driving, so by unwritten law, she was in charge of the music, though if the driver allows, whoever is riding shotgun can be in control of the tunes. When she picked us up, she was listening to "Drive Slow" by Kanye West, a relatively new song; like a lot of high school girls, she usually listened to music from the past year and never seemed to play much older stuff. Similarly, you could ask any high school girl, then or now, what her top five favorite movies are, and most of her answers would likely be fairly recent movies. That tendency might apply to the age group more than the gender, but my observation about movies and music is that the classics get buried when you're trying to fit in.

Fonz eventually took control of the aux cord and put on "Can I Kick It?" by A Tribe Called Quest, which took us all the way to the school parking lot and put me back in the mood to win the prank contest. Elaine parked and asked, "You guys won't be long, will you? I think I'll just wait in the car." Elaine shut off the car. The rain outside hadn't slowed.

"Yeah, Jon Ryan, how long is this going to take?" Fonz asked.

"We have to break in again. I guess we can use the skylight hole."

"Real original," Hernandez quipped.

"So I guess maybe fifteen minutes max? Thanks for driving us, Elaine. We'll be quick. I promise."

Fonz and Elaine kissed, and we looked away while we gathered our supplies. I took off my coat and draped it over my cardboard box to keep it from getting soaked, and Hernandez fixed his rope over his shoulder once again like he was a young, Mexican Stallone. We opened our car doors and bolted out into the rain toward the same ladder we'd used that Monday night to scale the building. Once we were on the roof, I carefully pulled a few staples from the plastic that was temporarily acting as Mr. Trout's skylight while Hernandez tied the rope to the ladder—the same impressive knot he'd used to hold us a few nights before. Then we descended.

I went down first. Fonz tossed my cardboard box down to me and then followed.

"Never thought I'd do so much rappelling in my whole life," he complained.

"Shut up. You love it," I bantered.

Hernandez and Weasel followed us down, and Weasel attempted to pull the plastic over the hole behind him to keep the office from getting soaked. A small drizzle was still making its way in, forming a puddle on the carpet near the desk, but it wasn't much, all things considered.

"Déjà vu. I assume based on the size of the box that we aren't painting again, right?" Hernandez asked. "Or do we need to cover the window so we can switch on the lights and just do my prank all over again?"

"No, guys. The light coming in from the window is enough. Like I said, this will be quick." I opened my cardboard box and started pulling supplies out and carefully setting them on the desk one by one in the dim office.

"What the hell is this prank?" Weasel asked in his high-pitched, weaselly way.

"It's a glitter bomb," I responded matter-of-factly.

"A what?" Hernandez asked. "So it *is* a bomb?"

"A *glitter* bomb. We blow up a balloon with glitter in it and then rig it so it explodes when the box is opened."

The boys seemed less than dazzled by the description.

"What is this, a twelve-year-old girl's surprise party or something?" Fonz asked. "You seriously had all week to come up with a prank after seeing all of ours, and you're just popping a balloon with some glitter in it?"

"We can't all murder a prized llama, buddy. Trout will probably come into his office in the morning before he goes to our graduation, right? He'll see a box in his chair; he'll open it, and then he'll be covered in glitter. This is my prank. It'll be a good one. Simple, but good."

"I didn't kill that llama," Fonz said, like I hurt his feelings.

Weasel and Fonz shook their heads and shrugged, but Hernandez came around, saying, "I guess I like it. What do you need from us?"

"Just keep a lookout. This will be simple."

"Damn right it's simple," Fonz said arrogantly. "No layers."

Hernandez nodded regrettably and said, "It does lack layers and complexity."

"Simple can be good, guys. The gas leak was simple, and I'd say it's favored right now for winning the best prank," Weasel said in my defense.

I finished organizing the supplies onto the desk while the boys watched carefully, yet unenthusiastically, as I prepped the glitter bomb. I stuck a small funnel into the opening of a balloon, and then poured three small glass containers of glitter in through the funnel.

"Where's the dynamite?" Hernandez asked, dumbfounded.

"There is no dynamite. The balloon pops, and glitter explodes from it. Have you never heard of a glitter bomb?"

"Sounds like some weak-ass shit, *ese*. No, I've never heard of this before. I figured a bomb must need dynamite or something."

I removed the funnel, blew up the balloon with three quick breaths, and tied it off. Very carefully, I placed the balloon into the box and duct taped it to keep it snugly in place. Then I slid a single nail into one side of the cardboard so that the tip of the nail was close to the balloon but not touching it. Finally, I closed the flaps, taping one flap to the balloon such that when the flap was pulled open, it would force the balloon into the nail tip. A veritable genius but harmless booby trap. I set the box down in the swivel chair behind Mr. Trout's desk and raised my hands to the sky like a magician revealing a final surprise. "Well, there it is, boys."

"Kind of anticlimactic, I'd say," Fonz belted.

Weasel nodded. "Yeah, so nobody will see this thing go off? Maybe at graduation we'll notice some glitter on Trout's bald head. Is that the idea? Well, those of you who are at graduation might notice. Should we take some video of the box sitting in the chair over there so we have something interesting for the record?"

"Oh, shit," I exclaimed and smacked my forehead. "My video camera; it's in the trunk of Fonz's car."

"Rules are rules, *pendejo*," Hernandez said to me like a disappointed mother. "How'd you forget that? It's kind of important. Do you remember the rules?"

"I think the car wreck threw me off. We had the camera in the car driving here. It's Fonz's fault for wrecking."

"What? Did you want me to plow into that deer? You're lucky I was driving. It's the only reason we're all still alive."

"Okay, fine. I'll use my phone." The quality wasn't great, but I took advantage of having a camera on my flip phone and snapped a photo of the cardboard box in Mr. Trout's chair. The extremely dim lighting caused proportionately grainy results.

"So that's it? We've got to climb the rope again now? Then I can go home?" Weasel asked, like he was ready for bed.

"Yeah, let's go," Fonz said. "Elaine's waiting. And I still have to get a tow truck for my car. Fuck."

Just as Fonz hopped on top of the desk and readied himself to climb up to the rainy roof, the door to Mr. Trout's office opened, and two silhouettes entered the room. The room was so dim it was hard to see, but strikes of lightning flashed through the window to briefly illuminate the faces of two Asian men we had never seen before.

"Um…" Fonz froze while standing on top of the desk.

"Get down from there. All of you move over here." The older man spoke calmly and herded us to stand by the window.

The younger man pulled a Tori Tanto blade from its sheath, which shimmered in the flash of distant lightning.

"Whoa," Hernandez said. "Are you guys, like, the new school security? We're sorry we broke in. Just some harmless fun. My name is David Hernandez. It's nice to meet you."

"I don't think they're school security, dude," I commented.

"Yeah, *dude*," the older man said mockingly.

"I can't tell if you're being friendly or condescending," Weasel stated.

"You all stole our diamonds," the younger one explained.

"We don't even have those anymore, man. We can tell you who's got them. They kicked the shit out of us." Fonz was doing his best to act as mediator.

"We already found them, *itachi*." The younger man held the blade up, readying himself to use it while the older happily pulled the four diamonds from his pocket to briefly show them off before returning them.

Then he pulled two fingers from the same pocket and tossed them at the boys. "These are fingers from the two useless drug dealers who took the stones from you. So what do you suppose is about to happen?"

"You all pay the price," the other man answered for us.

"Oh, um, what is the price, exactly?" Fonz asked with trepidation.

"You each lose a finger today. It is the way of jingi. Our moral code. But you are lucky. We will let you each decide which finger you lose. Because we are feeling generous."

We looked at each other in surprised, terrified anguish, and Weasel looked like he was about to cry. Fonz responded on our behalf. "Oh, um, sir—sirs, we are deeply regretful that we found those diamonds in the trunk of a wrecked car. That was our mistake, but since you already got them back, maybe we can skip taking a finger from each of us and chalk this up to a hilarious misunderstanding?"

The older man spit on the floor and growled like a feral dog.

"Um…" Fonz continued the futile negotiations. "What would you say to half a finger? I think half a pinky sounds fair."

Weasel nodded eagerly.

"Who's first?" The man with the knife moved to the desk and indicated where a hand should go so he could efficiently chop our fingers off.

Nobody volunteered, so the older man grabbed me and pushed me toward the desk. My heart raced, and panic sunk into my belly.

The younger man lined up his knife carefully like he was a calculating surgeon.

"Not so fast, assholes," a vigilante savior said menacingly from the doorway. We all turned and found Mr. Trout, covered in rain and brandishing a baseball bat, with the sleeves of his button-up shirt rolled up, looking as fed up and desperate as Michael Douglas at the end of *Falling Down*.

"This does not concern you, old man," the knife-wielding man said to him.

"This is my school. My office. My students. I'm tired of being pushed around. Being given the high hat. You set down the knife right now, and I won't break you into pieces." Mr. Trout was on fire with anger, and I was amazed he had turned into a stone-cold badass and had come to save us.

"Do you know who we are?" The older man laughed.

"My best guess is, if it weren't for you two, my dear friend Earl Derkatch would still be alive." Mr. Trout didn't wait for a reply or further negotiations. He swung his bat hard, and it connected with the younger man's skull. The kind of hammering to the temple that removes a year of memories in an instant. The man dropped his blade and fell, immobile, to the ground.

Weasel jumped on top of him and put him in a chokehold, unnecessarily, since he was already out cold.

The other man quickly grabbed the Tori Tanto blade with his left hand and lunged at Mr. Trout, who swung his bat wildly at him. The man grabbed the bat in midair with his right hand, pulled our principal toward him, and lunged in another attempt to skewer him. The blade pierced Mr. Trout's belly, causing him to drop his bat and fall to his knees, splattering blood onto his wet, white dress shirt. Our principal gasped in agony.

The man turned and pointed the blade at us, shaking his head in disgust. He gave a series of kicks to his cohort's belly in order to wake him.

The man slowly stirred and, even though the bat had thoroughly discombobulated him, struggled to his feet and whispered, "We were going to show you mercy and only take a finger from each of you. But now, you all die terrible deaths. Your own mothers will not recognize you." He leaned over and picked up Mr. Trout's baseball bat.

Tears streamed down Weasel's face. "No, please. A finger sounds great. Take any finger you want. I'll cut it off myself." Weasel dropped to his knees and placed his hands into a prayer pose.

"They're just kids," Mr. Trout pleaded between labored breaths. "Leave them be. Have mercy."

"This *is* mercy," the older man said, preparing to slash Weasel's throat as he knelt.

"Police! Put the knife down." The man spun around to see a cop pointing a gun at him from the doorway. It was

Detective Finnerty, the officer we'd talked to earlier that morning. Both of the career criminals lunged toward the detective, who didn't hesitate. Finnerty fired three shots in rapid succession: two into the older man's chest and one into the other's skull, killing him immediately.

The gunshots were much louder than the thunder outside, and the dark office was suddenly covered in blood and disfigured bodies.

Detective Finnerty asked us, "Are you kids okay?" Then he holstered his weapon and knelt down as we nodded. He applied pressure to Mr. Trout's belly wound and told him, "Hey, Stan? You're going to be just fine. An ambulance is already on its way."

"Oh my god, he stabbed me!" Mr. Trout was delirious.

"Yeah, it looks like he stabbed you. You're going to be okay, though. Just hang in there. One of you boys, come help me." Detective Finnerty waved Hernandez over and showed him where to apply pressure on our principal's stab wound. Then the detective grabbed the blade from the older Asian man's weakened grip and set it on the desk.

The man was still alive, but barely. He was coughing up blood and mumbling nonsense in two languages, but all I could make out was the phrase, "We solve problems creatively and take action on behalf of our customers." Then he drifted off to the other side.

"Thanks for saving our lives, sir. Those guys were mad about the rubies for some reason," Hernandez said.

"Diamonds!" I reminded him in irritation.

"You boys are either stupid or lucky," the detective announced while holstering his weapon and moving behind Mr. Trout's desk to calm down. "After everything that happened this week, you're still trying to do senior pranks? What the hell is wrong with you? Hey, what's this?"

The detective noticed the cardboard box sitting in the desk chair. Before we could stop him, he picked it up, gently pulled up one of the flaps, and—*POOF*. The nail popped the balloon, and glitter shot all over the room, especially in the detective's face. Just as designed. Mr. Trout smiled in agony and muttered, "Hah, a glitter bomb. Good one."

I flipped on the light switch, eager to be out of the dark, but that was when we all got a true glimpse of the horrors that had unfolded. The room was covered in glitter and blood.

Hernandez exclaimed, "Oh, man. They're really going to have to repaint this office again now."

"What do you mean *again*?" Mr. Trout asked, trying his best to hold on to consciousness.

"Oh, nothing. It's just a real mess in here, sir. Carlos is going to have his hands full."

The next two hours were a blur. Two paramedics rushed Mr. Trout into an ambulance on a stretcher. They said he was going to make it because the blade had missed his vital organs and arteries. Before they picked up the stretcher, Mr. Trout even told us he was sorry and that he'd allow Weasel to walk at graduation the next day after all.

Our parents were summoned. Statements were given. Detective Finnerty asked us all the same questions several times. Eventually, we were given permission to leave the school grounds on our own recognizance.

"Hey, Fonz, do you want us to wait with you for the tow truck?" Hernandez asked. I had forgotten all about Fonz's car being wrecked in a ditch.

Fonz was holding Elaine's hand, and she looked more shaken than him. "Fuck this day, man. I'll call a tow truck in the morning. I want to go home."

Overhearing the conversation, Detective Finnerty informed us, "A tow truck won't be necessary. I had it towed to the police station hours ago, even before I knew the full story of what's been going on. And it has been searched."

The detective chuckled as he explained how they'd found polaroids and a video camera in the trunk and examined much of it down at the station. Finnerty admitted that he obviously hadn't gotten to watch any of the footage himself yet, but according to others at the station, the tape in my video camera had helped explain a great deal. "You boys are almost kind of genius in your stupidity," were his exact words. He said I had been recording when the gunshots went off outside Sockolosky's house and that our time-coded recordings were critical evidence because they also showed Mr. Derkatch in the trunk of the SUV at the time of the llama snafu. According to Detective Finnerty, if we hadn't filmed ourselves trying to kidnap Rudolfo that night, Mr. Derkatch's murder would likely have remained unsolved. So supposedly, something we did that week had a positive impact on the world in some way. Or Fonz's prank attempt did, at least.

I thought about how ridiculous our polaroids and video must have seemed to the room full of police officers viewing them. Seeing us paint an office virtually the same color as it was. Watching us spray paint a deaf llama. Seeing the llama escape, flipping Weasel onto the pavement. Observing as we failed to save the llama. Flipping through photos of stink bombs and broken glass. Those were the images going through my mind: all the stupid shenanigans we'd recorded and photographed. I wondered what those sworn law enforcers had thought as they watched our mistake-laden, amateurish rip-off of *Jackass*. I wondered if any of those cops had laughed at our doomed prank attempts or if they were somber and judgmental.

It was after four in the morning and had finally stopped raining by the time we were released. As we walked to the parking lot, we voted unanimously that the gas leak was the best prank. We gave Weasel the $400 we had collected at the beginning of the competition, along with the honor of holding the title and privilege of being forever remembered as the class of 2006's official senior prank winner for Will Rogers High School.

CHAPTER 17

4:44 a.m.

Saturday, May 20, 2006

We said our goodbyes to each other and to Elaine, and our parents drove us home. My parents weren't mad at all about the fiasco. Not even a little bit. Evidently, they were just happy I was still alive. They didn't seem disappointed in my decision-making skills or ask what, in particular, had led to the damned diamond dilemma. In fact, all of our parents comforted and cherished us in the pre-dawn hours of the crime scene, relieved that, after receiving the dreaded post-midnight phone calls from officials regarding their teenage sons, they'd found us unharmed.

As we drove off, I glanced back at the institution designed to prepare us for adulthood, feeling a mix of emotions. On the drive home, my parents asked me multiple times who the Japanese guys were and whether I still had any of the diamonds. I could tell that they didn't really understand what had happened, but they thought they did. I gave short, vague answers until they realized I had no interest in discussing anything further that night. We spent the last bit of the drive in silence. Though I usually hated silence at night, that night I didn't mind. It actually helped me think. At the risk of

282

sounding corny and self-important, it felt a little like, in a way, the burden of creation itself had been placed upon us for a few days. Either that or we were just foolish and loony enough to thwart, by coincidence, the schemes of evil men and keep them from progressing in their nefarious goals and imposing their will on the present or the future. None of what I told myself that night made much sense at the time or later, but still, I ruminated on all sorts of theoretical, linguistical garbage often spouted by mystics and philosophers. I was just trying to make myself feel better by giving the situation grave, significant meaning. I thought about that philosophy book Mr. Derkatch had given me and decided that what little I understood from it either made total sense or no sense at all.

We arrived home as the sky slowly brightened in anticipation of the sun's arrival. Most people in our neighborhood were still sleeping and had no idea of the ordeal we'd put ourselves through that evening. My parents hugged me again after we parked and exited the vehicle, and they repeated to me how glad they were that I was okay. Then I went upstairs to my room and fell asleep. Powering down my brain took no time at all. I disrobed and climbed between the sheets, and my mind immediately shut down, as if I'd flicked a switch. I was out until early afternoon. That was when Heather woke me up, poking me in my chest and repeating my name over and over. Once my eyes opened, she told me that our mom had dispatched her to wake me and that I should come downstairs to join them for a late breakfast.

I told Heather I'd be down in a minute. She skipped out of my room and left my door open simply because she knew I hated when she did that. I grabbed my phone. I had a few texts from the boys, but I was thinking about Angelica. I decided to give it a go one more time. I started typing. Back then, several letters of the alphabet were assigned to each number key, so to compose a text, you had to press the number keys multiple times to scroll to the letters you wanted. For example, to type an S, I had to press the 7 button four times. Therefore, it was important to craft texts a bit more strategically. Plus, depending on your parents' phone plan, you likely paid a set fee per text message. The message I typed to Angelica read: "Sorry for last night. I've always really liked you a lot and thought it was my last chance to do something about it."

Almost instantaneously, I received a response: "Sorry, champ. She's still sleeping."

Fuck Jackson, that son of a bitch. I slammed my flip phone closed and set it back on my nightstand. I used the bathroom, showered, brushed my teeth, and went downstairs to find my mom cooking pancakes and bacon. Heather was already eating hers, and my mom fixed me a plate. My dad sat in his wooden rocking chair outside, reading the newspaper, presumably searching for any mention of my friends and me, or diamonds, or yakuza, or something. But nothing was in the papers yet. News traveled more slowly back then.

I wanted to get to graduation early, so I drove separately from my parents and went to Memorial High School's football stadium around 4:00 p.m. to find my friends, smoke a joint, and prepare for the ceremony. On the drive over, I listened to "Forest Whitaker" by Brother Ali on repeat and sang along.

Fonz, Weasel, Hernandez, and I got a lot of questions from students and teachers about all our wounds. Rumors were already floating around, but we had no answers. Mr. Trout was still in the hospital, but no one else seemed to know why he was absent. Somehow, the events from that week never made it into any newspaper. A few months later, a short paragraph about Bob Sockolosky being sentenced to prison was published, but nothing else.

The four of us walked the stage, received our symbolic diplomas (official diplomas were mailed over the summer), and took the obligatory graduation photos in our caps and gowns, which made our parents happy. Most of our class was jubilant and ready to celebrate, but I was tired and just wanted to go home and sleep. Most of all, I was hungry. After the photos and hugs were complete, I left by myself. I needed a feast, and I needed solitude. The guys understood, I'm sure.

The weather was perfect. The sun setting through the stringy clouds turned the sky multiple shades of orange, creating a hypnotic gradient of colors. I rolled all my windows down in the Bronco, blasted "Free Fallin'" by Tom Petty on my car's stock speaker system, and drove by myself to Ron's to get a jumbo bacon cheeseburger, plain and dry.

***

6:15 p.m.
Saturday, May 20, 2023
(seventeen years later)

My little sister, Heather, went on to attend medical school and worked at a hospital for a while before starting her own thriving practice as a primary care physician. She focused on her career and was single into her late twenties, but then she met a guy and rather suddenly got engaged, got pregnant, and sent invitations for a wedding in Tulsa, where she and her fiancé still lived.

So there I was at her wedding at Cain's Ballroom, a venue made famous by several iconic performers. The ceremony was short and sweet, and there was good food and dancing. Heather, a six-month-pregnant newlywed, was glowing. She was happy, she claimed, and I believed her. That day she looked as elated as I'd ever seen her. Her groom was a smart, tall man who worked in sales and seemed rather decent. Heather said he treated her well, and my parents and I were truly happy for her.

My path in the years after high school was not a straight line. Good things happened. Bad things did too. I attended college for two semesters. Then I applied to culinary school in Chicago and got accepted, so I dropped out and moved to Chicago for a reputable two-year culinary degree. I met a brilliant, beautiful woman when I was twenty-three. We got married, and she helped me start my own Italian bistro in the outlying Chicago suburbs, with a brick pizza oven, just like I'd always wanted. Really, it never would have happened without her. She pushed me to step out of my comfort zone and go for it. Those days were delightful, and I think about them often.

Deep-dish pizza was never my specialty, and trying to compete against deep-dish pizzerias in Chicago would have been insane for anyone, so I stuck to the Italian-American-style pizza and other cuisine that I did best, and the reviews were generally positive. Things went well for about five years. The business grew. My wife and I built it together, working alongside each other during the good years. Eventually, we started to resent each other. Or she started to resent me, at least. She wanted kids, and I didn't. That led to couples counseling, and that led to divorce. The business couldn't survive our breakup, so we closed down the pizzeria and lost the dream we had for each other. Since then, I've been working as a chef in an upscale Italian restaurant in downtown Chicago. I make it back home to Tulsa around once a year for the holidays. The burdens of a single, depressed chef can be tiresome.

As for the boys, we kept in touch throughout the years via social media apps and group texts, but I had been the one who drifted away, both physically and emotionally. Fonz, Hernandez, and Weasel never moved out of the state. After college, they all made their way back to Tulsa, and the three of them stayed tight. They continued to include me in their chats, occasionally sending me funny memes.

Fonz got Elaine pregnant a few months after our high school graduation, and his kid was already attending Will Rogers like his father before him. He and Elaine had broken up several times but always ended up back together. Finally, when their kid was about five, they got hitched and had been together ever since. Fonz started a business and ended up becoming the most successful toilet paper broker in the Midwest. No shit. A public company bought his business before he turned thirty. After that, he relaxed, started dabbling in the stock market, and enjoyed being a wealthy stay-at-home dad.

Weasel had gotten a job at the sign-printing warehouse where Obie, Pete, and Jake used to work (Obie and Pete were fired shortly after graduation because they were missing fingers that were crucial for the job, and I never heard what happened with Jake). Weasel's dad died a few years before Heather's wedding, and when I called Weasel, we spoke for hours, as if no time had passed. I was sorry to miss the funeral, but he understood. Weasel stayed in his dad's house and kept much of the same routine from his teenage years, presumably never wanting to grow up or change. He didn't get married or have kids. Hernandez, on the other hand, had some sort of IT job for a big oil company, a wife, and four children—all girls.

I had texted the boys to tell them I was flying in for Heather's wedding. They didn't know Heather well enough to attend the ceremony, but they asked me to text them afterward so we could all get some dinner or go bowling. I stayed at the wedding reception for a while and then congratulated the happy couple again, said my goodbyes, and went outside to call an Uber. I texted Fonz, and he replied, "We're at Weasel's house. Meet us here, and we'll go bowling."

I arrived at Weasel's a little before eight and let myself inside, as knocking had never been encouraged there. The boys were already in attendance, and they cheered when I entered, taking turns giving me solid bear hugs. Weasel was fully bald with a big beer belly, and he offered me a Bud Light. "Good to see you, man," he said with a big smile.

"Jon Ryan, you're getting a little tummy, buddy," Hernandez said, caressing my stomach. He was right. I had let myself go since I lost the restaurant.

"You too, *cabrón*," I said and gave him a belly slap of my own.

A professional tennis match was playing on TV—a newer, nicer television than before but in the same location as the old one. The couch, chairs, and dining table were all the same.

They asked all about my life and updated me on theirs. All three seemed happy, and I was glad.

"Hey," I said. "Do you guys remember that week we almost got killed by the yakuza?"

"Barely," Weasel responded.

Fonz nodded. "Yeah, I remember. At least I remember you convinced us to quit our jobs at Fuddruckers, and then I was broke all summer with a totaled beamer."

"Right," I responded. "But we were almost killed, right? We saw a llama get smashed. Mr. Derkatch died in my arms. It was a pretty big deal—to me, at least."

"Honestly, I haven't thought about that stuff in a while," Weasel murmured, focused on the tennis match playing on his fancy television.

"Eh," Fonz said, "I think you're overdramatizing it, Jon Ryan. The way I remember it, we did some stupid stuff in high school that we shouldn't have. We had a lot of those kinds of nights—the kind where we're lucky to still be alive. Almost getting our fingers cut off for some Japanese diamonds is barely in the top ten."

"Are you guys kidding?" I asked, flabbergasted by their indifference toward the memory. Seventeen years had passed, though, which is certainly a long time. A lifetime for some. After all, we were all just seventeen when we graduated, back when all the craziness occurred. "We were literally almost murdered by the yakuza. They were going to cut off our fingers and shit."

"Yeah," Hernandez responded, nodding while opening a fresh beer and holding it out to tap for a cheers. "And our history teacher might have been a werewolf. Who knows? We were young, and those days were wild, *ese*."

ACKNOWLEDGMENTS

Thanks especially to Sean White. Sean and I met in 2005 when we were sixteen and attending the Oklahoma Summer Arts Institute. He's always been a brilliant and hilarious guy. Then, in 2014, we tried to collaborate on writing a screenplay with the same basic storyline as this book, but we gave up after one draft for various reasons, including the process of co-writing, which was tough. That screenplay draft was the inspiration for this book, and I would be a fraud if I didn't acknowledge that some of my favorite scenes in the book were a team effort between Sean and I back when we were spry, young lads.

A big thank you to my editor James O'Brien, who is indispensable.

I must also thank J.S., Evan Strome, Michael Bolus, Alex Kruglov, Marc Richard Peters, Jon Ryan, Erik Johnson, Nic De Castro, Serafima Kobzeva, Aaron Ray, Zachary Brandt, Michelle Lochmus, Aaron Pettijohn, and my mom. Thank you all for your support and encouragement. It's much needed and appreciated.

AUTHOR BIO

Nathan Pettijohn is an author and entrepreneur. He is a contributing writer for Forbes on topics relating to what business leaders need to know about innovations in media and technology. Nathan's previous novel, *Public Opinion*, is a crime thriller. In 2011, Nathan founded Cordurouy, a digital strategy agency where he serves as CEO. He resides somewhere in South America with his dog, Raphael.

You can contact Nathan on social media at @nrpettijohn or via email at ivanstravensky@gmail.com.